OMEGA'S GAMBIT

FLORA QUINCY

LADY GARDEN BOOKS

CONTENTS

BLURB

OMEGA'S GAMBIT

~~ It is a knotty problem, and it will take some slick moves to mate these two together. ~~

London, 1795

Miss Viola Hartwell has one mission: ensure the Omega Property Rights Act becomes law. However, as an omega she is prohibited from participating in politics. Viola refuses to let her dynamic stand in her way and makes the risky decision to masquerade as her alpha twin sister. All she needs to do now is convince the reclusive Duke of Orley to support her cause.

In another part of town, Syon, Duke of Orley, has chosen the widowed Countess of Kellingham as his future bride in a marriage of convenience. But the omega widow refuses to meet any alphas. When the duke's beautiful new secretary offers a unique solution to his problem, he accepts.

What begins as a simple exchange of votes for a bride becomes a dangerous game of illicit desire and temptation.

DEDICAITON

Lockdown, you brought a lot of upsets but you also set me up
to start writing this novel.

&

The Wonder Women who were there when I started and
those I've met along the way.

A special thanks to C.S. for answering every question and her
unending patience.

AUTHOR'S NOTE

A quick note to those unfamiliar with omegaverse:

This sub-genre imagines a world where people are divided into three groups, known as "dynamics".

Alphas are dominant in all aspects of society. Male alphas have a physiological difference called a "knot", which plays a significant role in their sex lives.

Betas make up the majority of society and their biology is the same as ours.
Finally, Omegas are the rarest and most prized dynamic and are generally submissive towards alphas. They also produce "slick", which makes it easier for them to take an alpha's knot. Their biology means they have "heats" where they nest and are desperate for sex—particularly with an alpha.

There are other tropes including pheromones causing spontaneous erections and slick, people having unique scents, mating bites, and over the top possessiveness.

This scratches the surface of omegaverse and what makes it a unique sub-genre. Just like the rest of the romance genre, omgaverse comes in all shapes and sizes. If you like romance, you can find an omegaverse to suit your tastes.

In this omegaverse, gender does not play a role in sexuality. Rather dynamic influences a character's sexuality. This means MF, MM, FF, and any combination of genders is considered normal and accepted by society.

Historical accuracy was taken seriously... up to a point. Many words and phrases that might seem modern are not. For example, "steal my thunder" is a reference to an early eighteenth century story about a thunder machine for a production of the Scottish Play. Dildos is an even older world. It has been such fun doing all this research so that I could pepper the story with historical accuracies.

To conclude... This isn't some great novel written to give you pause, but a story meant to be a lot of fun and a bit over the top. However I over think things too much, hence the author's note. Enjoy. Don't ever take me too seriously. And remember that the best way to approach anything is with an open mind and a teaspoon of salt at the ready.

EPIGRAPH

"All the sacred rights of humanity are violated
by insisting on blind obedience."

Mary Wollstonecraft, *A Vindication of the Rights of Women*

I

VIOLA

" If music be the food of love, play on!" I waved my hand dramatically, as if an actress on a stage, and my body rocked slightly with the movement of the carriage as it hit a rut in the road. "But in all seriousness, I'm no musician. Nor am I interested in love or marriage or mating... Not today, tomorrow, or next week. So neither love nor music, dear sister. I must find some other occupation to keep me busy while I stay in London. Shall I write scandalous pamphlets?"

"Dear Goddess, what am I to do with you?" my twin sister Iris groaned with ill concealed weariness. We looked remarkably alike, with the same dark hair and medium build. The defining difference was that my eyes were violet, and hers a pretty brown. Still, we could fool people who did not know us well. Then there was the fact she was an alpha, free to do as she wished, and I an omega constrained by society's strictures. "Be serious, you can't engage in politics so publicly! Don't look like that, Vi. The law prohibits omegas from entering politics. You don't even have the right to vote.

Better marry and mate an alpha with political ambitions and be the power behind the throne."

"Never!" I laughed. "Tie myself to an alpha? To quote Beatrice, 'not until a hot January.' No, I want to change the law under my own name. Didn't Papa—an omega though you need no reminder of that—make a mark under his own name? All I require is a clever tongue and willingness to go as far as I can, do whatever it takes."

"By the saints, but you are a madcap. Do you want to make another scandal for our family?"

I shrugged. "Beatrice created a scandal because she was caught. How could she not be when she submitted her paintings to the Summer Exhibition as an omega! I don't plan on getting caught."

"Sister," Iris said with all the severity an alpha could use against an omega. However, it could hardly succeed. I was older by fifteen minutes. She'd only presented as an alpha four years ago, there were a further sixteen years of my being the elder twin. "Vi, please... I am leaving you with our uncle. In London, no less, where I am sure you will be a cat amongst pigeons. Promise me that when I go to Oxford you will behave? Until Christmas? A few short months..."

A grin tugged at my lips. Nothing like Hartwell alphas worrying what we Hartwell omegas could accomplish if given the opportunity. "I make no promises I can't keep. I'll try to be circumspect."

"Circumspect. You'll look around for trouble?" my twin teased.

"But I won't go looking for it," I stuck out my tongue.

"I give up. Game of chess?"

"Done," I pulled out the board and began setting the counters. Half the fun would be keeping the pieces on the board, for despite the good weather, the roads were rough. Then again—that *was* half the fun.

As our carriage pulled up in front of the house on Weymouth Street, memories of my childhood in Edinburgh came flooding back. To the time when our parents had been the toast of Scotland's intellectual establishment and had introduced their daughters to those great minds with no consideration for our dynamics. We'd lived there until I'd turned sixteen. Then my father, a notorious omega scholar and trouble maker, died in his sleep at the age of forty-three. My alpha mother, devastated by her mate's early death, had packed us up and brought us to England and her estate in Hertfordshire. Though a pretty house, with a large garden, I longed for the greater freedoms afforded omegas in Scotland and the anonymity of a city. In the countryside, your neighbours knew your secrets before you did. In the countryside, no scholars visited us. In the countryside, omegas stayed home, quiet and wholly concerned with domestic arrangements. London, however, promised a change. A wider circle of acquaintance. And surely my uncle, who was a member of Parliament, would host his friends and discuss the issues of the day late into the night. I'd be able to talk with men and women whose liberal minds matched my own.

But, on stepping into the narrow hall, I saw my mistake. The house was as quiet as a church. My aunt Maria, my father's younger sister, stood at the head of the stairs looking down at us. She dressed demurely and clutched a handkerchief in one hand, which she often brought to her mouth in a strangely child-like gesture. Her greeting was not cold but neither was it welcoming. Distant, rather. I knew there existed a tension between our families—Mama openly disliked my uncle and disliked more that I would be spending time under his roof while she took up a diplomatic posting in Paris. They'd never travelled to Scotland to visit, and we rarely saw them in Hertfordshire. Still, I was taken aback by the strange household I now found myself a member of.

After settling, Iris and I joined our aunt Maria in the drawing room. This was an unexpectedly cosy chamber, with an overflowing work basket by a chair full of cushions next to the cold fireplace—the room gave the impression of a nest, my aunt's retreat. I liked it, my first positive impression since arriving. My optimistic smile was quickly wiped away as my aunt began to outline my stay.

"Now, I must explain the conditions of your visit," she said in that soft omega-like voice of hers. "You shall be presented next Spring per your mother's instructions. In the intervening months, you'll be fitted for a new wardrobe. As you aren't formally out, despite your age, we will not have many social engagements. Visiting, receiving callers, and some small omega only private dances. My health is indifferent, but I shall endeavour to find a chaperone for you if you desire to go out more. Otherwise, you can read and write as much as you choose. Your mother says that you are much like my brother, rest his soul."

"That ain't bad, is it!" Iris smiled encouragingly.

"No political dinners?" I breathed. The one thing I'd looked forward to about living with these strangers. "Surely my uncle must host..."

"My health is indifferent, and I dislike noise," my aunt snapped, a spark in her otherwise gentle eyes. "When my husband desires to spend time with his political cronies, he visits his club or dines out. Thankfully, that is often."

"But..."

"I will do my duty and bring you to events I deem appropriate. Do not fight me on this, Viola."

"But..."

"Viola, you *will* listen to her," Iris barked. I didn't need a mirror to know the look of horror on my face.

"Did you just...?" I blinked. My sister had never alpha'd me before. "I can't believe you!"

"Vi... You haven't been presented. You are an omega," she tried to soothe me with a purr.

"You barked at me!" I cried. "You barked and then you purred! How could you?"

Nearly tripping on the stairs, I ran up to my small bedroom, locking the door behind me. What had happened to my sister that she now used her dynamic's power over me? We'd never, ever made distinctions in our household. Ever. And now, within a heartbeat, my closest friend turned into a stranger seeking to manipulate me, to bend me to her will.

I glanced about me, helpless to understand my situation. The room was stuffy, and even when I opened the window there was no breeze. Not in the city, I realised. I looked at my little desk, already covered with books and scraps of paper with my various thoughts sketched out, ready to be refined and prepared for the book I intended to write. But it might as well be thrown in the fire. Without an audience for my work, how would it ever get out into the world? No one would read the political scribblings of an unknown omega— no alpha would take me seriously, and betas had their own worries. Even my father had written under a pseudonym before he had married my mother.

The lock clicked, the door opened, and I recognised the scent of another sister—mint and something that could only be described as frosty mornings. Since I'd last seen her, my middle sister Hippolyta had chopped off her red hair, allowing it to curl prettily about her head giving her a cherubic countenance. But it would be a mistake to assume Polly was meek or mild. More correctly, she was lethal, dangerous, and wonderful. Despite being the smallest of us, Polly carried herself with cat-like grace.

"What are you doing here?" I sniffed, refusing to admit I'd been crying.

"I came to see why you threw a tantrum... Iris sent word," she said lounging in the doorway, arms crossed over her chest. I huffed, not believing a note from Iris could have reached her so quickly. There lay the great mystery. Hippolyta always knew what was going on. Her preternatural insight was a fact of our lives we never questioned, so I supposed I should just accept her explanation even if I didn't believe it.

"Lay low, Vi," she frowned when I didn't reply. "Iris is off to university. Beatrice is in Paris with our Mama. Though I hope they come home soon given the political situation. The Reign of Terror might return at any moment. Attend closely Vi, with no alphas, you lack protection. Our aunt and uncle don't know your wild ways."

"You'll be here." I knew she spent her time in London... But she wasn't an alpha.

"I've responsibilities that mean I won't be able to look out for you as closely as I would like."

"Being a modern day Robin Hood isn't a responsibility," I pointed out. "Wealthy alphas will always hold the power no matter how many times you steal from them."

"I'm not talking about that," she said, her tone sharp which told me she'd reveal no more.

"I'm not a child," I growled, hating that none of them trusted me. I was twenty. Accomplished. Skilled. Capable. Yet was shoo'd away and forced to sit pretty in a house that lacked *life*.

"Of course you aren't! If you were, you'd be in Paris," Polly frowned. "Vi, we just... You are our only chance at a scandal-free alliance for our family with the world. We need you. We, all omegas, we need your brain to win our fights in the light while the rest of us work in the shadows."

"You and Beatrice are older... And she has made her curtsy!" Though we both knew that meant nothing. She'd rejected several excellent proposals before devoting herself to her art. "Why isn't she the one marrying and mating some influential alpha?"

"We gave up our influence when we followed our passions. You are... You are far cleverer, far more capable of changing minds..."

"If I am..." I bit my lip, the papers on my desk caught my eye. "You know they'll keep me prisoner here. Nothing but an omega to marry off as suits them."

"You'll marry and mate who you wish. Don't worry about that, Mama will ensure that... She promised Bea. You could publish your writing," she pointed out. "I have the contacts."

"And who'd read it? Anonymised? With an alpha's name? No. I won't let one of them—even if it is my pen name—take credit."

My sister shrugged. "You've always been good at coming up with a clever excuse not to do something."

"Polly, you are the worst," I laughed ruefully.

"Come here," she opened her arms. Of all our family, she was the least affectionate, turning her embraces into gold dust. I went willingly, wrapping my arms around her smaller frame. "You are a silly wench. Stay the course, bring them down... Marry, mate, be happy... For our peace of mind and because Bea and I won't be able to do so."

"You'll find love and a mate," I mumbled into her hair. "Just perhaps not in a conventional manner."

"No Hartwell omega is conventional," she chuckled. "Even our aunt may surprise us. Be patient with her. I've been watching for a while and things are never what they seem."

"Sisterly advice?"

"Sisterly advice. Now, go and make your peace with Iris. She feels miserable for barking at you like that."

Polly kissed my cheek and left me pondering our conver-

7

sation, but Iris could not be put off. I went to find her in the drawing room. Luckily, she was alone, at her feet the remains of an ugly porcelain shepherdess.

"Vi..."

"Iris... That really was an ugly figurine. But I doubt aunt Maria will be pleased it is broken."

2

VIOLA

Some six months after Viola's arrival in London.

O ut of my bedroom window, I could see the frost on the streets. It was January, which always reminded me of my father's death. Inexplicably, I wished for the evening when, with girlish romanticism, I had watched my parents, loving mates, sit on the sofa, their hands clasped while they listened to us recite our lessons before telling some mad story of seeing sea lions in the surf.

I sighed with longing for those happy days, with weariness for my current situation. But life moves on and I must face facts: Even after six months, nothing had improved at Weymouth Street. I learnt from the housekeeper that my aunt's health was genuinely poor, but even at my uncle's urging, she refused to see a doctor, preferring instead to bear her illness stoically. I'd begun to suspect that there was a battle of wills between her and her mate but could not find the cause except that they were unhappy, perhaps even disliking each other. It made for long, boring days and interminably long, silent evenings, with my uncle almost always out and my aunt bent over her embroidery.

My sanity remained intact, thanks to correspondence with my sisters and mother, and my hours spent writing about the subjugation of omegas and the inequality of the dynamics. It was solitary work, and I missed the company of like-minded people. It was only when Iris returned to us for Christmas that I finally realised quite how lonely I'd become.

My boredom found some relief in my sister and her friends. One such friend was Arthur Jones, who had gone up to Oxford with my sister and had haunted our doorstep since the Christmas vacation. They returned for Hilary Term in a week's time, but today we discussed the new bill being considered by Parliament.

"It will give unmated and unmarried omegas the rights to own property without an alpha co-signer. Not so free as betas, but an improvement, is it not, Miss Viola?" Mr Jones smiled. Of course, I knew this. I'd been following its progress as closely as an omega watched over a newborn.

"What is the bill's chance?" I asked, pretending enough ignorance for him to feel superior to an omega. He was a handsome alpha even if he considered my interests in politics shallow rather than deadly serious—though I hoped I would never have to kill someone for my politics. In short, I liked him because there was no one else to like better.

"They lack the votes, but it will be close. Ten would do it. There are several on the fence waiting to see where certain peers will sit on the topic."

"Which ones?" I pressed.

"The Duke Orley has not expressed an opinion, and he's six seats under his patronage. Though, he is in Town, so we might expect him to sit silently in the House of Lords. There is a hope he will follow Bedford, but the duke spends his time in the country and rarely comes to town so we don't know which way he will go."

"Perhaps the Parson Duke will demonstrate that he isn't quite so parsimonious with the votes he controls," Iris laughed at her own joke. The duke, however, was serious business—six votes was nothing to sneer at.

"He would not be enough," I frowned. "He has six seats under his patronage. We'd need to be certain of all Gale's and persuade at least a few more of the governments' less settled members... What shall we—"

"We? You keep your nose out of it. Exile would not suit you, Vi," my sister frowned.

"You would take up and campaign for this bill? That is very admirable, Miss Viola." Mr Jones spoke with a great deal of warmth. My omega, however, did not respond to his blatant overture—his scent made no secret of what he desired. Though handsome, we did not think him powerful enough.

"Thank you," I managed and glanced at my sister, who grinned like a Cheshire cat. Did she think to play matchmaker? But my twin was neither so crafty nor much interested in my personal affairs. Which could only mean she enjoyed my embarrassment. Damn her. Dammit, again because I was suppressing myself in front of a strange alpha. That was when I noticed they were both dressed for riding. I'd added cabin fever to the long list of complaints I'd begun in my latest letter to my mother. "I suppose you want to be on your way..."

"Next time, Vi, get permission from our aunt and join us on our ride," she said with a friendly flick to my nose. "I'm surprised you've not gone mad cooped up as you are."

"Not until the weather is better," I said with regret. "It seems we omegas must only ride on fine days, lest our hair becomes wet and our appearance ruined by the wind."

"I expect you would look brilliant in any weather," said

Mr Jones as he took my hand and held it a little longer than was strictly necessary.

I murmured my hope that they had a pleasant if damp ride. Dammit. What was this place doing to me, that I must act like a girl just out of the schoolroom? That I bit my tongue around alphas I knew I could tie up in knots with my words! I could not pick the problem apart and it was no gorgon knot to take a sharp blade to. Dammit.

But now I had something to think on—The Duke of Orley and his votes. They called him the Parson because he was a vegetarian, teetotaller, and seemed allergic to gambling. That being said, he was a noted sportsman—or at least that is what Iris had let slip one afternoon after watching him box at Jackson's some weeks before our conversation about the bill. Iris didn't practice the Fancy but had gone along to watch a bout between the duke and the war hero Colonel Jack Fordom. The duke had won, but it had been a near thing. The crowd had declared the bout would be remembered one hundred years from now.

"He's a bruiser and ugly," she'd reported. "But there is something about him that commands the room, and it don't have anything to do with his title, for he doesn't throw that around. Wouldn't have known it was him if our uncle hadn't pointed him out."

I'd no interest in boxing or the duke until I knew that he had votes for the taking. My mind tripped along as I began a new letter to Mama. Within a fortnight, I had her reply.

My darling Viola,

I am pleased to hear from you and that you are no longer in a murderous rage at the modiste for making your dress too much in the modern style. It is not her fault you have long legs and that current fashions make you look taller. If you chose to wear men's clothes, I would not stop you. Beatrice does.

I rolled my eyes. I liked wearing dresses. They were often the only things that made people remember I was an omega. Compared to most omegas I was a giant, matching the height of a tall beta woman. It was not fair. Everyone had expected both Iris and me to be alphas, especially when I did not have my first heat until I was sixteen. Instead, I'd presented as an omega, and felt awkward in a body that did not match my dynamic's ideal.

As for Orley, there isn't much to tell. I never knew his parents. We were already in Edinburgh. However, his grandmother was a fixture in society her whole life. She raised him. Dearest, I would not, however, approach him about votes. Viola, consider your own feelings if he refused to see you. Consider that going too far...

I crumpled up the letter and tossed it over my shoulder. She meant well. I looked to where it had landed on the floor, then rose and smoothed the page.

Consider that going too far, rushing your fences, will do nothing but frustrate you. Instead, perhaps find other alphas who are more out in society and easier to approach. Gloves off, Orley will not speak to a young, unknown omega about politics, nor would he like being bullied into doing what you want. Some tact, my dear, is what I recommend. Then...

I heaved a sigh and stuffed the letter into my desk drawer knowing I would only get frustrated as she urged me towards a different path. I'd honour my Mama's advice by not burning her letter as I desired.

While I tried to cool my temper, I absently traced my finger over the cover of the book of poetry I had found amongst my aunt's few books, and a plan began to form, designed to convince His Grace of Orley to support the bill.

The greatest hurdle: getting close to him. If I wished to approach him, I needed to hide my dynamic. Perhaps I'd take on Iris' identity, borrow her alpha scent by wearing her clothes. She would be in Oxford, and I in London. The duke did not know us, did not go out into society, so the disguise would be perfect. And I, as Viola, was not out. If he chose to go to a ball, I would not be there. Yes, it could be done.

Now to convince Iris.

The clock had just struck one in the morning when my twin returned to the house on Weymouth Street. Being rather the worse for drink made her susceptible to my plans. For when she was foxed, she loved to urge me along on my madder schemes—and this certainly was the maddest.

"Iris, when do you intend to return to Oxford?" I asked tugging off her form fitting coat.

"Oh, by Tuesday surely," she weaved a bit on her feet.

"Do not travel on Tuesday," I reminded her of our old nurse Samantha's distrust of Tuesdays, saying her granddaughter Trudie preached that the world would end on a Tuesday. We Hartwells took this apocalyptic warning to heart. Always reminding each other to put off decisions and actions rather than risk Tuesday's curse. After all, our father had died on a Tuesday.

"Then I'll return on Wednesday. What does this have to do with anything?"

"Let me borrow those clothes which no longer fit or which you plan on discarding as they are no longer in fashion? I'm bored to death here and won't be presented until the Spring. Then I will be invited to balls. I was thinking that dressed in the scent of an alpha I could at least slip into a few lectures at the academy. Perhaps even the gallery to watch Parliament? Watch the debate?"

"Do you promise that is all you intend to do, Vi?" she

asked as she struggled out of her shirt, which had caught on her hair.

"Of course not. But isn't it better that you know as little as possible? You know Mama would rather I do it dressed as an alpha instead of getting caught as an omega. I drink Queen Anne's Tea every morning to suppress my scent. Remember the scandal when Beatrice was caught submitting her paintings to the Summer Exhibition? She attempted that only wearing men's clothes without the protection of an alpha's scent. And that is how they caught her... Her heat... But never mind that for mine isn't until June."

"I wish you wouldn't call it a scandal. You know that she and Hippolyta do it purposefully. Just to create the—Fine. The scandal."

"I do not intend to create a scandal. The opposite in fact."

She grabbed my chin and turned my face to the light of the single candle in the room.

"Vi, you are my twin. I shall back you in any plan you might have, but you are an omega nearly twenty. That changes things. Your choosing to dress in a man's clothes is one thing. But doing so and stealing an alpha's scent? That is dangerous. Possibly illegal, if you are caught in the wrong place. Until we can change the laws of the land, you are still at risk without a spouse or mate bond. I want everything for you. Not just for you and our sisters to have all the same rights as an alpha, but also to find a good and loving mate as our parents had. There could be nothing more beautiful than that. Mates working towards the same goal. Doing this? You might jeopardise that beyond saving."

"I hate it," I whispered and wiped an errant tear away. Anger drew forth tears more often than sorrow. "How can the world be so unfair?"

"Don't tell me you regret being an omega?" she asked

softly. Our father's death had hurt us all, but there were times when I thought Iris missed him the most.

"Never! It is an honour to carry on our father's legacy! I just wish I could do more."

"You were born in the wrong time, sister. Very well, take my clothes. I'll send you more and leave what things I can to let you hide your scent. But let our uncle know. I've a fear you plan on entering one of the clubs? Have a friend in the clubs and you might be saved. But, Vi, don't tell me more. I'd rather not know. I'm still an alpha. The impulse to protect you is deep and strong. So it will be with a mate. Be warned. You will not be able to manipulate another alpha so easily."

"Iris!" I threw my arms around her. "Thank you. I promise you will be proud. You won't have to worry!"

She rolled her eyes, she knew better than to take me at my word.

I waited until the evening after Iris had returned to Oxford to approach our uncle. It was a rare occasion to find him in his study, for he avoided omegas like we were the plague. I entered on his command and was struck by how different he looked here than when I saw him with my aunt. In command and relaxed. While my aunt presented a picture of omega beauty, my uncle's height wasn't balanced with any of the usual bulk you found on most alphas. When they stood next to each other, he appeared lacking. But sitting in his sanctuary, he looked like a king on his throne. His hair was thinning, and brushed back in an attempt to give it more coverage, but his clothes were well cared for. He might not have the fortune to support his wife in the style she had been born into but he clearly went to one of the better tailors in town.

"Viola, I should warn you that I've already spoken with Iris," he began before I'd the chance to speak.

"Yes, sir."

"Sit please."

I sat in one of the stiff-backed chairs in front of his desk. As he leant forward I couldn't help crushing my skirts in my hands. I so rarely felt like an omega in all our physical limitations but I did now. I knew he could arrange it that I could not leave this house. I believed he would not, but alphas had that power. That *legal* power.

"Straighten your back. If you plan on pulling off this mad scheme of yours, then you'd better stop cowering like an omega when an alpha projects any anger."

"I hate it," I hissed. My anger all towards myself. In stiff increments, I sat up and met his eyes head on.

"I cannot imagine what it feels like," he leant back into his chair, all aggression vanished. In its place, there was a teasing, but not unkind, smile fluttering about his lips. "But I suspect that if you have even a quarter of your father's spark and intelligence, you'll set His Grace on the back foot."

"You'll help me? How'd you know about the duke?"

"Yes, but only if you follow my instructions," he said. "And your mother wrote that you'd asked about the duke's politics. The connection was easy to make."

"Oh," I slumped back. Then straightened once again into the correct posture my father had taught me from the moment I could balance a book on my head. This would be how I must be from now on. No cowering before an alpha. No folding in on myself and making myself smaller, less of a target.

"I think we will work on your posture. You are now too stiff. No young alpha would have a problem slouching and lounging about. Sure, you must act quick and respectful with the older alphas, but don't worry about the formalities all the time. We are alphas after all."

"I won't succeed, will I?" I slouched in defeat.

"You will. With my help," he chuckled. "And so long as you never remove your clothes in front of anyone... You'll not be able to fake a mate stain."

He was right. Other than a bark, which I could (perhaps) fake, alphas possessed a unique to each alpha port-coloured mark, called a mate stain, on their body that appeared when they presented. Of course, male alpha's developed their knot, and females of the dynamic a tie, but there'd be no reason I'd ever be in a position for some to see if I had a tie or not.

"Why are you helping me?" I wondered aloud. My plans were dangerous, they could jeopardise his career.

"Why boredom, my dear. I suffer from boredom. I suspect you do as well. Now, first. I shan't be introducing you at the clubs. He don't visit them so you have little chance of meeting him there. Rather, you will apply to be the duke's new secretary—I hear he requires one. He'll take you on if I put you forward."

"I—"

"More to the point, I desire to help you catch his heart. He will be a difficult man to influence, even more so because he is an alpha without much interest in politics. However, he is ripe for the picking, as his politics are without any real direction. Confronting him where he is most at ease will help your suit. Once you've captured his heart, you'll make a good political wife and mate. We could use one like you if we're to gather support for our proposed reforms. To have the Duke and Duchess of Orley would be a great coup for the opposition."

"I don't want to win his heart!" I gasped, horrified that he would think I had romance in mind. Then again, as an alpha, perhaps he could not imagine my ambition to be more than the base sexual congress between an alpha and omega. "I have never laid eyes on him and had not considered meeting him until I learnt he was in town and had the votes we needed to pass the Omega Property Rights Act."

"Just politics then?" his eyes sparkled as if he didn't believe me.

I gaped at him in shock. "Of course! What else? He has the votes we need. If I can just get close, within his orbit, then I can do it. I can convince him. I am not a broodmare for breeding the next generation of alphas."

"No, my dear, omegas aren't broodmares. But remember that doesn't change the fact. You are an omega, and he is an alpha. Spend too much time around Orley... Things might change."

I shook my head. My uncle underestimated my ability to ignore alphas and their supposedly natural power over omegas.

3

SYON

I was a bear in a cage anytime I was required to be in London.

The food bland, the people lazy and content to spend their time locked inside their cramped rooms rather than risk the refreshingly brisk winter wind. Yet here I was, the house draped in black crepe, the knocker off the door to let everyone know visitors were not welcome. I was in mourning for my grandmother. My last blood relative of any importance was dead.

My grandmother, the dowager duchess of Orley was dead. Dead. I'd yet to accept that. Killed at the age of eighty by, in her words, a trifling cold. No figure in my life loomed quite so large as she. There might be alphas who had no respect for the abilities of omegas to manage—and manage well—estates as great as ours, but she had until I was old enough to take up the reins. My grandfather had died before I was born. After his death, my father obsessed over my mother's indiscretions rather than instruct his heir or look after the estates. So it was my grandmother, her three alpha mates, and Lord John, my grandfather's omega mate, who'd raised me. But their pack was gone. My grandmother's mates died in a yachting accident. And Lord John, the man who had given me my first pony, had only died three years ago.

Now I was alone.

And who was I but the Duke of Orley, named Syon at my grandmother's insistence. But no one had called me that in almost twenty years. Not since my father had killed himself over my mother's so-called honour not long after my eighth birthday. It had been Orley ever since. I almost forgot the sound of my name unless I spoke it out loud.

"Syon," I whispered into the silence.

The loss of my grandmother created a dull hollowness in my chest. As the only living member of my family, as the woman who'd raised me when my own mother had fled the country with some German prince... Yes, I missed my grandmother far more than the omega who'd given birth to me. Her firmness and straight speaking. She'd never hidden the scandals attached to the name Orley. Not my parents' disastrous mating and marriage that had my father blowing his brains out when his mate eloped with another man. Nor my grandparents' own scandal—the duke and duchess of Orley not mating had been the *on dit de jour*—which had blossomed into a happy pack full of laughter and love. There were other scandals, but the last two generations had impressed upon me that a happy life meant not making my wife, the mother of my heirs, my mate—at least not right away. We could find emotional satisfaction elsewhere so long as we followed my grandparents' example. Passion and instinct could and should be put aside.

I would find a woman to marry and give me heirs, but not mate her. She could find mates, lovers, whatever she chose after an alpha child had been born. I would have the same freedom. I'd even allow mating if either of us chose to mate the same sex before the child was born. So long as everyone knew that the child was mine, I was not concerned with our sleeping arrangements.

"Damn you, grandmother," I laughed as I looked over the letter she'd written me on her death bed. Of all the letters she'd penned the one to her beloved grandson was the shortest, barely covering a single sheet. Others were thick packets, double-crossed in her tiny, precise handwriting.

Orley,

> *Marry now. Find a wife. An omega and a woman, for a man will not be able to give you an heir. I'm forever grateful that John had a hand in the raising of you. It made him very happy, though I am sure he never breathed a word of it to you. Let her be beautiful, for my sake, as I do not wish for a fish to have her portrait hung next to mine. Let her be cheerful, for yours. You smile so rarely and that is not good for procreation. For her sake and yours, do not mate her until you both know it is the correct decision. My marriage was happy because Orley and I looked elsewhere for love, for mates. Your father was not so wise. He married that woman and mated her. She brought him to the brink of madness with her dalliances. I blame her for his death. Thankfully the bitch is dead. But she gave me you so I cannot hate her.*

> *But, beloved grandson and most excellent duke, think of your duchess as a wife and not a mate. At least not until you are sure of your mutual happiness, which I wish for more than life itself.*

> *DDoO*

> *P.S. I've instructed my goddaughter, Cordelia Markham, to call on you. I believe she can help you to find an appropriate omega.*

Her voice came through in her letter. This was the woman I'd lost, and my heart ached for the first time since I'd heard of her death.

Now all that mattered was to find some omega to marry. An

weaker dynamic. How could I, when I did not seem to register the small gathering of slick she felt between her thighs? And she, a mated widow nearing fifty! I suppressed a chuckle. If only she knew. I could not smell her or her slick even if I was within arms reach. But I could read people and her face told me everything I had no interest in.

My dispassion would have scandalised many omegas, for what omega did not want an alpha to respond to them? I had noticed her attraction the moment she entered—flushed cheeks and fluttering fingers over a thin mouth spoke as loudly as scent. And I gave the matron credit. Her beauty had matured, not faded. Her fair hair still glistened in the afternoon sun. In all, if I had been so inclined, she would be just such a woman an unmated alpha might dally with—the wild passion of her heats would not be so severe and as she had been mated there would be no worries that she would form ideas for the future. But I was not so inclined. Once I had made my mind, I did not waver or become distracted as a weaker man might. No, I ran towards my goal with the singular determination of my dynamic. My goal was a wife, not some affair with an omega, who so easily wilted at the sight of a powerful alpha.

"Your Grace," she murmured and dropped a submissive curtsy as if she'd not curtsied a few minutes before. I nodded and indicated she should take a seat on any one of the chairs littering the space.

"I require your help," I said, still standing, curious to see how she'd respond to my request.

"Your Grace?"

"I look for a wife. Omega, of course. Let me be clear, a wife. I shan't take a husband as I marry not for love but an heir. Perhaps I will take a mate, but for now, I'm not interested in that. I am not out in society much so don't know the current market. I'd like you to bring me a few names. I'll look them over and pick one."

"Your Grace?"

"D'you have any other words than 'Your Grace'? If not, then get out of my sight and I'll find another. I don't need a simpleton to help—"

"Your Grace!" Mrs Markham flushed a deep red. My lips twitched, I'd angered the omega—for that was anger, not arousal, colouring her cheeks. "I object to being called simple."

"Simpleton," I couldn't help but correct her.

"Simpleton, not that it makes a difference." She surprised me with a soft laugh. "I am shocked by your request and did not know how to respond in a civil manner."

I took pity on her. "I'm not civil. But I don't see why it'd make you uncomfortable. I'm sure my grandmother had some thoughts on the matter, even if she didn't draw up a list for my... edification."

"Nevertheless! Please forgive me, but, to take on such a task! You are still in mourning."

"You think I've forgotten? If I'd the time, I'd look myself. I want to get this managed quickly. There is nothing in the law—" I bit off the last for I did not like the fact I was defending my actions to a mere omega with no connection to me but she'd been my grandmother's goddaughter.

"And you expect her to take on the role of Duchess immediately?" she asked, her eyes going from subservient to assessing. I repressed a grin. I would need to watch her like a hawk which I should have expected of my grandmother's goddaughter.

"Obviously. Some help can be given by Mrs Danvers, the housekeeper. But she cannot be insipid or without a brain between her pretty ears. My grandmother requested no fish."

She choked. "That is a... It is a lot of to expect of a debutante."

I smiled. "I don't want a child. Just a wife. What could be more simple? What omega wouldn't want to be a duchess? Bring a list of candidates within a week. Exactly at the day and hour we were expected to meet. That will be all, I think. Happy hunting, Mrs Markham."

Her jaw clenched briefly and her curtsy was decidedly rigid. I liked her. She would find me the right wife.

"I'll take you to your carriage," I ushered her out, suddenly feeling very jolly. "I'm headed out myself. I'd planned to ride, as you can see. But had to send my horse back to the stable. No matter. I'll go to Jacksons and practice the Fancy. I feel like putting my fist into something."

"I am afraid I don't have the same joy in blood sports that you do."

"Not for lack of wanting to punch an alpha or two in your time..."

My sally earned me a twitch of a smile.

A WEEK WENT BY IN THAT MANNER WHEN THE HOURS SEEM to stretch for an eternity and the days flash by in a blink of the eye. I had both remembered and forgotten to expect Mrs Markham. So it caught me off guard when Horne came to me with the news that she had arrived with her daughter. I'd cursed all omegas for their unfortunate timing as I'd been on the brink of going for a ride. But it could not be helped. I had asked Mrs Markham to find some appropriate omegas. Of a sudden, I remembered a meal with my grandmother in my youth. We'd been at Ayleigh, and I about to go off to university. "Marry for the future, as we did in my day. And if you meet someone else? Well, Shakesperia said that music be the food of love, play on." Such was her careless way of giving good advice.

"The Drawing Room?" I asked with some asperity.

"As Your Grace says."

I did not waste time, for I wanted this meeting over with so that I could get on with my day. I hoped it would pass quickly. I cursed under my breath. Damn all omegas, except my sainted grandmother.

"I bring you news, Your Grace," Mrs Markham said with a hasty curtsy as I entered. Today she was dressed more extravagantly as if she had put aside plans to meet me. She'd brought her daughter, a plain beta called Hero. An odd name for an odd almost bird-like child who fidgeted with her pelisse as if unused to wearing such a fine garment.

"Here is a list."

I took the paper from her and glanced over the surprisingly long list.

The Hon Miss Divinia Cole
   Miss Arabella Smith
   Lady Olivia Clare, widowed Countess of Kellingham

I stopped after the third name and frowned at what I saw. "Tell me what you know of Lady Clare, Kellingham's widow. I am surprised to see a widow on the list."

"Lady Olivia Clare, wife of Lord Augustus Clare," she said without hesitation. "They were unmated. He died without any heirs. I thought perhaps an older omega since you expect her to begin her duties right away."

"Is she pretty?"

"Very. And a good woman."

"How do you know she ain't barren?" That was the relevant question, however crude.

"The late Earl had no natural children," she replied her

cheeks darkening with embarrassment. Then with a boldness that came through on occasion: "He left her to a terrible fate. Six years of marriage and never mated her during a marital heat."

"I sense you have more to say," I growled, unafraid to exert my alpha dominance on her. "Is she out of mourning?"

"Not yet... But... She has declared she will not marry again. That is to say, she will not suffer men or alphas to be near her except the alpha daughter of her vicar who acts as her temporary guardian. I suspect that perhaps Lord Clare was not kind to her."

"Lord Clare's past behaviour has no bearing on my suit." I tried and failed to keep the bite out of my words. Now that I knew her fate—that she would be left without a penny to pinch, if the widow of an earl knew how to pinch pennies—I had irrationally, against all logic, decided that I would marry her. I would play the hero to her distressed damsel.

"Your Grace! She needs care!"

"Madam, the widow will be thrown out of her home when her period of mourning ends. She will not be cared for by some alpha children. She will be a pauper. Not many alphas, regardless of circumstances, will have the means to pay the Omega Fee for a Countess. Do you think she has a better option than the one I can give her?"

I crossed my legs and glared at the omega perched on the very edge of the sofa in front of me. I could sense she was beginning to fret. If she'd had a good mate, the alpha would have taken her aside and calmed her. But instead I, Syon Duke of Orley, was left to deal with the fidgeting hands that crushed her gown in a most unbecoming manner. She agreed even as she threw a distressed look to her silent beta daughter.

"Then find a way for me to meet and woo her. When she hears my suit, she'd be a fool to refuse."

"Yes, Your Grace," came in a whisper.

"Keep me informed," I concluded our discourse as abruptly as I had the first meeting.

"Your Grace, if I may? I hope you realise that choosing a wife is not the same as buying a horse."

"No, madam. I choose my bride because of what I can do for Lady Clare. I buy a horse because of what he can do for me. Just because I will mount both doesn't mean I value them the same."

"Then may I say you are riding for a fall."

"Touché, Mrs Markham."

She rose and left with a haughtier bearing than she began our meeting with, her daughter trailing behind her. The little beta glanced over her shoulder before following her mother out the door.

"Good day, your Grace," she breathed so softly I nearly missed it.

I slumped against the window, my eyes tracking the carriage carrying Mrs Markham as it left. If only there were a cousin to take my place. But there were none. Like the late earl, I had no alpha bastards or cousins with any claim to the title. I must go through with this farce if I wanted the dukedom to survive and after twenty years the duke, I took pride in the title. Pride in everything that surrounded me. Moreover, should I die without an heir, my tenants, servants, the people who depended upon me would find themselves at sea with no guarantees to their future.

Shakespearia had it right, "Uneasy lies the head that wears the crown."

4

VIOLA

One particularly mild day, a new neighbour of my aunt's, the recently widowed Mrs Markham, arrived in such a havoc of omega pheromones that I nearly choked on the too sweet scent. Her beta daughter, Hero, trailed behind her. The girl was eighteen with blonde ringlets tied back with a blue ribbon and the largest blue eyes I'd ever seen. I'd never heard her talk above a whisper, but how could she, when her mother possessed such a dominating personality?

"Well, what is this?" my aunt asked, her wrinkled nose demonstrating her vexation at the other omega's bad manners for flooding the drawing room with her scent. I crossed to the window and cracked it open to thin out the overwhelming mix of omega florals.

"You'll never believe what I've become a part of!" the matron sighed dramatically full of news and busting to share it with us. But there was something tinny in her voice that made me uneasy. She'd not paid this morning call to innocently gossip. There was a method in her madness that I wanted no part of.

"Of course I won't know whether to believe it or not until you tell me, my dear Mrs Markham!" my aunt put her embroidery hoop down in an exasperated manner, her good mood vanishing in the instant.

"La, my dear Mrs Florey, you might not even believe when I tell you. Come, for what I have to say... Oh, it is shocking. His Grace the Duke of Orley tasked me with finding him an omega bride."

"But why?" I asked, surprised to hear that the reclusive duke would advertise his intentions so publicly. More shocking that she would share the information with us. Of course, he held the balance for the bill and strangely I wanted to hear more of him and his plans. Everything would help.

"The late Dowager Duchess was my godmother, for remember I used to be the very beautiful The Honourable Miss Constance Field! But the Duke! He sees it to be his duty to provide himself with an heir. Naturally, she must be an omega and of exceptionable beauty and breeding. And a woman to give him heirs," her gaze turned to me. I did not like that look, as if she hoped to provoke me to utter some indiscreet remark.

"That surely is not so great a challenge. There are many such ladies and all happy to become a duchess." My aunt had no interest in the to-ings and fro-ings of those outside of her immediate circle. In that, we had found a kinship. I had grown grateful for the discovery over the past half year, for she had no interest in dragging me to pay morning calls or introduce me to what eligible alphas resided in town when Parliament was in session. My mind might be bored, but I didn't have to listen to aimless omega gossip or learn to flirt.

"Oh, that is not the half of it! He does not wish to mate his wife," Mrs Markham threw another sly glance in my direction. She had some plot, and instinct told me to be alive to any schemes she might have. Why she might be interested in *my* opinion on the matter bewildered me. Something strange passed over her face and she tilted her head to the side as if she was a bird considering a worm. "Miss Viola, what are your thoughts?"

Why did she stare so? Did she seek to put me out of countenance, so that I might utter some indiscretion? I mimicked her tilted head. I was as much a bird of prey as she. "The duke may do as he will—what alpha doesn't?—, but I pity his future wife. She shall be denied the protection of a mate bond. And what if either of them finds a mate? Will it lead to divorce or will he take a mate on the side? Will she be left 'Duchess' in name only? For a mate will always take precedence over a mere spouse. She'll be a womb to him."

I bit my lip. I'd revealed far more than I'd intended. Dammit! If I wanted the duke's votes then I'd best stamp down on my desire to flay him alive. Not mate his wife? Oh, it made my blood boil.

"Would you like to know who he chose?" she leant forward as she asked the question. Her eyes cunning and assessing.

"What? Like a pair of new boots?" I scoffed.

"He compared it to buying a horse. The widowed Countess of Kellingham shall be his bride."

"Oh? I do not know her." A bald-faced lie. Though I hadn't the pleasure of her acquaintance, she had been the subject of Beatrice's scandalous paintings. I knew her story as well as I knew my alphabet. Words had not formed but the basics were there.

"No, you would not," she said not unkindly. It was not my fault that I had yet to suffer the indignity of being presented at Court. "But know this, the Earl's line ended with him. The properties returned to the crown, and the widow friendless because she was a wife and not a mate."

Nothing I did not already know, but hearing it spoken out loud ignited my anger on the widow's behalf.

"The Earl had no alpha relatives?" I asked—oh, how I hated pretending an ignorance to the world around me! How I longed to just speak my mind, be unashamed of my knowledge.

"None, and no natural children either. I understand the duke will marry Lady Clare, breed her in her next heat then leave her to raise the children. What a life for her to live! Don't you think, Miss Hartwell? An omega such as her? Truly blessed to go from Miss to Countess to Duchess so easily!"

Every instinct in me, every principle I held near to my heart, revolted at the thought of this poor omega subjected to the indignity of becoming a mere womb to a powerful alpha who had no care for her well-being or her future should he die, leaving her without the protection of either a mate bond or the guarantee of an alpha child. What would happen if she gave this duke omegas or betas? Would he mate-bond another woman, in hopes of finding heirs? It turned my stomach. I pressed my lips together in a valiant effort to keep my feelings in check. Was Mrs Markham taunting me? Daring me to say something indiscreet, more indiscreet than I had been earlier. No, I would not do it. "You will excuse me. I have a headache."

I crossed to the door but had not left before hearing my aunt, her omega sweet voice carrying easily to my ears. "I thought the Countess was refusing to entertain another marriage or to spend time with any alphas?"

I snorted. Her tune would change once she discovered herself the object of a duke's interest. Perhaps that was uncharitable, but omegas could no more resist the pull of a virile alpha as a virile alpha could resist us. Our natures worked against us with every breath we took. My jaw ached with how tight I clenched it. I needed Orley's support for the bill. I loathed the thought of interacting with an alpha who would not see past his own needs for an heir.

OMEGAS—OH, VERY WELL, TO BE SPECIFIC, AS MY PAPA would wish, that great omega poetess Shakespearia (for Charles Hartwell subscribed to the belief that such a way with words could only come from an omega)—say that "the apparel oft proclaims the alpha." Those words, from her play Hamlet, are said with uncomfortable honesty by the beta Polonius to his alpha son, who is about to return to the French Court. For while the speech is full of ridiculous maxims that set one and another off, at the heart of the plea there is some truth that cannot be denied. While betas must keep themselves muted in the world, alphas have quite the opposite pull. They are a dynamic that must wear their strength and position in society openly. They must posture and parade around to maintain their standing. Were I to be asked in a more serious moment I should say I pity them for that. Peacocking to prove yourself seems like an exhausting way to spend one's time, and as I looked down on the clothes Iris had left me, I considered how lonely the lives of alphas might be. I knew she wore men's fashions to assert herself as a female alpha. She struggled more than our mother because she was slight, small compared to other female alphas. Dominance was the game they sought to play. It sparked a feeling of sympathy for this unknown duke I was determined to influence. In offering marriage to the countess he only did what he thought necessary, what his dynamic and position in society demanded of him. No different from an omega's assumed desire to raise children and nurture those around them. I brushed the feelings aside. What point to project any of those concerns onto someone

I'd never met? One who seemed to lack any natural passions or desires.

Once again steeled by unwavering purpose, I removed the simple gown I wore and thanked my dear Mama for having no interest or time for fashion. I could not think of a single garment I wore—including the front lacing stays—that I could not dress myself in. My trick would be better protected without the need for a maidservant to lace me in or help fit into the fashionable gowns the way my aunt required. Much less dress me in the masculine fashions. My women's weeds might be out of date, but what did that matter? I could not see the need to create such a vision when my work was that much more important. Best keep it simple.

I stood in my room, skin covered with goose pimples, and looked at myself in the long mirror. They were a popular necessity in the rooms of every fashionable omega and revealed every imperfection I suffered—at least according to the current standards of beauty. My hair was nearly black, and I stood almost tall in my stockinged feet. The height of a beta woman, certainly, and not the petite diminutive omegas that the portraitists of the day sought for their models. But such was the lot of omegas and alphas born to the unusual pairing of omega men to alpha women. I could better get away with my ruse as a smaller alpha—especially when it was known who my parents were. Still, Iris's clothes were a smidge too big for me, and I had laboured over altering them to better fit my smaller frame. I could not thank the fashions of the day for they were no help in concealing my hips, which flared in the way every woman would wish. I hoped that it would not be remarked on for my height and build were of greater import. The final touches were to hide my scent by using all the products alphas preferred. I had even purchased a box of perfumed snuff, which I could pretend to take and would help in my goal to disguise my own scent. Most importantly, I must refrain from too strenuous exercise and bathe in lemon water. For this first attempt at pretending to be an alpha, I decided to forgo wearing Iris's unwashed shirts that would do the most to mask my scent. As her twin, I could not even notice the smell the way another alpha or omega could. To my nose, they smelt unpleasantly unwashed, but a necessary evil. Pulling my hair back into a club tied with velvet ribbon, I descended to the drawing room where my uncle waited for me along with his beta valet and butler who had both been brought in to my charade—though the reason they were given for it in no way touched on my true motives.

I entered, as my uncle had instructed, without the usual knock gently bred omegas were trained to give whenever they entered a room. Pushing the door open and allowing it to bounce on its hinges, I strode in.

"Good, you are dressed for riding," was the first thing my uncle said. He stood by the fire also dressed for riding, one booted foot resting on the grate. "Your aunt feels unwell, so you'll be with me tonight. Wear your sister's puce satin. I will introduce you to some friends of mine. They were also friends of your parents and will keep your secret. And think it a good joke if you are discovered."

"Sir, that is too much of a risk!" I exclaimed. What I planned was dangerous. A fact I was increasingly aware of now that I stood dressed like this in front of an alpha and two betas.

"We must test you amongst unfamiliar alphas. How many have you met?"

I clenched my teeth, accepting that he was correct.

"Let me see. Turn for me, young mistress." Drews, my uncle's valet, pursed his lips together.

My cheeks heated but I did as he asked. "I feel... I mean I've worn men's clothing but not for many months."

"You've done well. Though if you must go into society, permit me to have the tying of your cravat?"

The tension broke and I found myself smiling. I had no notion of whether this would work or not. But for the first time I knew, amongst these men, my dynamic didn't matter. The greatest complaint to be had was merely the tying of my cravat. "I would be honoured, Drews."

From the drawing room, I found myself on horseback riding my favourite grey filly through the streets of London and learning the mode of greeting the dynamics as an alpha. We did not stop to speak but moved on with a nod. My task was to observe the niceties of alpha behaviour and by the time we returned to the narrow, not quite fashionable house on Weymouth Street, I was exhausted from the experience. As we dismounted, Mrs Markham came out of her house across the street.

Following my uncle's lead, I smiled and doffed my hat. "Mrs Markham. Good day to you."

"Iris Hartwell! And I thought you had returned to Oxford. Have they sent you down? Your Mama and sisters will be most displeased if you do not complete your degree."

"Fear not, no Hartwell would ever be sent down from Oxford," I jested. "Some business recalled me to town unexpectedly."

"Well, I am glad to hear that you plan on honouring your parents. Is Miss Viola at home? I had hoped to ask her to sit for a portrait," her smile sly and eyes seeing more than I would wish.

I flushed realising that she meant me! Though why she would want to paint me was a mystery.

"I did not know you painted," I looked to my uncle uncertain how to proceed.

"Oh, an amateur to be sure. Nothing like your eldest sister."

"Viola will be pleased to sit for you, I am sure," he told her. "I do, however, believe that she is out with my mate. I am sure Iris can pass the message along."

The omega's eyes turned to mine. I bowed, hoping that she did not catch sight of my unusual eyes, for if there was one thing that could destroy all my plans, it would be those violet orbs which betrayed me more readily than the clothes I wore or the dynamic I pretended to be.

"YOU WILL NEED TO KEEP YOUR WITS ABOUT YOU," my uncle said as we took a carriage to St James' a few hours later. I didn't need to be told that. I was about to walk into one of the exclusive Alpha only clubs. Iris was not yet a member, but my Mama was, and she had plans to put her forward when she'd finished at Oxford. My uncle, however, saw nothing wrong with bringing me along earlier in the evening before things became wild.

"If I tell you, leave," he muttered as we passed through the doors.

Though projecting a young alpha's easy confidence, I had never been more terrified. What good would *wits* do me if my nature betrayed me? I had chosen the shirt that had the strongest smell and had anointed myself with oils intended to mimic an alpha's musk. But I had not expected my own physiological response. I felt almost faint with the pheromones that lay stagnant in the rooms we passed through until we reached the relative privacy of a small library where my uncle had invited some friends for cards.

"What's here? Do you bring a stripling with you? What for?" asked an alpha with a florid complexion and poorly powered hair. His name was Marshall and a member of Parliament aligned with the liberal, Whig opposition, as my uncle was.

"The girl had some business in town... A trip to the tailor. Can't have her look like a provincial," my uncle gave a disapproving but amused shake of his head. The more I saw of him, the less he was the man I'd grown up knowing. Was this relaxed and bantering man the same one who sneered at his wife and mate?

"Well, child. You are Hartwell's get?" the lone female alpha smiled. She was dressed in the height of feminine fashion with her pale blonde powdered to perfection. Tall and willowy, I saw the same traits in this woman as my own Mama. The easy, almost lazy power that infused every one of her words and actions. Would Iris be like that? Would I look at my twin and feel this unpleasant instinct to defer to her?

"Viscountess Gale, cub," my uncle prompted me, and I bowed as was required.

"That is what they tell me," I kept my tone light, comfortable. "I admit I'm finding town..."

"Overwhelming. And the club too, no doubt," she laughed. The others joined in. But they did not laugh at me. It was sympathetic, which I had never expected. "Yes, so many grown alphas in one place can bring out the rougher side of us. Best go home before the pack becomes too wild. You won't want to provoke one of them."

"Them?" I cocked my head to the side and felt a bantering ease infuse my being.

"The ones who hunt down those wet behind the ears. Greenhorns who are easy pickings. Besides, once it gets out who your parents are—"

"I'm not ashamed of my parents," I snapped. The words were out and an uneasy silence hung in the air. I was caught, I realised. No young dynamic would dare challenge—and so openly—mature alphas and powerful members of the aristocracy to boot. They would come for me and discover what I had so recklessly dared to do. "I—"

Another alpha, much older and in a chair close to the door began clapping. "Well said, pup. I thought you might be a weakling given your size but seems you have teeth and ain't afraid to bark. You are among friends here, fear not. Your parents are well respected in our circle, no need to feel shame."

"I challenge anyone who throws... It won't matter who, I will challenge them," I found myself—once again!—talking over an alpha. I didn't know what to think and feared for a minute that my heat was upon me called forth by over-whelming alpha pheromones. Heats were one of the few times omegas became aggressive with alphas. If my heat came here, my uncle would not be able to protect me. With so many alphas about there would be a riot. I would be raped by whichever alpha had conquered the others. There would be no other outcome. I might die in the chaos.

I took a deep breath, I needed to leave.

The others must have noticed something. Pray let it not be my omega's scent!

"And how," growled a new alpha who stood in the door. "How would you propose to do that, little alpha?"

He was handsome with sharp grey eyes and a full mouth. Though now it twisted unpleasantly. No denying it. I felt a small part of me, the omega that I hated in moments like this, weaken towards this darkly brooding alpha. I looked to my uncle hoping for some guidance but his face was still watching the new alpha who was easily the tallest in the room.

"The duello," I managed to get out, more intimidated by this alpha than the others. He was dangerous. Controlling. Dark. Powerful. "I am accounted good with a sword."

"It wouldn't be your choice," the interloper pointed out.

The other alphas stayed quiet. At first, I thought it was out of fear of this alpha dressed in a suit of rich grey velvet and a short sword at his side.

"Pistols then. It matters not."

The viscountess snickered. "You are put into a difficult spot by young Hartwell. Do you, do any of us, challenge such confidence from such a diminutive firecracker?"

"Faith! To think to have that spark when I was her age," the old alpha laughed. "Paxton, you are well taught. Prick the cub and it bites. Girl, come. This here is Lord Paxton and no enemy."

"I've heard of you," I admitted like a fumbling schoolgirl reprimanded for getting a lesson wrong. "Luciano told me you were a student of his. That it would be a success to have a hand as sure as yours."

"Pretty words. But I hardly believe that you have danced with the master," Lord Paxton smirked, his eyes narrowing. He was an alpha of shining, cold silver—I could not imagine anyone meeting him and not coming out the worse.

"He retired to... He retired to Hertfordshire and was our neighbour. I have danced with him. As have all my sisters," I refused to back down especially given my audience.

"Of course! Hartwell!" He threw up his hands as if coming to some profound realisation. "How could I forget that Beatrice Hartwell is your sister?"

That seemed hard to believe for despite the differences in our colouring and stature we looked like sisters. Had he therefore sought me out, sought to antagonise me because of Beatrice?

"Speak with that tone about my sister again, and I shall take offence."

He stood head and shoulders above me, but, in the heat of the moment, that was nothing. My family, my omega sisters we had all worked hard to be more than the weak dynamic we were seen as. "Beatrice on her worst day would be able to take you with swords or pistols."

Lord Paxton's eyes widened. Beatrice was the most omega of my sisters. Feminine in both form and face. Put a rapier in her hand? She could and would go up against the strongest alpha. With pistols, she was even more deadly, for that required less strength or stamina.

"Stand down, stripling. Paxton meant no harm. Isn't that so?" Viscountess Gale invested her words with enough bark to remind us all who the top dog in this room was.

"I meant no offence," he gritted out. "Your sister... The lady is singular."

"I don't like the sound of that." This time it was my uncle. I looked over my shoulder at the alphas who now stood at my back.

"Fine, I'll back down. An old pack growling over an omega—"

I lunged.

But a firm hand on my collar prevented me from tackling the alpha who seemed to have a death wish when it came to my sister.

"Paxton, go now before I release the pup on you. You'd deserve—"

"Pass on my compliments to your sister. She is a fine woman."

I locked eyes with Paxton and something almost like regret flashed across his face. With a bitter smile, he bowed and walked off.

"That was reckless," the florid alpha holding my collar shook me as if I was a child. "But by damn, it did my old bones good to see one of his crowd back down. Well done, young Hartwell. Though keep that temper close and pray Paxton does not hold a grudge. He ain't one to be trifled with."

"He spoke of Beatrice!" I protested.

"You're like to hear worse. You've three pretty omega sisters. Alphas will be sniffing after them. By all means, protect them but do not challenge every alpha who chooses to test you," Gale said. No doubt a warning.

"DAMN!" I shouted, my frustration overcoming me.

A firm hand landed on my shoulder.

"Go home, Iris," my uncle urged me. I nodded, knowing I needed to get away from the persistent scent of alpha. Perhaps my mother was correct. Alpha scents at their strongest sparked aggression in omegas, no matter how close to a heat. I had learnt one thing in my short foray into a temple of alpha dominance: there was fire and anger, there was defiance in even the supposedly gentlest of dynamics.

I was lucky not to run into Lord Paxton as I walked through the rooms that had begun to fill. Making the street I turned the wrong way, hoping that by taking the longer route I could better cool my head. My confrontation at the club had shaken me. More than once I had been on the brink of exposing myself. The danger was immediate, and if I didn't control myself I would, I knew in my bones, risk losing my life.

THE INCIDENT AT THE CLUB RESULTED IN A BLISTERING lecture from my uncle the following morning. He claimed he would never take me to one of the London clubs again because he could not trust my temper. My temper! To imagine an alpha telling an omega they were too fierce. I did not know what to think and instead of arguing—for I knew I never wanted to go to an alpha club ever again—I turned my mind to learning how to be the most believable alpha. Everything from alpha-alpha friendships, to how to dance like an alpha, and any number of other details I might be expected to know. Most embarrassing was the need to learn how to react to an omega. How to puff out my chest and swagger. How to press up against a pitiable omega when one wanted their attention. It was both intriguing and alarming how little respect alphas seemed to have for omegas. How the propriety drilled into omegas from the moment they presented was so carelessly discarded by alphas, particularly male alphas whose arousal was considered not only acceptable but even a compliment! My uncle assured me that while these might be an alpha's instincts, civility and social mores were considered the hallmark of the best alphas. To even suggest that an alpha would lose control around an omega was madness, tantamount to the worst insult to that alpha's honour. Duels had been started for less. When I asked if my run-in with Lord Paxton qualified, I saw once again the amused man behind the dissatisfied facade. "Of course! Should anyone question your ability to defend an omega, remember that encounter. By the by, be glad to know that Paxton has not made a story of it. You are safe."

Which led to one thing that stood greatly in my favour. I had been trained in both fencing and shooting so if I found myself in the wrong—or more terrifying needing to call someone out in all seriousness!—at least I had some way to protect myself. But even with this assurance, and my uncle's promise to save me should the need arise, my stomach was full of butterflies. What if I was found out? What if the duke did not accept me as his secretary? What if he threw me out when I began to pressure him to change his politics?

More quickly than I would have liked, I found myself walking towards the Duke of Orley's London residence. With the help of Drews, I was dressed exactly as a young alpha who had aspirations for working as a secretary was meant to dress. In a pocket I held my letter of reference; in my heart, I told myself that what I was doing was right. I was ensuring omegas could own property and manage their own interests. If I saved an omega from a marriage that could only bring her misery, so much the better. My cause was just. My path? Yes, that was unsure. Every time I thought about how I would beat the odds.

I remembered playing chess. My next step was a gambit. A chance, a risk that had me sacrificing a pawn—my omega name and nature—in the hopes of winning the game.

So my first step into Orley House was full of false confidence.

5

SYON

The first impression of my new secretary—hired at the recommendation of Florey, who had approached me, begging that I take on his niece—was not good. She stood in the library door, by all appearance a poor excuse for an alpha, so young and small that I almost mistook her for a schoolgirl. But no child carried herself like that. A straight back and easy air, dark hair with beautiful violet coloured eyes. To be fair to the youth, she was of medium height, like a beta perhaps, with good shoulders and a bearing that exuded confidence. Then she moved, and I saw the secret to it all. A fencer, no doubt trained by one of the great instructors in an art increasingly less popular. Modern fashions favoured pistols, which took little skill and lacked the sheer power of a sabre in hand. When it came down to it, a quick foot and nimble wrist were as deadly as a long arm and strength. Perhaps when I knew her better, we could cross swords. Yes, the thought pleased me greatly. Even so soon upon meeting her, I wanted to bend this creature to my will.

"Come, girl," I beckoned her further into my sanctuary. I had no time to beat about the bush. My time was too valuable, and the need for a helping hand too great, for in recent years my eyesight had deteriorated. These days I struggled to keep up with my correspondence without suffering a headache. Not something I wished to broadcast, but which I must accept. "Why'd you want to work with me? Your uncle was keen to put you forward despite your youth and complete lack of experience."

"Because of my youth and lack of experience, Your Grace," she said, her voice light yet there was a husky quality. On an omega, it would have been pleasing. Instead, it only added to the small alpha's irregularities. "My father was Charles Hartwell. Perhaps you know him? If you do, then you know my family's politics. My chances of a career in politics..."

"Is that your aim, alpha Hartwell?" I asked. Yes, I knew of her family. Her mother was an alpha who could not but be respected and was currently attempting to establish diplomatic relations with the revolutionaries in France. Her father, well, even in death Charles Hartwell could not be ignored. Perhaps her omega father and alpha mother explained why this stripling was not as large as one might expect in an alpha, even a female one.

"Yes," she confirmed, folding her arms across her chest, her chin tilted as if she didn't appreciate my prying into her plans.

"And do my politics—"

"I believe in learning every position, Your Grace," she interrupted, with more coherence than I'd expected since she spoke through gritted teeth. The youth flushed and something inside of me responded to that flair of... What? Embarrassment that could so easily be mistaken for arousal on, say, an omega, which this alpha was not. No omega would dare speak over an alpha in their own home. They might rush their response but never interrupt.

"No need to snap, child," I warned. "A student of politics then. And staying with your uncle?"

"Yes, Your Grace. I admit I am anxious to keep an eye on my youngest sister, Viola, who is presented this year."

"I do not need you to explain your domestic arrangements." Though it was not surprising she'd want to stay close to her omega sibling.

"Of course not. May I ask what tasks... That is if you will take me on."

"That is the plan. But must you ask what you will do? You shall do whatever fulfils my needs," I smirked. "But to ease your mind, hot head, you answer my correspondence, letters of business, anything I do not wish to do myself. However, there is a task that, while not of primary importance, must be dealt with. You will do some, ah, research into the Countess Kellingham. I realise that is not what you might normally expect of your duties, but my secretaries are involved with all my business. At present, the Countess is the primary aim. To marry her is my meaning if you can't parse it."

"The Countess?" she frowned as if I belonged in Bedlam. "You want *me* to look into her?"

"What engagements she has, which social events I might meet her at when she comes out of mourning in the next few weeks," I continued as if Hartwell hadn't spoken.

"Your Grace, I should warn you that the Countess is known to me a bit through my aunt. And from suffering omega's talk..." her lips twisted.

I smiled in sympathy. How could I not? Omegas could prattle on about nothing.

"I know the Countess has forsworn alphas and men. You say your aunt knows her? Use your skills to persuade and convince her to get access. Should you desire to go into politics, tasks less savoury than this will be asked of you. Eventually, you shall ask it of others. Not the wooing of a spouse, but jobs you might normally turn your nose up at. Politics ain't pretty business but dirty dealings, researching your opponents, and using the knowledge to your advantage. It's why I hate the whole race of politicians."

Her eyes flashed. Oh yes, this little alpha would afford me many hours of pleasure.

∾

HARTWELL PROVOKED MY TEMPER WITHIN A WEEK OF HER arrival.

"Would you be so kind as to explain to me why I must hunt down my secretary in my own home?" I barked on entering the drawing room.

She scrambled to her feet and attempted but failed to straighten the already poorly tied cravat at her neck. I'd come down to the library after my morning ride to find it empty. No dark head bent over some piece or other of correspondence. No violet eyes glancing up or quick smile before returning to work. Instead, I must find her here lounging at a lady's writing desk and looking at home. As always, she was peculiarly arranged so that her body sat parallel to the desk, with the paper lying in a similar manner. Her left elbow, for she wrote with that hand, resting on a small book and with her right hand she moved the paper progressively upwards as she wrote. One might think this impeded the flow of her writing but it was not so. Her words appeared on the page with such rapidity that must be witnessed to be believed, and, when it came time to review, there was little to complain of. This was no instant genius, but by her own admission, she would sit in silence, staring at a blank page, deep in thought before beginning. As if she composed the entire piece in her head before committing thoughts to paper. It was probably the only time she paused before forcing her opinions on others. Her mouth was different, words pouring forth like blood from a mortal wound. An alarming experience one could only imagine became easier to understand with time.

"The light was poor. This room is south facing," she fiddled with her cravat. It was loose so I could not understand how it might bother her. Watching her fidget, it occurred to me that I did not know her scent, and yet there was an underlying hint of pheromones that soothed my temper, a surprise for sure given that Hartwell was an alpha.

"Are there not windows, even a candle, in the library?" I asked after a moment, dumbfounded by this strange change in location. She lay down her pen and tidied the desk.

"There is no economy in using candles when the sun is out. And I couldn't move the desk on my own. So I asked your butler Horne and came here instead."

"I can afford whatever candles you might require. Or call a footman to move the desk for you," I felt like pulling my hair. Surely the Hartwell estate was not so small that they did not use candles in the dead of winter. Unless they wrote so prolifically that they never once needed to use a candle as automatic as it was for them to fill pages with sentiments of liberal passion and righteousness.

"I could not take advantage..." she pressed her lips together. "I am not used to such extravagance. I am used to sitting in the window."

"Then we can move your desk. It is not such a great thing, little alpha."

"There are betas shorter than I!" she snapped. "I am... I know I am the wrong height for my dynamic. But please do not call me *little alpha*."

"Then what should I call you?" I asked, amused by her sensitivity.

"Hartwell. I prefer when you call me Hartwell."

"As you will."

"You are not what I expected," the words burst from her. While I had grown resigned to the readiness with which she pronounced her every thought, this admission demonstrated her youth in a charming manner. With her politics, thoughts on the management of the estate—so far as she was privy to my correspondence—all that she spoke with a surety that no longer surprised me. Then in other moments, her impressions on something or other, some person, some book she found on my shelves, a comment on her home life, which I'd begun to suspect was more complicated than she let on, she showed her newness to the world. There existed a purity in her soul that, given her choice of profession, might be destroyed with very little work. I did not want that. I did not desire another cynic to populate the world or become a politician. Now that I had felt the fresh breeze of Hartwell, I desired to protect it in hopes it would blow away the stuffiness I found so oppressive.

"How'd you mean?" I asked, holding back a smile. There was something about Hartwell I liked in an obscure way. Not in any intimate way... I shut that thought down before it had a chance to mature.

"I thought you would be proud. But you are no more proud than you ought to be. You take your responsibilities seriously. Your tenants are fairly treated, though perhaps your time spent in the country accounts for that." she glanced out the window as if something caught her attention before looking at me once again with those unusual purple eyes. "You ain't cold. They call you the Parson Duke. But again, again, again! you defeat my expectations. You ain't mean with your money or time with your tenants and dependents. I said that already. You might not eat meat and be a teetotaller, but you are addicted to sport."

"If I'd known you would hardly take a breath between periods, I'm not sure I would have hired you. Oh, do not frown at me cub... Hartwell," I corrected myself with a chuckle. She flushed, lowered her head, and proceeded to look up at me through ridiculously long lashes. A coquettish tactic for an omega. Charmingly innocent on this peculiarity I had introduced into my life. "But do not hold a mirror to catch my likeness before examining your own."

"Oh! You ask me so charmingly to decline some invitation or to tell your steward to take on some new task... Then you must go and wrap censure in silver paper."

Impulsively I tilted her chin so that our eyes met. By all the saints, one could drown in those violently violet orbs, which conveyed every feeling in the cosmos. I could believe the poets, who said eyes were the window to the soul. But now I needed her to see the sincerity of my next words. "You. Are. A. Scamp."

She gasped, and a little pink tongue licked her lips, which I followed with a strange clenching feeling in my chest I had not experienced in a while.

"Come. Let's have that desk moved. I won't have you working here for fear you urge my people to some mad scheme. I must keep an eye on you should you start a rebellion in my absence."

My words urged action, but we stood there a little longer in a strange battle of wills. There were few peaceful instances of physical contact between alphas. This, however, felt so natural that I did not wish to break away. It took restraint not to allow her to stay here and move my own work here. I was surprised to find myself considering such an indulgence. But this was my house, and I would be the one to hold my ground and not bend to youth. I had expected some upheaval to my home with the introduction of this young alpha, but nothing could have surprised me more than my ready acceptance of her daily presence. Such was the ease at which she slotted into my routine that I considered returning to the topic of the widowed countess. Since that first day when I'd taunted her with the idea that she would be responsible for easing my way into the countess's life, neither of us had raised the subject again. I forgot it except in passing. Then forgetting again when I was in Hartwell's presence. When I remembered, it did not surprise me that she hadn't raised the issue either. I made plans to do so the next day, but before I had the chance my surprising secretary had a bone to pick with me. I bit back a smile as she stood before me, the speech she had written, which I had read and balled up ready for the fire, tight in her fist.

"You... Your Grace must see how very important it is for this bill to pass," she ground out.

"And why is that?" My gaze flicked to her face and stayed to observe the play of emotions. Those violet eyes were addictive and soothed my soul more effectively than any cure known to man or the Goddess. Even when they flashed with anger and barely suppressed frustration, I found a perverse comfort in them. "Well, secretary mine..."

"Lady Clare," she bit out. "Lady Clare, the countess you seek to marry. If this bill passes she, my sisters, all omegas will be protected should they become widows without a mate bond... Or should they have no alpha children or siblings to inherit what parts of the estate that are not entailed."

Her chest heaved when she finished. I leant back, observing Hartwell as if I'd never seen such a strange creature before. One both far-seeing beyond her years and yet blind to the realities of our society.

"Sit," I ordered. Her jaw clenched. There was rebellion in her eyes. I nearly chuckled. She looked ready to rip my throat out. There would be no warnings before she moved to end my existence. I would be dead in a second if she had her way, and all because I ordered her to sit as if she had not delivered such an impassioned speech. "Sit. I will talk to you of this bill and why its outcome shall not alter my plans."

Ever irascible, Hartwell, instead of taking the chair in front of my desk, came around and dragged one of the side chairs over, allowing its legs to pull against the fine Abyssinian carpet. "Petulant child. I seek to open your eyes, not lecture you."

"Well?" She crossed her arms and sat back. "Instruct me, Master."

Master had my blood heating, though perhaps not in the way she would like. The vision of instructing my secretary took a turn in my imagination. Let her learn how dark the desires of a fully grown alpha could be. I'd put that mouth to better use. Have those violet eyes flash with a different kind of passion. I would school her, and she would say thank you.

"You've read the bill?" I asked, already knowing the answer.

"Yes."

"You've read it and *still* do not see that it won't come into law until after her period of mourning."

"But that is no matter!" she said. "Our laws do not prohibit *ex post facto*. They can come into effect prior to their passing. I can list... I admit this is not well-conceived for many reasons, but in this case—"

"Do you really believe that the Crown would willingly give up such an estate as Kellingham?"

"Are you arguing with the law?"

"That isn't how the world works," I growled. "The Crown will do what they can to hold on to the estate. And," I scrubbed at my face. "And we must consider that Clare died almost a year ago. They shall take it into account and use it against your petition. A prohibition on *ex post facto* is central to common law."

"But..." her face fell. I moved to stand before her.

"If perhaps it had been a month, we could have petitioned the Crown. But a year? No. I'm sorry," I rested a hand on her shoulder. "Come have a drink."

"You don't drink."

"That might be, but it don't mean I don't keep a cellar for recalcitrant secretaries," I poured her a glass. "Drink."

"Tell me. If I were to offer the countess in exchange for the votes, would you accept?"

"Votes?" Her proposition blindsided me.

"For the Omega Property Rights Act. I want to see it passed more than anything."

"No."

She gave a stiff nod and returned to her desk, keeping her head down for the rest of the day.

By the middle of February, the weather had become unseasonably mild. On the chance the roads were passable, I dreamt of escaping back to Ayleigh. I could bring Hartwell with me since I still needed her services. We could gallop across the fields, or I could take her shooting. As I lay in bed, the wicked part of me fantasised about giving up my quest to find a wife. There were plenty of omegas in the world. I was not so ancient that I needed a wife now. It could wait a year or two. No, better get it over with—like a tooth being pulled. The immediate pain would be worth it in the end rather than risk infection.

So instead of my carriage, I ordered one of my stallions, Orsino, to be saddled. The poor beast wasn't used to life in the city and probably craved a morning gallop as much as I.

At this dawn hour, Rotten Row could be found empty of casual riders. Only those who wished for an undisturbed gallop exercised their horses. I took the moment to enjoy the silence of a winter morning. Despite the lack of bite in the air, there was a fine mist creeping within Hyde Park and drifting across the path. The sharp look of a frost on the ground and cold light shining in a cloudless sky. Freedom rang through me for the first time since my grandmother's death.

I watched a pair go by and recognised Hartwell. I nearly called out to her, but seeing her companion gave me pause. A dark-haired woman in a well-fitting riding jacket who on sight could only be Hartwell's sister. I pulled to the side, jumping down to fiddle with Orsino's bridle so that I might better observe them. The most obvious being their similar build and dark hair. I wondered how often they'd been mistaken for identical before Hartwell had presented as an alpha. Interestingly, Viola Hartwell's posture displayed none of the natural shyness one expected of her dynamic. I could not catch their conversation, but there was a directness to her body language that gave the impression of a strong will and purpose I'd never once seen in an omega. Even my grandmother had kept a veneer of subservience when dealing with alphas. Not so Miss Hartwell, who carried herself more like an alpha than omega or even beta. As to her seat, it was better than my secretary's. Though Hartwell did not seem uncomfortable, her twin appeared to be born to sit in a saddle. Even when her filly danced, she laughed at its antics and chided her alpha sister for trying to catch her bridle. Her mount spun, eager to run and across the stretch our eyes met. At this distance, I could not tell if the omega Viola shared Hartwell's fine violet eyes, but on seeing me, she instantly took control of her mischievous mount and took off in the other direction. Hartwell shook her head and galloped after her.

I found my mouth twitching into a smile. *Now* I understood her passing comment that she desired to watch over her twin. Viola Hartwell was wild. Nothing like the kind of omega I could imagine as my duchess.

6

VIOLA

"You must see... Here. Here," I stabbed at the sheet in front of the duke. I'd been good enough to bring a draft of my book for him to review. But all he wanted to do was discuss the winter lambing, even though there had been no news since we'd concluded the business last week. I suspected he was doing it on purpose. Could alphas be more insufferable? "See. Omegas do not lack the qualities of any dynamic. They merely are slaves to their nature, as alphas are. Their bodies smaller, to be sure, but their minds as great."

"As great?" he blinked lazily. I gritted my teeth. At times I wondered if he deliberately provoked me or if he was stupid. The latter, of course, was ridiculous. His mind was agile and exciting. In the past fortnight, I'd engaged in more debate about topics that mattered than the past six months combined. The duke excited me beyond his natural, physical allure. I flushed. At times I marvelled he could not scent the faint trickles of arousal I'd come to expect when I was in his company.

"As great," I emphasised. "Why, my sisters are better versed in—"

"Latin, Greek, and practically every philosopher known to mankind. Better than half the alphas who sit in parliament?" he offered.

"I do not deny it," I said stiffly. Oh, it made me cross when he threw my own words in my face. His ability to recall, near word perfect, every conversation we'd ever had was wasted on him.

"Don't resent me because of my superior memory, you brat. Don't look surprised that I can read your thoughts. You complain about it enough. Claws in, Hartwell," he smirked. His crooked nose should have made him ugly, but when he was in this teasing mood, the great Duke of Orley was almost boyish in his handsomeness. I wanted to keep him in a mood where the difference in our ranks melted away and he opened up to me. I flushed as an unreasonable thrill coursed through me. They came on whenever he addressed me as he might address any other alpha. *Hartwell*. An equal of sorts. I preened before realising his smirk had grown while he'd been observing me. I pressed my lips together... Provoking alpha!

"My upbringing is such that I shall ignore you insult. May I recite what my sister Viola said this morning? Over breakfast," I felt the need to add.

"You'll bother me until you do. Stand in front of me," he waved. I could see his thoughts as clear as day. "Stand there—
"

"Like a schoolgirl?" I asked, hurt that he could make me feel so small with a simple command.

"No, wild one. Like a member of Parliament," he beckoned me forward. "Do you think your abilities that of a mere child? Do you believe I think so little of you? You are more like to lead our country than wear leading strings. Which is it to be? Schoolgirl or Prime Minister?"

It would be role play either way. A taboo I never thought to consider, yet his offer had my heart rushing with desire.—

Not a carnal desire, I blushed at the thought. No, this was the aspiration to step outside my dynamic. This alpha was, unknowingly, giving me a chance to make-believe.

We grinned at each other.

"Then take your place, Prime Minister Hartwell."

I moved in front of him. Closed my eyes, calmed my pounding heart as I conjured the—I drew a blank.

"I do not know what it looks like," I admitted. I peeked at him through my lashes. There was no derision. Just a soft smile of understanding. How could he understand? No doubt he had been to a million places I as Viola would never step foot.

"The stage is less important than the words," he told me. "Speak, Hartwell."

My throat felt dry as if I had swallowed sawdust. Our eyes met. And it came upon me that this was the stage that mattered. He was the alpha I must convince. How could I forget? It was the votes he controlled, rather than his admiration, that I needed to win.

I could. I would.

"Viola spoke thusly over well-buttered toast and tea," I paused that he might appreciate the ridiculousness of the picture I painted. "Omegas, said she, are the rarest dynamic, and like precious stones, are hoarded and jealously guarded. But in shutting the omega away, the beauty, the brilliance withers as a jewel left in a box grows dull. To truly be appreciated, a jewel must be worn in the sunlight. Allowed to dazzle all and demonstrate to all its value. So spoke Viola Hartwell, omega"

"A shallow comparison," he remarked.

"It is not," I snapped. I'd been struck enough by my own words to rush away and write the sentiment down and refine it, commit it to memory. "What Viola says is true! Or are you too proud—"

"The sentiment, I admit, is compelling. Very compelling. But not all value a jewel, no matter its brilliance. Others will covet it once seen and then shut it up."

"You reject—"

"I did not say that. More—your sister must think of a better comparison... Come. You try to find one."

"You insult Viola," I growled. He insulted me. By Our Goddess, this alpha would have me losing my temper, and then I'd be in a fix. For all our comfortable discourse over the last weeks, he would not accept me for who I was. That I was Viola, an omega and aspiring rabble-rouser.

"Think of a better," he urged. "'Tis' of no import who finds the better comparison. Get the damn thing right and worry less about who came up with the words."

"Sharp steel," my eyes glinted. "An omega and a sword are the same. I think of my sister and I think of good steel. The point driving home, sharp enough to kill. If you do not use it? If you keep it in a scabbard the steel will dull. It must be sharpened like wits. An omega is only good if she is matched with an alpha whose skill is good enough to wield her."

"Good enough. Omegas are the blade rather than a sheath for an alpha to put his sword in," He cleared his throat. Then I realised the sexual nature of his comment... A man might sheath his cock in an omega's slick hole—my cheeks flared hot at the thought of his knot and how it might feel, how it might stretch me. The duke was a virile, attractive man and alpha. I was a woman and omega, young and inexperienced. My cravat felt tight, and I tugged at the collar.

"I did not mean—" I bit my lip, unable to put my thoughts into words without embarrassing both of us.

"That is more than enough of sheaths and swords, I think," he smirked.

"Have you given thought to my proposal?" I asked. "If I can't convince you to support the bill with my words...

Perhaps I should with my actions. A quid pro quo? The countess—"

"Enough! Get back to the work I pay you for."

I was quiet the next day, unable to look Syon in the eye, afraid that he would see my inner turmoil. Did I want to press him on the bill? Bring up the trade I was willing to make? I'd stayed up the whole night thinking on it. One person for many? Could I do it? But he had his own concerns and barely spared me a look until I stood to leave.

"Don't come tomorrow. You look tired," he didn't look up from the letter he was writing.

I swallowed, unsure what to do with his kindness. He was kind. He was good. What secretary received the same courtesies I had come to expect as my due? If he treated his duchess half so well as he treated me, a mere secretary, then I should be doing everything I could to marry him to the countess. If I got in the way of a marriage that could prove happy even as it saved the countess from penury, then I should be putting all my energy into achieving that outcome.

"You are too good to me. I will be here," I frowned at my shoes, confused by the emotions I had no name for.

"Hartwell, if I tell you to stay away tomorrow, you will follow my command. I go to Newmarket. Take the time off to buy some new neck clothes. You mangle them beyond recognition."

"Why? It is not the time of year," my head shot up in confusion. The first races were months away. I reached for my cravat. Even without seeing it, I knew it would make Timms, His Grace's valet, turn green with nausea. "And I don't mangle them."

"Do my movements concern you?" he chuckled. "More to

the point, does Newmarket vanish simply because the races aren't taking place?"

"No, sir."

"What? Hanging your head like an unrevealed schoolgirl? Something is causing you to act out of sorts. Tell me."

I gave into that firm tone. Perhaps not so much because he was exerting an alpha's will on me, but because I wanted to unburden myself. The story of my emergence into society and interacting with other alphas, omegas even, came pouring forth, coming to an abrupt halt with the admission that "The more I see of the world, the more I recognise my idealism, my own—"

"And what is so wrong with that, pup?"

"How old are you?" I glared at him.

"I will be nine and twenty this year. Not so old."

"Yet you have been to university, have been on the grand tour, have spoken in the House of Lords. In short, you have lived. You must think me wholly incapable and yet you are kind to me. To hear Viola's ideas..."

There was a pause. It could have lasted a moment or an hour, I would not know, for our eyes held so steady, even while my heart galloped within my breast. It had been a few short weeks in his company, yet I felt at once comfortable and at sea with him—very well, I was not sure what it literally meant to be at sea but the expression was known to me enough that I felt confident using it to describe my feelings at this time.

"Is't so strange? Perhaps I wished someone had been a friend to me at your age?" he asked.

I felt my cheeks flush. Had he called us friends? When there existed such a gulf in our situations, our stations, our dynamics. Everything separated us. There he sat. All languid grace as he lounged in his chair confident that there was none to challenge him. He could not be more correct. Yet he called us friends. A title I suspected was more precious than any other in his lexicon.

"It is late... I should go," I mumbled, knowing if I gave voice to my feelings, I'd break this serenity. When he didn't speak I realised how badly I had wanted him to ask me to stay. To have dinner with him. To not leave him in this grand and silent house.

"Come out with me tonight. I feel you need a night away from..." He waved a hand. As if it were quite common for a duke to take some young alpha—his secretary, no less!—with him to some exclusive club. "I think you do not play. That is not good for a young alpha, especially one who so demonstrably lacks any Town bronze. They call me the Parson for not indulging in pleasures of the flesh, but no one is the worse for learning whether you desire to partake or abstain."

"I—" I choked. The thought of going to another alpha only establishment had me nervous. "I mean, I am expected at home this evening."

"You are always expected this evening. Tonight you will do as I say."

I growled in annoyance. "You have no say over my free—"

"You are my secretary and reflect on me. If I choose to introduce you to a club, you bow and offer your humble thanks. Your protestations that you are not worthy of such regard..." he grinned. That smile was more lethal than his bark. If he had forced his alpha will, exerted the dominance we both knew he had, I would have caved. I would have had to submit. But that teasing twist of his lips commanded me just as well if not better.

"I will not rise to that bait. I will go with you," I snapped. But inside, my heart was singing. I hated myself for cherishing my time with him.

∾

HE CHOSE TO TAKE ME TO A GAMING HELL, FULL OF ALL THE young bucks and corinthians and betas with deep pockets. The house itself was a discreet building, but there was no doubt of what this place was once we climbed the shallow steps. A large, pugnacious alpha stood at the door, and the duke greeted him with a familiarity I'd not expected. When I asked, he pointed to his nose and said with some amusement, "That fellow ensured no lover would enjoy looking at me."

I wanted to protest, for he was distractingly attractive to me, which made me nervous with each passing day. It was only the great amount of work that he insisted I do which kept my stolen glances to the bare minimum.

Almost the second we stepped into the brightly lit room on the first floor, the duke and I were separated. Some unknown alpha led him off, while I floundered in a haze of strange alpha pheromones. As quickly as we were separated, I made up my mind to find him and not leave his side unless he explicitly ordered me away. My decision made, I threaded my way through the alphas until I spied him across a table where dice was the game. Near enough to call out to, I relaxed. My friend.

Yet, as I was about to draw closer, a beta woman dressed in a scandalously low cut gown pressed up against the duke's arm and trailed her fingers along his back in a well-practised gesture. The feeling in my stomach was not pleasant. Something warred within me, and I unable to determine why I wished I was the one caressing or being caressed. I kept my face still as I watched her attempted seduction. And in that deep meditative space, I missed my name being called.

"Hartwell!" The bark broke through my tangled thoughts.

"Viscountess Gale," I bowed. Relief unlike I'd ever known flooded my senses at the sight of a familiar face. "Apologies."

"You seemed lost in thought. What might it be?"

"Do you think that the women and men here practice

their seduction in front of a mirror? It seems like their actions are more for those watching than the subject of their... Shall we say caresses?" I spoke carelessly. My words purposefully crude, though I wished them back as soon as I had spoken them. What omega would speak so forthrightly? Even my sisters, who were wild and had kept themselves free of the weight of an alpha—literally, I smirked—would not speak like this.

"Both, young alpha," came a tinkling laugh. A beta wearing an even more provocatively, her breasts winning the battle with her gown. slipped her arm through mine. "Sarah is my name. What is your pleasure? To watch or to participate?"

"Both," I said, without any of the natural embarrassment an innocent such as I ought to feel. "I watch these alphas make fools of themselves and learn that I do not wish to be thought a fool."

"Away with you, pretty thing," the viscountess shooed. "I wish to talk to this firecracker, not watch her flirt."

"You know where to find me," she smiled coyly.

"In my dreams?" I parried. Her green eyes widened, pupils dilated. My own heartbeat harder with my breast, and my nipples tingled with something like desire. She leant close and kissed my mouth. It was soft, warm, and oh so sweet when she slipped her tongue between my lips. For a hundred heartbeats we kissed, slow and teasing, until she left me panting while she ran her lips along my jaw to my ear. Her tongue tracing the sensitive shell until she could take my earlobe between her teeth and bite. I hissed softly. We'd not touched except to kiss. I'd not felt the heat of her body pressed against mine, but my every nerve was on fire. She'd stolen my first kiss—my second, third, and tenth—, and I would gladly repeat the experience if given the chance. She might rob me of a thousand kisses and more, til, as the poet said, *no one would be aware of how many kisses there had been*, and I would consider myself richer for the experience.

"Your dreams, your bed, wherever, however you want me," she whispered. "And should you need an escape, I'm a friend to Hippolyta. Our Queen of the High Toby."

She backed away from me, her little white teeth pressing into her plump bottom lip, before spinning around and snaking her way through the crowd.

"My goodness. Sarah seems enamoured," an alpha standing next to the viscountess chuckled. A quick glance was enough to tell me he was her son. They shared the same high cheekbones and heavyset eyes. I took him to be in his thirties, not an old man to be sure, but older than the duke who was still focused on his conversation with some alphas I had not been introduced to. The beta still hung on my duke's arm. I smiled. He did not seem interested in her flashy beauty.

"I fear I am just her mark for the night," I inclined my head.

"To be the mark of a pretty woman is not such a bad thing," his mother smiled. I could see her assessing me. "I wonder, when will we see your sister presented? Is she to stay locked up until her debut?"

"What is she like?" the viscountess' son asked.

I growled low, furious at how... Casually they gossiped about me, about any omega.

"Easy, Fredrick. Hartwell does not like her sisters discussed in public."

I swallowed down the burning desire to tell her that she had brought them into our discussion. I looked up the moment I had myself under control, and my eyes caught the duke's. He gave the smallest of nods, an acknowledgement that I had kept my temper. My body slowly began to unwind as I realised I didn't need to jump to my sisters' defence. That I could allow them, myself even, to... To what? Be ourselves?

Independent of these alphas who wished to admire us, like the jewels I'd spoken to him of earlier. They did not appreciate that the metaphor had changed. We omegas were now steel sharp enough to make them think twice of meddling in our lives. Dammit, he was right about the metaphor—though I'd never tell him.

"Viola goes out with my aunt," I said evenly. "I believe she goes to small, private parties."

"So she meets no alphas," acknowledged the handsome alpha. "You must call me Fredrick. I think we should be friends. Perhaps through your friendship, I will have the good fortune to meet the fair Viola Hartwell, of whom the world has not seen but of whom much is heard."

His smile was for his mother and not me. I ground my teeth together. It was not hard to see the game they wanted to play. Viola was the scandal-free omega sister. I was the Hartwell sister who was valuable to the alphas. The one whose political pedigree... I frowned at the realisation. There was political power in marrying Viola—Hippolyta had told me as much. The purity of my father's politics, the increasing need for a leader for the opposition—fresh blood in the party is what my uncle had said the other night. I was the fresh blood. Not as Iris the alpha, but as Viola, the omega who would give her mate children and secure a political legacy, a dynasty. I looked for the duke, suddenly missing his reassuring presence. Around him, I could relax and be myself, rather than constantly worrying someone might guess I was an omega or listen as alphas bought and sold omegas as easily as they laid bets against the bank. Within his sphere, under his watchful gaze, no harm could come to me. To put it plainly, unknowingly, he had stepped into the role of my alpha guardian. The realisation did not alarm me as it should, but his care was too natural so I did not question it.

The duke did not let us stay much longer after my conversations with the Gales, but grabbed my arm and drew me away. He released me only to struggle into my greatcoat as if I were a child.

"I do not like it," he hissed as we left the disreputable establishment. His hand pressing against my back as he steered us away.

"What don't you like?" I asked. He'd seemed happy enough earlier.

"Gale and her son. Using you to get to Viola. Apologies. To Miss Hartwell. To use her as a pawn in their political ambitions. They might run with your uncle's political pack, but because it suits their ambition. Do you truly think Gale wishes to die a viscountess? She looks up. Your sister is merely a pawn in her game."

He echoed my own thoughts, but I'd hoped he would have a different interpretation of the conversation. He'd set me right before, if only he could do it now.

"Surely the daughter of a more powerful alpha..."

"A pretty wife with a pedigree and connections such as your sister possesses? And your mother getting a title for her diplomatic work in France? Both are as valuable as a fortune, which the Gales do not lack."

"I won't let them," I assured him. "I doubt any of my sisters would allow themselves to be used like that."

"Fool, you don't understand," he growled and swung me towards him. It was late and cold, yet I didn't feel the chill because his heat warmed me better than any furs could. He thrust his face into mine. "You need an alpha to protect you. Do you understand my meaning? Viola... Viola is going to be bargained away by your uncle for political gain. With your mother out of the country, there is no one to protect her. If she doesn't accept their suit, they can as easily compromise her."

I scoffed. "Even if my uncle wanted to, Mama would not

let him. Your Grace, trust me when I say that my uncle loves Viola, my sisters as if they were his own. But Mama and my uncle Florey are not on good terms. She'd block—"

"Oh, your manners are too nice to see what others would do with Viola." He snapped. My heart however hovered in a state of pleasurable shock that he said Viola so naturally. I could almost imagine he spoke to me, knowing all and accepting me as I was. "Be sure that Gale and her son believe that Viola will set them above others in the hunt for leadership of the opposition. I've no doubt they hope to marry and mate her by the end of the season, especially with your pet project going to a vote in a few months time."

"Your Grace!" I gasped. "You think... Viola? I doubt she has that much value before her debut... Though I do see the argument... I just don't believe that one omega could be such a powerful piece on the board."

"You speak of a chess game? A fair comparison. She'll be their gambit so that Gale can take the part of the queen. Now answer me. Does Viola look like you?"

"Yes," I did not know where he was going with this.

"So she is beautiful. Don't blush, Hartwell. You know you're beautiful. Sarah was rubbing against you like a cat in heat. Don't think that kiss you shared did not go unnoticed. If you were an omega... Never mind that. Should Viola have a fraction of your attractions, alphas will... Why are you looking at me like that?"

Had I been looking at him? I had been trying to look anywhere but at him... The duke had called me beautiful! No alpha had ever done that before.

"Was I looking at you?" I managed to ask when he continued to stare at me.

"Yes. The same look you had after Sarah stuck her tongue down your throat. Can't believe you kissed her like that. You looked…" he cleared his throat. "Remember I don't want to see you tomorrow."

Without any warning he turned down the next street, leaving me to watch his retreating back. He'd provided food for thought. Would alphas move so quickly? Forego the Marriage Mart in favour of deals behind the scenes? Compromise me, negating my mother's influence.

My fingers brushed my lips, which still tingled with the memory of Sarah's kiss. What would the duke's kiss do to me? Would I be as lost? As… No. Dangerous enough I even considered it.

7

SYON

"Then take up my offer. The widow for votes. If we get it passed, then my sisters... After last night— Dammit, but my sisters must be protected. Especially with my mother out of the country... Viola can help. You intend to marry her by the end of the season or her next heat, whichever is soonest. The countess, not Viola. You don't wish to marry Viola."

"You want them like that?" I asked, amazed she was willing to sacrifice one omega for the gain of the others. "I'll speak for you. But I will not force them. You convince them and with my influence, you will have your votes. Be sure of my support, Hartwell. It is yours," I promised. Never before had I put myself out to help another, much less a stripling who had me pulling out my hair in frustration half the time we were in the same room.

"But that still leaves the countess. Let me... I could do it." she laughed full of joyful humour or desperation, I could not tell. Neither I nor my plans were a joke. I was in earnest wishing to help the countess, but Hartwell wanted a quid pro quo.

"How dare— I can do my own wooing. All I wish is for you to find out which events she will attend," I snapped. We'd been arguing all morning. "This is no joking matter to me."

"Oh, Your Grace! Please excuse me. I do not laugh at you. Rather this," she threw a hand about her. "This situation could not... I came here to be your secretary and now I offer to act as your go between? Really duke, it is too much! Farcical... My suggestion that I woo her, I mean." Hartwell stopped abruptly and a definite crease formed between her finely shaped dark brows. I could almost see her mind flashing about hither and thither with thoughts that went too fast for me to follow. At last, those sparkling purple eyes met mine. "Your Grace... all mirth aside, I think that if you charge ahead like an alpha you will not meet with success. An alpha's wooing is too rough. Yet... I never in my wildest imaginings thought I could provide a solution to your problem. Perhaps if you had asked me yesterday, this morning even I would have told you something else—even suggested putting pen to paper! Love letters. But the devil has me and I, if you shall permit, will speak my mind?"

I was struck dumb again by this odd alpha. Florey had warned me his niece was a young woman with an almost too serious disposition. This creature in front of me defied description—she sounded crazed, not sane, but as ever she piqued my curiosity. My visage must have been stormy though, for she swallowed and tugged at her cravat.

"I meant no disrespect," she tried to chuckle, to bring back that levity she'd used so carelessly before. "And know you would be in the right to throw me out without reference. But I did not, on the honour of my family name, in the name of our friendship, laugh at you. I just can hardly believe my solution to your problem, for it defies all my good sense and reason. You are correct. I should be convincing you with the strength of my argument rather than bribe you with the countess' hand in marriage—I admit I am wrong. However, I can still help you to the altar, and I think you should accept my help."

"Well, tell me, whelp. And it better be good if you wish to keep your hide, for today you push my patience more than ever." Though I could not help the smile that tugged at my lips. Faith, but the scamp was original. Yet her tune had changed so fast I worried she was up to some scheme that would end with us both in Fleet Street prison.

The fool gave a graceless bow. But when she had risen, our eyes met, and I saw just how serious she could be.

"Your Grace. I propose the unthinkable. Something I would not want spoken of here, would not leave these walls for I take advantage of my dear sister. Though you are a greater man and alpha than I, I fear my sister's anger more than anything you could do to me."

"Spit it out. None of your poetry," now curious to learn whatever scheme she had devised within such a short space of time.

"I, under your direction, shall woo the lady for you."

I grinned. She was mad.

"And how will you meet her? She will not see alphas."

"Why, dressed as my sister. The fair Viola always wears skirts. It is known, Your Grace. Your business cannot be bandied about. So I will not ask her to do this for you. I will pretend to be an omega." Her lips twisted into a wry smile as if knowing how ridiculous her proposal was.

I buried my face in my hands, but could not contain my mirth. A laugh erupted, much to her surprise. This young alpha was an Original, and, as little as I liked to admit it, I liked her despite, nay because of her graceless ways. I more than liked her. Our time together had been brief, but she'd yet to bore me, an all too often occurrence when I spent my days with all dynamics bowing and scraping afraid of speaking out of turn. There was a plainness to her manner, despite the poetry and almost careless deference. If there was a thought in her head, it would be spoken willy-nilly. Novel, to be sure. She fascinated me without any artifice—a worrying state of affairs if she were an omega, a temptation to look away from the countess.

"What do you get from this?" I couldn't help but be curious. It was a dangerous game to play. An alpha intruding on an omega went against all my principles. I'd be happy for Mrs Markham, but an alpha? It bothered me.

"My sisters forever play pranks on me. Why shouldn't I play one on them? Stand up for the honour of alphas everywhere?" she snorted with a wry grin playing across her beautiful face.

I sat back in my chair, head cocked to the side as I considered her plan. Sure enough, there were poems and songs of alphas and omegas cheating their way into a lover's heart by transforming into the opposite dynamic. Even rumours that it had been done, and successfully. But when attempted—some omega wanting to take on the natural role of an alpha—the omega was caught in the lie. They could not carry off such a ruse because their scent and slick would reveal their dynamic sooner or later. Nature had its plans for the dynamics. The point was raised, and Hartwell grinned back at me.

"Your Grace should trust me. I've grown up with the best of omegas and know the ins and outs of their behaviour." She stepped forward, a hand reached out in supplication. "And no one would expect me to produce slick amongst omegas..."

I cleared my throat, almost embarrassed by her jocular reference to eliciting slick from a roomful of omegas. Did there exist an alpha like Hartwell? The answer was plain as a pikestaff. Never, nor would there ever be an equal to my secretary.

"And you expect me to believe that you will honestly court her in my name? That you will not woo her for yourself?"

"Yes. And should she suspect that—"

"That you are an alpha..."

"Then I shall tell her the truth: I am an alpha, wooing in your name. Not so difficult, I think?" She smiled coyly. Yes, I thought. She could convince a grief-stricken omega, wild with the loss of her husband.

"I'd like to see you in this disguise first. I'm not convinced you will pull off the dynamic change," I said, after some thought. She flushed again. Surprised and somewhat, I realised, embarrassed by my request. "If I cannot be convinced by your disguise, how do you expect an omega, whose sense of smell is even more sensitive, will accept the deception?"

"Will you keep me on as your secretary regardless of my success?"

"Yes." I knew I could not live without her help. For Hartwell, despite her youth and seeming carelessness, made an excellent secretary. Though having been rusticated from Oxford, her understanding was greater than many who had graduated with honours. There was a rough idealism to her, and I determined to urge her to return to complete her degree rather than attempt to make a career in politics without the experience—quite frankly, the connections—that university would afford her. Idealism was well and good for youth, but hard-headedness was needed if she sought to establish a more liberal government, which would provide omegas with opportunities and legal protections from aggressive alphas.

Her shoulders dropped, and she flashed me a sheepish smile. "I admit, Your Grace, I'm more interested in working as your secretary than I am in flirting with an omega or sitting through morning visits."

"What?" I laughed. "I saw you kiss one of London's most desired women. She blushed and watched you until we left... Or did you not notice?"

She glared at me, her nostrils flaring. I know she struggled to believe herself attractive, a feeling I knew too well. And rather than give her a reason to pick another fight about her looks or quite frankly erotic kiss, I ordered her back to work.

∼

A FEW HOURS LATER, GROWN RESTLESS FROM SITTING FOR SO long, I abandoned Hartwell and walked over to Manton's, one of London's exclusive shooting galleries. In one corner I found a dissatisfied looking Lord Paxton checking a pistol with Colonel Jack Fordom, a black-haired war hero with a gallows humour that held many at arm's length. The two alphas were like silver and cold iron, as pretty and lethal as the guns they so accurately shot with.

"Orley. Didn't expect to find you in town," Paxton set his pistol down and flexed his hand. I leant against the wall and watched them at their game, for it seemed they were competing for some prize. "Will you demonstrate your aim? Jack is looking to embarrass any and all."

"Embarrass? Ha. Orley is more like to embarrass me than any. Except perhaps Bea... Miss Hartwell," Fordom aimed at the target and less than a breath later hit the bullseye.

"Hartwell?" I frowned. "Related to Iris Hartwell."

"Not her again," Paxton snarled. He glared at his guns, deep in thought. "I ran into the child the other night. Fired up like a dog with a bone when I mentioned her sister."

"That's not my impression of her," I inspected the pistols laid out on the table. My intention to observe, engage in some conversation, and then leave was set aside in my interest to learn more about the Hartwells. "She's too young to do more than blow a bit of hot air about."

"Oh? And how'd you come to know young Hartwell?... Your Grace," Fordom asked, throwing my title in at the last moment and shooting me a sharp glance. We'd sparred earlier in the year. I'd suspected he'd thrown the bout out of some deference to my position in society... Now I wasn't so sure for he didn't appear to be an alpha to lose to anyone.

"She is my new secretary," I summoned a lackey and asked for my pistols to be brought over. "It's no secret."

"Ain't like you to hire a stripling."

I shrugged, yet I felt no need to explain myself to them. We might know each other, but neither of these alphas were my friends.

"She was lucky to have a handful of ancients with her the other night." Paxton aimed and a shot rang out.

"She is a fencer," I remarked as Paxton, clearly still riled by his run-in with my new secretary, lost another point. "I've a mind to try her hand."

"What, to take on a girl just out of leading strings?" Fordom asked. "Is she as pretty as her sisters? Beatrice and Hippolyta have their mother's fiery hair. Do the twins also carry all those curls or are they dark like their father?"

Did he realise he'd revealed he knew the Hartwells far more intimately than he wanted to let on? Dark like the father? The omega had died some five or so years before, and Fordom was only recently returned to England.

"Dark hair and violet eyes," I scratched my chin watching them. "She's slight for an alpha but does not lack courage. Speaks her mind."

"Regretting taking her on?" Fordom smiled.

"You should throw her out." Paxton snarled. He had taken my secretary into an intense dislike. It would be amusing to see them together again, and by his looks, Fordom agreed.

"If you see the fair Miss Hartwell, do let me know," Fordom's eyes didn't leave Paxton's face and sparkled with mischief.

"Which one?" I grinned enjoying a new kinship with Fordom when he taunted Paxton.

"For all that is holy. Be done with it!" Paxton threw his hands in the air. "Play or not. But let us leave Beatrice out of this. You aren't worthy to—"

"So you do still care," Fordom's eyes flashed. "I was not speaking of Beatrice, the wretched albatross, but the youngest Viola."

I watched the two and remembered with a suddenness that they were known for taking lovers together. Perhaps their problems with Beatrice Hartwell, who had red hair and caused her sister to lose her temper, were of a far more intimate nature. My guns arrived, and Fordom, clearly bored of teasing his friend, steered the conversation to less troubled waters.

I DID NOT THINK OF BEATRICE HARTWELL AGAIN, UNTIL the following week when my Hartwell barged into the library, a footman carrying a portmanteau. With each passing day, I became conscious that she was a beautiful woman who'd turn heads with a flash of her sparkling, mischievous eyes and easy confidence in both manner and body. To be certain, a captivating and dangerous woman.

"Your grace," she said with a bow. Noticing the footman was still present she waited until I signalled he should leave. "Shall I prove myself? As an omega? I hope I've already proved myself a sufficient secretary."

"Very well," I waved her to continue.

"A screen perhaps?" She fiddled with her cravat. The

nervous tick always brought a smile to my lips, but I'd not taken her for a prude after that kiss the other night.

"Aren't we alphas?" I asked, curious to see how far she would take it. My curiosity was piqued. I conjured up an image of a lithe body, leanly muscled, and perfectly proportioned. My feral side blossomed with anticipation at seeing her stripped bare. "We are alphas."

"Mystery," she cleared her throat. "Watching the transformation will take something from it. Don't you think?"

"Is't something else?" I frowned sensing there was more than preserving the illusion.

"I am not such a fine specimen of alpha. But," she took in a deep breath. "An alpha must have her pride."

"What do I care for that?"

She sucked in her lips, hesitating before confessing a little too quickly. "I have an injury. My leg..."

She pointed to the offending limb.

"Yet you fence..." It seemed preposterous since this lithesome woman moved with grace one rarely saw in an alpha.

"I fight to win fast. A long bout and I would falter."

No need to press her further. Alphas disliked discussing their weaknesses. As we waited for a screen to be brought I felt a strange sympathy. By no means was she an impressive alpha, but there was some quality in her manner that attracted me. At last, I admitted my response to her was not an objective appreciation of her face and form. Something deeper than that... For it wasn't just my blood that ran hot when she was near. I smiled more when she was near. I liked the sound of her voice, the scratch of her pen, and her predilection for split infinitives.

"How long will you be?" I asked as she disappeared behind the screen.

"Not long! You would think ours a strange household. My sisters are as like to wear breeches and ride astride as not.

And they've dressed me in their garb for a laugh or to play some prank. My sister Viola and I are very like, which is why I am confident this trick will come off. But she only ever wears skirts. We are of a height... She don't think she is omega enough. I hear the countess is different... A perfect omega."

I crossed to the fire and stared into its depth trying to remind myself why the countess was the solution to my problem. To put it down to being a female omega, who could provide me with an heir, wasn't the entirety of it. I felt anger that she had been left exposed. The dead Earl had been the worst kind of alpha not to consider his young bride. But then I remembered my father—what little of him I remembered—and my mother—what little of her I wanted to remember—and the answer hit me again and again. To mate someone without due consideration to compatibility was a fate worse than death. True, my beliefs hinged greatly on my grandparents as well. They had not mated but instead found mates later. My grandmother spoke fondly of the six of them spending weeks on end together. They had been happy. If they had not been other than they were, they could have formed a pack of four alphas and two omegas. But a duke or duchess must ensure it was their bloodline that carried on. And if I bonded a wife to me, and she found someone she truly wished to mate? It would be uncomfortable for all of us. An unwanted bond was a burden to all and could lead to ugly jealousy—just as it had with my own parents. That would be... I did not want to think of it. I kicked the smouldering logs. There seemed no fair way out but to take the countess, who once her time of mourning had ended would be thrown onto streets. If I married her, she would have a home and place in society. Perhaps later we would be able to grow close and the possibility of mating could be raised once again. But for now, she needed the protection of a husband, and I could provide that.

"Your Grace?"

I spun at the sound of an unfamiliar, sparkling, undoubtedly omega voice with all its song-like tones. But it could not be, for my secretary Hartwell stood before me. The white gown was cinched tight, hinting at a trim waist and flared hips that were most pleasing. The loose trimmings around the neck revealed her breasts—I'd not thought of her breasts until that moment. She'd let her hair free from the simple queue and was running fingers through the loose curls. My fingers itched to take on the task.

"Well, Your Grace? How do I look?"

I did not have an answer and was immediately grateful for the high backed chair I stood behind because, by all that was holy, I was hard and needing for the vision in front of me. This not-Iris laughed and dipped into a graceful curtsy before gliding towards me. Still, I could not speak. My eyes traced along every line of the face and figure that I longed for on a primal level I'd never before experienced. The vision moved closer until it stood next to me. Those unique violet eyes met mine, and I was able to accept the truth. This must be some hallucination on my part. I froze, unable to explain what happened next. Not in ten long years... It was impossible, but I scented her. Violets and vanilla filled my being and belonged indisputably to an omega—one that made my blood run hot and base need cause my erection to press hard and heavy in my breeches.

"Whose scent is that?" I rasped out, unable to believe I could smell. I, who would not smell horse manure if I stepped in it. Since nineteen, I'd scented nothing, but now, the most heady scent in the world caused my body to thrum with need. I reached down to adjust my hard cock, to squeeze and hope to ease the ache in my knot and balls.

"It belongs to Viola," her eyes sparkled with mischief.

"Your twin," I confirmed. Almost certainly too young for me, since I took Hartwell to be at best seventeen or eighteen. And there would be no doubt to *her* innocence. I found myself screaming at my instincts which sought to claim the owner of this scent. If I thought Hartwell too young, her sister, not yet presented at court, was, without doubt, a forbidden fruit I would need to avoid at all cost. I was a peer of the realm, an alpha capable of controlling himself. Throwing away the plans I'd made all for the chance at a schoolmiss? Unthinkable. Especially a sister I had silently sworn to protect from any unsuitable alphas—alphas like Gale.

"Do you think it will do?" Hartwell asked. She took a step back, her body tense, those fine shoulders rising up to her ears. Almost, almost I could convince myself it was the act of an omega uncertain around a virile alpha.

"Yes, an excellent facsimile of an omega," my words a rough growl, for I had breathed in and now my body thrummed with primal desire to conquer. I needed her gone before I did something that would embarrass us both. "You may go now. I have letters..."

"Oh, do you need my help?" Delicate fingers tucked a stray lock behind her ear. At last, I saw the smooth column of her neck where her mate gland would be if she were an omega. Thank the Goddess I had enough control to stop myself from reaching out to touch that soft skin, to scent her, chasing the first scent... A decade and it must be my secretary's omega sister that I must smell.

For the life of me, I wondered how she could continue to sound so calm and unaffected by my own aroused scent—I may not smell it but I knew that it had spiked the minute I'd laid eyes on this Viola Hartwell mirage. Those eyes. I focused on the one thing I knew: Those violet eyes belonged to my Hartwell and no one else.

"No. Change and I will see you tomorrow," I growled.

I gave her a swift, abrupt nod and left the library, going straight to my room, hoping to find some peace away from that intoxicating scent. Fuck, my aching cock! I gave into temptation and squeezed it hard through my breeches. I'd never had such a strong reaction to an omega's scent before. I would not show any weakness to relieve myself, but when I crossed to the window in an attempt to let in the cold crisp air I saw her leave my house. Hartwell was once again the charming young alpha dressed in men's clothing. The tricorn hat over her dark hair and tossing a friendly comment over her shoulder to Horne my long-serving butler.

I turned away more confused and more aroused than ever. The way my body responded to her in all her guises only hardened my resolve to marry the countess. I could not in good conscious take... I spun away and almost tripped over my feet to get back to the library. The screen was still there. I edged towards it, my heart pounded with equal parts hope and dread. Behind it, the dress she'd worn lay crumpled on the floor—a white stain on the richly coloured carpet. I brought the delicate cotton, better worn in summer than this cold February, to my face and inhaled. A growl escaped before I could control it. I needed to ensure I was never in the same room as Hartwell dressed in her sister's clothes. For those sparkling eyes, that smart mouth paired with the smell of—I inhaled again—violets and vanilla. I wanted to lick every inch of her omega twin.

But I couldn't. She wasn't for me. If I wanted to secure the future of the dukedom and save an unmated widow from destitution I could never test my resolve by spending any time around Viola Hartwell.

8

VIOLA

It. Was. All. Too. Much.

I maintained a carefree bearing until I made it to the safety of my bedroom, where at last I could confront my reaction to the duke while wearing my own clothes. He'd scented me as Viola, and I had melted like butter, feeling more like an omega than ever before. Rejoicing that an alpha as great as the Duke of Orley had responded to my scent.

Not for the first time, it struck me how dangerous an alpha like the Duke of Orley could be to an inexperienced omega like myself. Tall, broad, strong, unrelentingly attractive. Hair like honey washed throughout with red sheen. Intelligent eyes that flashed beneath heavy brows giving him the look of a perpetual scowl, even when he was amused or pleased by something I had said. He possessed an unfashionably firm jaw with full lips, though you wouldn't know it for how frequently he pressed them together in annoyance. He thought his broken nose ugly, but to me it revealed a dangerous element. That twisted nose manifested his primal and feral strength. His every look and word demonstrated that he could master anyone, omega, beta, or alpha, and come away the winner. And then I had to contend with how his scent thickened when his temper sparked and he put out more of that alpha musk. I covered my face with cold hands in hopes of calming the heat that suffused my body.

I dreaded facing my physical reaction to the duke. The cloths folded with sawdust that unmated omegas wore to absorb unexpected slick were nearly soaked. Yet the duke had not reacted as most alphas might. His self-control was nearly as intoxicating as the rough sound of his voice. I threw the cloths away for the maids to deal with as if removing them from my sight would banish the shame of reacting so strongly to an alpha. It had not been the same at the club, or even the first time we had met. I could only conclude that his reaction to my real scent had triggered such an embarrassing rush of slick. His own scent had become heavy with arousal, and as I'd left I'd seen how his erection had pressed against his breeches. My fingers traced along my breasts, down my stomach to press against my exposed sex. I snatched them away at the final moment before I gave in to my temptation to touch.

"It is not your fault," I told myself. He was, after all, an alpha responding to the traces of my scent on the dress, the muted smell of slick that had flooded between my thighs. Any unmated omega would cause an alpha to release a strong scent of his own seeking out a receptive home for his knot. There was no blame on either side. We were trapped by our natures. Nothing was more natural, and yet I recoiled from my own body's response. Could I really have felt desire for him? An alpha who'd ordered me to ferret out information on the woman he intended to marry. As if a duke's secretary shouldn't be focused on writing letters and conducting business for the duchy. Then I'd been so bold as to suggest I woo her in his place. He wished to marry another omega, I reminded myself. Not me, another.

My body betrayed me at the memory of his cock and fresh slick gathered between my thighs. That alpha scent so much richer than any I'd experienced before. Like sun-warmed leather and cloves, playing my every nerve raw. Not knowing whether I wished to stay in touching distance or run, had me hanging upon his words and slipping out of the guise of Iris and back to Viola. Young, naive, and for the first time alone with an alpha I was not related to. While I had learnt how to be an alpha amongst alphas, learnt the way they behaved, I had no good knowledge of how omegas should behave with alphas. Was the rush of slick normal when in such near proximity? Should I perhaps end my plan? My fears battered at my resolve. I reached for pen and paper to write a letter to my mother seeking her advice. Yet I could not find the words. Mama was loving and kind. She would urge me to be honest and not play about like this when I could instead be straightforward. She would tell me to appeal to the duke, to put forward arguments to convince him of my position without once putting me in danger.

But Mama, an alpha, would not understand.

I wish I had spoken with my sisters about being an omega around alphas they were not related to. For now, I knew the depth of my ignorance. How was I to temper my response when an alpha looked at me the way the duke had been staring at me? Was there some trick? Beatrice would know. She was the oldest, eight and twenty. She had been out in society, danced and supped and flirted with alphas before claiming she had no interest in marriage or mating. Her knowledge would be invaluable. But she was in Paris with our Mama. My shoulders slumped. How had I forgotten that Mama was no longer in the country?

One thing though was as plain as the nose on my face. I

would not dress as an omega around the duke. If he responded so strongly to a whiff of my true scent when I was wearing fresh clothes, then what would it be like if... It didn't bear thinking of. Dammit.

You liked it though. You liked when he looked at you with hunger, my traitorous heart taunted. *You liked the desire reflected in his eyes*.

How could I not? He was the first person, male or female, alpha or beta or omega, who had looked at Viola with desire.

I shoved the thoughts aside. Something would have to be done, but first I needed to change out of Iris' clothes. I regretted leaving my favourite dress with the duke, but I could not trust my omega instincts that wanted to hoard the dress that would have carried the virile alpha's scent. What if I had attempted to build a nest around the smell? I could have found myself in dangerous waters... No, I would not think on it. I changed quickly into my own things, hoping that skirts would help me return more to myself. I could get some writing done, I decided. Clear my head a bit.

An hour later I came down the stairs to find my uncle's butler hovering.

"A visitor for you, Miss. A Mrs Markham."

"Oh!" My hand fluttered near my mouth. Would she be able to tell the difference between me in my dress and how I had appeared to her the other day? Or would my disguise prove weak against a woman as watchful as she? "Is she... Has she been waiting long?"

"Just arrived. I ordered tea," he smiled.

"Thank you. I am not sure if I would have remembered that," I admitted. It struck me that I'd never received guests on my own.

"Go in, Miss Viola. She is not so frightening."

I had to laugh at that. How could I be afraid of Mrs Markham when I had spent two evenings surrounded by alphas? When I'd spent every day for near three weeks with an alpha I lusted for? I straightened my shoulders. If I could be an alpha amongst alphas, I could be an omega with another omega.

"Mrs Markham, I am sorry for keeping you waiting," I smiled and dropped a slight curtsy. "I am afraid my aunt is out and cannot be here to greet you."

"Worry not, child. It was you I wished to speak with. Your sister Beatrice is a friend of sorts. I have wanted to meet you alone for quite some time. And to see up close if your eyes are as striking as she has claimed. They are. Quite remarkable, my dear. Quite remarkable."

"My eyes!" I laughed at the absurdity. "Would anything about my appearance be *remarkable* if not for my violet eyes? Forgive me! I am all mirth and no..."

"I know Beatrice well enough to expect, nay, hope that you are as singular as she. Come forward. Let me see you better. I admit my first visit... I had my reasons."

My eyebrows jumped that she spoke with an open intimacy, going so far as to imply her behaviour that first time we met was an act—though to what end, I did not know. I walked towards her and knew we were assessing the other. Before me stood a middle-aged woman, whose beauty had faded attractively. She carried herself with an omega's grace and floated rather than walked, which when paired with her sharp, direct eyes made her something out of the ordinary— she was dashing. Alphas would look twice at her on the street, but something more compelling than beauty held my attention. What she saw in me, I was less sure of. Surely not much beauty—at least not the type that most omegas dreamt of. Now that we were alone I saw her for who she was: she presented as a typical, flighty omega, but it was an artifice. Now in a more private setting, she was plain speaking. I saw how she and Beatrice could be friends. Regardless of these duelling personas, my impression that she was crafty proved accurate. She as good as proved it by coming here knowing my aunt was out. And then there was the business of announcing she knew Beatrice, was on familiar terms with her.

"You pulled off the act quite well," she murmured so low that I almost did not catch her words.

Denial was all that I could do.

"No, child. Fear not. I am sure you have your reasons to dress as an alpha—pretend to be your sister Iris. But it is a dangerous game. Especially if you are living here where people will visit and know you. Though you are not out..."

"I am aware of the risks," I told her, not quite believing that she believed me. "My reasons are noble. Unlike you, who wishes to match Orley with Lady Clare despite knowing her intentions never to remarry."

"Orley? Are you so familiar with the duke?" she questioned. I flushed. No secretary addressed their employer—especially a duke—in such an informal manner. A slip of the tongue, I told myself. Nothing more.

"I am his secretary."

The older woman frowned and led me to the window.

"What do you see outside?" She asked. I shook my head not understanding. "Look. What do you see."

I looked. "Betas, a few alphas."

"What else?"

"What else?" I frowned. "Carriages, horses, houses. The rain," I smiled as the pavement began to darken with fat drops.

"And who owns it?" she pressed

"Alphas."

"And do you see any unaccompanied omegas?"

"Of course not!" I scoffed. "They do not let us—"

"Yet you wander the streets in your disguise without fear. Your world has been one of privilege. You have been taught more than most omegas. More than most alphas and betas too. For some reason, you have decided to dress as your twin and go out into the world. Risking everything, I might add. Yet when you looked at me, here in the perfect safety of your uncle's house and with an omega, you hesitated. When we first met your guard was up. Why is that?"

"You didn't want me to see the injustice in the fact that as an omega I cannot go about my life like one of them?" I asked, confused.

"You know all that. Have been raised with your eyes open to injustice. But do you know why you are afraid to be an omega?"

"I'm not—" I snapped my mouth shut as I remembered how desperately I had wished for an omega to talk with, air my concerns, and ask for advice. "I... At home, I do not know many strange omegas. And our neighbours in Hertfordshire rarely acknowledge us because of our family's reputation."

"Do you respect omegas who are less educated than you?" she asked.

My cheeks heated in embarrassment. I would have never aired such thoughts out loud, but the memory of how I so easily dismissed my aunt and her friends, even Mrs Markham when we first met, spoke louder than I had ever expected.

"You have never been confronted by your own prejudices. Tell me. Have you spent more time in the company of alphas or omegas since your arrival in London?"

"Alphas," I admitted. "I'm not out in society. I've not been presented. Any omegas I meet are here when I am with my aunt, and she is quiet."

Her lips thinned and her face folded into a frown. I

looked away, back to the street, which had mostly cleared because of the now steady rain.

"I would like to offer you my help," the older omega said. "Your aunt is well-meaning, but I fear she cannot give you the guidance that perhaps you need. I offer my help as a friend to your sister. I can prepare you to go out in society in your natural dynamic. You needs must learn how to be an omega."

"Mrs Markham... I do not care to be a good omega. Or a good alpha, for that matter! I am nothing but who I am and I take pride in that."

"The world does not take pride in dynamics acting out of turn."

"Dammit. Why!" I bit my lip, embarrassed at my outburst. She claimed some friendship through my eldest sister. Her quick eye, her experience in the world made me certain that if there was an omega I could open up to, she could be the one. Yet Mrs Markham had purposefully provoked me to respond by talking about the duke's plans as if he were uncaring, which I now knew to be untrue...

"He is going to marry her with no intention of taking her as a mate. But I understand his reasons," I decided to see what her response would be to my position. "They are honourable. *He* is honourable."

"Is that all?" she gave me an ironic smile.

"Could there be another reason?" I narrowed my eyes. A stab of uncertainty cut through me. Was I revealing too much and to a near stranger?

"Perhaps."

"Or not." I allowed the bite to enter my voice. I would not be played the fool by her. "You were the one who raised the issue, madam."

"We both want the countess taken care of," she sighed. "I recommended her to the duke. Perhaps I was hasty in doing so... I meant it for the best."

"I have every intention of helping the countess. And convincing the duke to give his support to the Omega Property Rights Act. That is the reason I entered his employ." I kept my eyes focussed on her face. I caught the flash of surprise when I revealed my motivation for approaching the duke. "I dressed as an alpha, because he would not meet me as an omega."

"And how do you intend to help the countess while you are persuading him of your politics?"

"I haven't thought of a solution," I lied. "Perhaps I will encourage her to consider his proposal. I can go as myself."

Mrs Markham threw back her head and laughed. "So lie to him and pray that your plan will just emerge? You are a greater fool than your sisters combined, and believe me when I say that they are fools of the highest order."

"I am not a fool!"

"Why not seduce him as yourself? He is quite a catch," she smirked. I nearly rolled my eyes at her absurd understatement.

"I have no plan to marry or mate him. He is... I am his secretary." The words were no sooner out of my mouth than I saw an image of the duke as he looked at me when I was myself.

"Heavens save me from alphas and omegas both," she shook her head.

I fiddled with the collar of my dress. "You don't understand..."

"I understand well enough. Certainly well enough to know anything I say shall only strengthen your resolve to go along with this harebrained idea."

"Will you help me to woo Lady Clare for him?" I asked.

"Marrying Lady Clare to the Duke of Orley? After what I have learnt today? No, I cannot support that match. Both of them would be miserable. I would like you to sit for me,

93

though. I've a mind to catch your portrait before the world knows your face."

Not help me? Oh, I wanted to scream. I could not understand how her mind worked! "Who are you? There is something illogical about how you jump from here to there with no—"

"I want to be your friend. And help you in any way I can... I couldn't help Beatrice," she said as if that explained everything. The clock chimed the hour. "I must be off. But fear not. Consider the matter of whether you need my help or not. Come visit me Thursday next."

THE NEXT DAY WAS A BITTERLY COLD SATURDAY, BUT somehow I convinced my aunt to take me along with her to sit with the countess. My aunt had insisted I wear a yellow silk that made me look anaemic, but if that was the price to be granted a meeting with the Countess of Kellingham, so be it.

That Lady Clare would reside at Kellingham House for the entirety of her period of mourning was a boon for her. That the grand residence was directly across from Orley House, courted disaster. If His Grace the Duke of Orley, Marquess of Darenth, Viscount Mote (and many more titles I'd yet to memorise) saw me, chose to greet me, thinking I was Iris, only for my aunt or another member of our acquaintance to contradict him... What then? My lie would be exposed and in the most horridly public manner, embarrassing all, but most especially that proud alpha I'd come to admire so much. I had not appreciated the dangers of visiting the countess when the duke could easily see me in dresses and assume that I was Iris in disguise. But it would be necessary, and surely he would not forever be on the lookout to see who was coming and going. Besides, the square was large enough that he would not know if it was me or merely another nameless omega. It gave me a headache to consider all the possibilities. I'd reached no conclusion when the butler opened the drawing room door and announced us.

"Mrs Florey and Miss Hartwell, your ladyship."

The countess was a young woman, not quite three and twenty, with fair hair and rich brown eyes, unattractively dulled and made unbeautiful by the dark circles beneath them. Still, her lady's maid had done what she could, and the countess wore a little rouge on her lips and cheeks. The attempt at livening her complexion was ruined less by the Lady's looks than by the fact she remained in deep mourning blacks despite the Earl having died nearly a twelvemonth before. If she had been in health, I knew she would be the example of omega perfection. And even in grief, her voice had that magical quality omegas cultivated from their first heat.

"My niece wished to meet you," my aunt murmured. She'd not been pleased when I'd suggested making the call, and played with her handkerchief more than usual. When the countess did no more than offer a tentative smile, my aunt added. "She is the youngest of my dearly departed brother, Charles Hartwell. Perhaps you have heard of him?"

"I'm sure I have but cannot remember. What is the name again?" came the artless and frankly stupid response.

"Hartwell. My father was Charles Hartwell," I tried to smile but couldn't hold it for long. This was the omega the duke had chosen? That Mrs Markham had suggested? Other than her beauty, there was nothing to recommend her. Though I now recognised how my own prejudices coloured my opinion, could the duke, a man of substance and a deep thinker, really be happy with her? Did he desire a stupid bride? One who'd defer to him in all things? We argued daily.

I admired how quickly and effortlessly he could produce precedents where some liberal bill had led to setbacks in omega rights. It grated, yet I found my own thoughts sharpening with each battle of wills we engaged in. But many alphas would prefer a stupid omega... *He only wants her to breed and give him alpha children*, I chided myself. No reason to feel annoyed with his taste, when his reasons for marrying the woman in front of me were to save her from the legal injustices omegas faced.

It took near an hour before I found the opportunity to sit with her and quickly realised how poorly I had judged her. While her understanding was not great, she blossomed in more private settings, making it a simple matter to direct the conversation to the possibility of her marrying again or looking for a mate. The precariousness of her position had been beaten into her, and she demonstrated a kind of quiet resolve when she spoke of finding her place in society. This strength flickered on and off as if sunlight through clouds. I determined to bolster this by increasing her belief that her life could have meaning, that she could find a mate despite the recent tragedy. If not a mate, a careful husband who would give her kindness and respect.

"The Earl married me because he thought I would give him an heir. Not because he loved me," she said in a small voice. "My father, a beta... He..."

"Do not distress yourself," I begged.

"He *sold* me," she whispered, distress colour her voice and her scent turning bitter. "The Earl did not love me. Love is not necessary in marriages among the aristocracy..."

"And what would you think of an alpha who did love you?" I asked unsure how hard I should push the clearly distressed woman in front of me.

"An alpha? Oh? I mean. If the alpha was as kind as you

have been... Not that you are an alpha," she offered me a trembling smile. "But alphas are not kind."

"They can be," I gave in to instinct and reached for her hand. "My Mama and sister are kind. I... my sister works for the duke of Orley and says he is the best of alphas."

"Oh," tears sparkled in her eyes. "Lord Clare... I will not speak ill of the dead. I am sure he did not mean to be unkind. I am weak and stupid. I did not give him an heir."

"Was he unkind to you?" I asked softly. I moved closer and tipped her face towards mine. I felt so much older than her, which instead of making me feel strong, only made my heartache for the things she must have endured.

"He was so much older. And, I understood what an honour it was that he chose me to be his bride... But he... I think I must have disappointed him a great deal."

"Olivia!" A sharp reprimanding bark came from the ancient beta companion who had been hired as her companion. "What are you doing in that corner? Come here."

"Please," she whispered to me. "Please don't leave me. Come back. Please. I am so lonely."

She held my hand until the very last minute before she rushed to the side of the vulture who watched me—no, watched her—with such hatred.

"What do you think you are doing?" a female alpha I hadn't noticed before snapped at me. Standing I turned to look at the newcomer. She stood tall in her men's clothing—only her status as an alpha allowed her that privilege without public censure. The stranger's hair was almost white it was so pale. Then there was her figure, lean and muscled and proportioned so perfectly that I flushed. It was nothing like my reaction to the duke, but there was no denying the fact she was the kind of alpha omegas fought over. A flash of jealousy had me gritting my teeth. In the years since I had presented as an omega, I had come to better understand the drawbacks of my dynamic. The nurturing and supportive home life, stripped away to the cold judgement of society and the restrictions of the nation's laws. In my few weeks as an alpha, men and women had not given my hurried stride or open manners a second glance. I'd been myself, free of judgement or censure. Even our beta king would not be granted the same instinctual respect and deference as this young alpha.

"I was being friendly. I thought Lady Clare wasn't permitting any alphas..." I gave a false smile.

"My father is the vicar at Kellingham. I am Caroline Wilson. I've known Olivia—Lady Clare all my life. She is mine to protect."

"Are you staking your claim?" I sneered. How I wanted to strangle every alpha for their unrepentant arrogance when talking about omegas.

"If you were an alpha, I'd call you out for taking that tone with me," the words weren't even laced with threat. Just a statement of fact that had my eyes pricking with tears of frustration.

"I'll take my leave," I bit out and walked to where my aunt sat with a round male omega. Neither of them looked very happy with the seating arrangement, so I was not surprised when my aunt bounced up and told me she thought it time for us to leave. I was grateful too. But one last glance at the widow, and I knew I could not leave her to this suffocating sadness forced upon her.

9

SYON

One morning Hartwell arrived earlier than usual, her face drawn and something like anger causing the muscles in her shoulders to tense before she took a steadying breath and released whatever plagued her. I cursed for noticing such details, but since her arrival, I'd caught myself hunting for hints of the omega she'd dressed as. Not just any omega but her sister Viola. The dress I'd stolen after that day was carefully wrapped in tissue and placed at the bottom of the closet in the duchess's nest. I could somehow excuse holding on to it when I kept it in an omega's quarters.

We'd been working in silence for some time when she stood abruptly and walked to the other window before spinning around to stare at me with those fierce eyes.

"Are you sure you want to marry her?" she asked. "The countess. Could there not be another omega in the world you could pick?"

"Why do you ask?" I felt my lips twitch. "Don't tell me you've already seen her and decided to take her for yourself?"

I meant it to tease. After all, she was heir to her mother's fortune which was respectful and certainly good enough to support the young countess. I considered that if she couldn't afford the omega price, I would help her. However, even as I thought the words, I realised my mistake. I did not love the countess, but if Hartwell married her I would lose my secretary. "Surely you are too young to think of marriage?"

"Omegas are married at my age," she snapped. "But no. I've no interest in omegas. She is a shell, Your Grace. I cannot... I have met her. I admit she is as pretty as a picture, the model upon which all omegas should be formed. But there is no life in her eyes. Her alpha guardian growled at me. And! An old crone is sneering down her nose at the countess. I did not like it. I do not like it. I urge you—"

"So you are saying her life is not happy?" I stood and crossed to where she had rested her forehead against the glass. She had a soft heart if she thought widowed omegas lived happy lives.

"More than that—" she slammed a hand against the windowsill.

I purred for her on instinct. I wanted to soothe her. "Then surely becoming my wife would be a solution? It would offer her protection from the hell she is living in."

"I know. Being your wife would be... It is her best hope."

"You had not thought of that before? I thought we had agreed to that."

"Your Grace! How could I? You've said that... You want a wife and mother to your heirs, not a mate. What would you be doing but put her in yet again the same situation."

"She would give me alpha children who would care for her," I touched her arm. "There is no reason to think she is barren. The Earl had no natural children. An alpha like him? He'd be rutting anything with a womb. Designation wouldn't matter to him so long as they gave him an alpha heir. He was a nasty piece of work, you wild puss."

I froze when I realised what I'd called her, but thankfully her mind was full of the countess and not my slip of the tongue.

"You can't guarantee that!" She spun away and thrust hands through her hair bringing it loose from the black velvet ribbon that held it back. "Don't you see—"

"Enough!" I barked. The sensitivities of youth had their place, but she took it too far. And in a conversation I believed us to have come to an agreement on. "Perhaps, having been surrounded by so many omegas, you think that there is some romantic notion to all of this. But amongst the aristocracy marriage is not as simple as it is for the lower classes. Mating is not so simple. The reason the countess is in this predicament is because she bore no alpha children. Not because she lacked a mating bite—would you really want her mated to one such as him? Do you think the world cares for your romantic notions about mate bites? They do not. I will allow you to have some emotions about this; you are young and raised amongst omegas. But I shall not tolerate this behaviour from my secretary. If you think to continue in this manner I shall send you on your way. Are we understood?"

There was a moment when I thought Hartwell, raised by omegas, would submit like an omega. How wrong I was. She straightened her spine and crossed to my desk where she picked up a bottle of ink and dashed it into the fire. A pretty display of temper to be sure. Those eyes flashed with anger, and it called to some primal need to dominate her. I wanted to put her in her place, on her knees cowed to my superior alpha. Another part of me was on edge, curious and excited for what she would do next. Another still wanted to comfort her in her distress.

"Your Grace... You are wrong if you think I am not aware of the place omegas hold in our society. Do not forget I went to meet the countess dressed as Viola, covered with her scent. I endured an alpha sneering at me and could do nothing but bow my head and retreat like a good omega. If you think for a moment that I am determined to let this go you are mistaken. If what I had to go through is the worst of what my sisters suffer... I will not let it stand. My father and mother taught me better than that. You and any other alpha would use that young woman, that frail beauty as a broodmare. And when I tell you, Your Grace, that she will be ripe for picking the moment she comes out of full mourning, I do not lie. A simple sign of kindness will have her in love. There is nothing I would not do to protect that innocence."

By the end of her speech, she was panting, and if possible those eyes were even brighter than before. I wanted to smooth that furrowed brow. Instead, I lowered the pitch of my voice, spoke to her as I might a young filly just becoming comfortable with a saddle.

"Then give her to me. If I marry her, she will be protected. She can stay in the country or Town. She will want for nothing. I will allow her the life she wants. If she wishes to mate another alpha, she may. But she will have my blessing to find love where she can."

"So long as she gives you alpha children," she snapped, her face flushed.

"After she gives me an heir. Is that so bad?" I asked knowing better than to take the bait she offered. Why Hartwell was so desperate for a fight I could not fathom, but it seemed best to ignore it. Turn her thoughts in another direction. It was several moments before she spoke, and when she did the fight had drained from her. I took that stubborn chin in my hand and tilted her head back until she was forced to look at me.

"No," she sounded so resigned. "If Iris hadn't been born— Ha! Well, if my parents had no alpha children the others...

You've no notion of my sisters. They are wild and determined to drive our Mama to an early grave."

"Your older sister had something to do with the Summer Exhibition, I believe?" I prompted, glad her thoughts had turned to a more, shall I say, pleasant subject.

"You put it very nicely, Your Grace," she chuckled, and the weight on my chest lifted. I did not believe she was completely satisfied with what we had been speaking of, but now at least her temper had cooled. "Beatrice paints. Hippolyta... She enjoys hunting."

"And your twin?" I couldn't help asking. That scent of violets and vanilla still haunted me.

"Oh? She is Viola. An idealist I suppose," Hartwell worried her bottom lip between neat, white teeth. My eyes focused there, almost not hearing her. "She used to write letters to the cabinet when she was a child. They were beautifully written—she has the most beautiful handwriting according to the last three Prime Ministers—but until my uncle enquired at cabinet they were left unread."

"And what did she think of that?" I smiled into the face I looked forward to seeing each morning.

She barked a laugh. "Your Grace? Viola couldn't escape the praise that her handwriting was so fair until she parcelled out the fact the Prime Minister had only seen them at our uncle's insistence. Then she determined to flood Parliament."

"With letters?" I asked. She shook her head and I realised she meant Viola had planned to flood parliament in the most literal sense possible. "Where would she get the water? The Thames?"

"Of course."

I looked at Hartwell, really looked, and was alarmed by my response. The desire to take her hand and assure her face in my hands and kiss away her worries. The Countess would become my wife, and be spared a miserable existence as an unmated, childless widow of a peer. Then Hartwell could go back to Oxford, complete her education, travel, and return for a brilliant career. I would sponsor her. We could be... friends. We could only ever be friends. Yet "friend" seemed so inadequate, as I'd grown to realise I wanted more.

"Your Grace?"

"Apologies, I was woolgathering."

"Shall we return to business? I am sorry for... My outburst was inappropriate."

"It is close to your heart. Your passion is admirable." I gave in to impulse and took her hand in both of mine, patting it. "Everything will be fine, Hartwell. You've your votes. We'll rescue the countess." My lips quirked at the image of us, knight and page riding off on some ridiculous quest. "All's well that ends well. Isn't that what the *alpha* Shakespearia wrote?"

"Omega," she grumbled, but I caught the hint of a smile in those violet eyes.

I FOUND MYSELF AT MANTON'S AGAIN, HOPING TO GAIN some mental space from Hartwell and the memory of her face as she wrote letters in my name. Yes, I needed to get the young alpha out of my head because when I'd teased her about her handwriting as pretty as her sister's, she'd gone red, the flush disappearing down her neck. I had almost given in to the temptation to pull her never neat cravat free and see just how far down her neck her blush went. The flutterings of attraction bothered me one day and felt so natural the next. I put it down to the subtle whiffs of Viola that seemed to constantly hang around her. I could sniff out Viola more clearly every day—an addict desperate for the taste of juice of the poppy.

"You've been coming here more often than I remember,"

Paxton said as he watched me take aim, a faint frown marring his handsome features.

"What? Am I not permitted to leave my own house?"

"That's not what I mean, Orley," he sighed. "You spend so much of your time in the country that seeing your face in London on more than one night in a year is an oddity."

"I plan on marrying," I told him, seeing no reason to hide my purpose for being in London.

"Oh? And who is the lady?"

"It is still in negotiations," I smirked.

"Not one of Hartwell's sisters? I beg you not to get involved with that family more than you already are."

"And what is the tale there?"

"Beatrice Hartwell is a menace to polite society. Dressing as a man in an attempt to have her paintings shown at the Summer Exhibition. I saw them. Her work is without equal, but I've never witnessed such careless, reckless disregard for personal safety. An omega in a room of alphas! What's more —the paintings... She went too far. *An Omega's Progress* depicting—thinly veiled, mind—the Countess of Kellingham's journey about an indigent farmer so poor he sold his omega daughter off to the highest bidder. And now she is a widow without a penny to her name."

I snarled. I'd known my intended bride had not been born into a noble family but it seemed her tale was even more tragic than I'd known. Hartwell was right. She needed a light hand rather than my own brand of wooing.

"Ah, Paxton on his favourite topic? The delectable Miss Hartwell?" Fordom sauntered over. Next to Paxton, he appeared stocky, but I'd sparred with him at Jackson's and knew him to be all muscle. I'd put my money on him were he to enter the ring against any professional. He raised his quizzing glass to his eye and faked being startled to see me. "Orley, but this is a rare pleasure."

"Keep your mouth shut," Paxton growled. "The Misses Hartwell as a collective unit are a menace to polite society."

"You used those same words not a minute before. Are you certain you do not protest your dislike too much?" I asked. "And to answer your question. No, the Hartwell omegas are not where my interest lies."

These alphas did not need to know that it was the alpha Miss Hartwell that truly called to me.

Fordom smirked at us. "The pair of you tied up in a family that delights in causing scandal. Two alphas, both alike in the indignity of omegas stepping out of their allotted roles. Taken down by the Hartwells. Miss Beatrice Hartwell shall be your downfall Pax, and Miss Viola Hartwell for you, Orley, since I have heard she is as dangerous as Beatrice."

"And Hippolyta?" Paxton asked.

"I have already retired from the lists. Hartwells ain't for one such as I. As for Hippolyta Hartwell..." Fordom laughed. "They don't call her Queen of the High Toby for nothing. Beatrice is by far the most level headed Hartwell omega to have drawn breath in this century... And the most beautiful."

The last seemed dragged from him as if it pained him in that moment to recall her face.

"You speak of the Hartwells?"

I turned to find Caroline Wilson, an alpha a few years below me at university, standing just to the side watching us. She was the eldest child of a vicar, and the last I'd heard she planned to join the army... Yet here she was.

"What of it? An odd family, wouldn't you say?" Fordom smirked.

"Damn officious," she spat. "I met Viola Hartwell at Lady Clare's the other day. A shrew."

I found myself growling—so this was the alpha who'd sneered at Hartwell while dressed as an omega. But it was Paxton who squared up to her.

"A shrew? You're lucky Iris Hartwell is not here. She would challenge you before you took your next breath, and she a mere cub barely out of leading strings."

"And I'm meant to be scared by that?" Wilson scoffed, but she left without another word.

"What a trio of fishwives we are," Fordom chuckled. "Just the other day Pax faces down the infant and now he threatens to let the little one loose. You, Orley, must be next to defend the Hartwell name."

I WOKE THE NEXT MORNING ACHING WITH NEED FOR violets and vanilla. Violets and vanilla. The first scent I'd smelled in so long that I thought I'd go mad with aching need no matter its source. I'd promised myself not to ask after Viola, but that control almost vanished when I entered my study to find Hartwell at my desk looking over some documents. She'd taken her bottom lip between her teeth and was worrying it.

"That is un-alpha-like behaviour," I snapped, mad I had spent at least a minute staring and warring with the need to take the task upon myself or soothe the abused lip with gentle kisses.

"Oh, sorry. I suppose I am but a child in your eyes..." she murmured without taking her eyes off what she read. "Did you have a look at the latest bill they wish to put before the commons? It is rather peculiarly worded, don't you think? Pitt must have a new secretary. Have you heard anything like that?"

"And why would you think the Prime Minister has changed secretaries?"

"Oh, the syntax. My father used to have us read all the bills pertaining to omega rights. All the bills, actually."

"Even you?" I asked, confused. Alphas presented earlier than omegas, so it made little sense for Hartwell to have sat in on lessons with her sisters when she should have been at school. "Didn't you go to school?"

"Hmmm... No. My parents could not bear the thought of us being away," she was still distracted by what she was reading. I took the time to observe her in greater detail. "I presented later. They thought we would be the same dynamic. We presented at the same time. One of each. My father believed it had something to do with the fact we were born of a female alpha, male omega pairing."

"And you? Do you believe your father's hypothesis?"

"I am to read natural history and biology, Your Grace," she chuckled and finally turned her face towards me. "I would say that my father had no proof... I should say that I respect him too much to argue with his ghost on a point he had spent his entire life working on. I too am interested in the assignment of dynamics. I plan..."

"I thought you wanted to follow a career in politics."

"I do," she hastened to assure me."But first I will spend a few years looking at mating pairs. An odd kind of work to be sure."

I smiled. It was odd, but then the Hartwells seemed to be a family of singular tastes.

"You had an interesting childhood," I observed.

"Very. We were in Scotland until my father died. We all went to the parish school, and my father taught at the university because omegas have that freedom... Edinburgh is a beautiful city. The most beautiful I know."

"Do you miss it?"

"I prefer the country. Beatrice prefers town. Hippolyta is a cat, dissatisfied with wherever she is."

"And Viola?"

"Viola..." she paused and looked back at the papers she

held. "She wants to be with the people she loves... I've never considered it before. But what of you, Your Grace? I know that at some point you must have been a child."

"Naturally. But nothing like your own. Perhaps you've heard about my mother and father?"

"Only whispers. My parents were not gossips. My aunt, only about the comings and goings of her neighbours. My uncle could not care less."

I fought the childish urge to roll my eyes. Her uncle might not care for social standing but he was a shrewd man and a political creature to the bone.

"My parents were married and mated. My mother's affairs with other alphas and betas drove my father mad with jealousy. The year I was meant to start school, he blew his brains out. Officially it was a duel. But he could no longer take the shame of being an alpha cuckolded by his mate."

"Oh. I see."

And I knew she did. That quick brain pulling the pieces together and understanding why I would not mate my wife.

"Which is why you choose to marry and not mate. Though why not mate at a later date? When you know each other better."

"Perhaps I've no interest in turning into a feral alpha. It would take a remarkable person—one I could not imagine living without—to convince me to take a mate. One who could not live without me. I would mate them no matter the dynamic or sex. Do you understand me?" I could not explain why it mattered but I needed her to... To what? Agree with me?

"I should not have pried. We have work to do, Your Grace," she cleared her throat.

"You are avoiding my question," I pointed out.

"I do not understand it," she sighed, her eyes unhappy. "I

would not fight with you for the world. I am sure that your reasons make sense to you but to me, they are a mystery."

"Because I do not wish an unhappy mating on anyone. My grandparents were happy because they married for respect, the legacy of the dukedom. But they mated those they loved. I grew up with a pack who were a single unit. Should I force a mate bond on an omega? A mate bond she or he didn't desire? Or one that I didn't desire? Is that love, do you think? Or respect?"

Hartwell, so quick with an answer to every question put to her, stood looking at me. Her cheeks were stained pink, and she pulled that blasted, plump lower lip between her teeth. I gripped the arms of my chair. My alpha rode me hard, urging me to make plain to her exactly how I felt about mating bites. If I just got my teeth on her neck, she might better understand the permanency of something she had not asked for. That is if an alpha would respond as an omega did. As our eyes locked. I perceived the dilemma of my reaction to my secretary. As an alpha, I really ought not have this response to another alpha. It was not unheard of. But alphas needed defined hierarchies, making an equal relationship between two alphas challenging without the tempering influence of an omega. Yet here I was, satisfied to allow her to play as she would, make small challenges to my authority, all because I knew it would take very little for me to exert my dominance. We could work, I realised. With her youth and, despite those sparks of temper, natural submissiveness. We could work as mates. And for that very reason, I must fight my urges. For desiring to mate her while I planned to marry the countess went against my own principles. What omega would accept that scheme? For if I were to take her to my bed, I would never deny her access. An omega bride would have to accept we were one. All of which made this an impossible game of if's and could be's.

"Get back to work," I said, at last breaking eye contact. She walked back to her desk and sat, her focus seemingly back on the letters of business she'd been tasked with. But every so often, when I was caught in a mindless perusal of my young secretary's face, her eyes would meet mine. Enthralled by each other before one of us looked away.

"Your Grace, I believe it is time for me to return to my uncle's," her voice rough as if roused from a deep sleep. I looked at the clock and saw the late hour and shooed her away before I gave in to the impulse to invite her to stay for a light meal or game of chess.

That night I sat up weighing my options. I could not do without the best secretary I'd had, though I would never tell her that. It was more satisfying to watch her not realise her own brilliance. And at the same time, I needed to right the course of our relationship. Put her in the role of secretary, perhaps protegé. Invite her to some dinner and introduce her to other alphas she could make connections with. For if I kept her too close, I would never be able to give her up. I walked into the duchess's nest, a place I had visited every night for the last week. I had come to London with a clear plan in mind, but now I felt almost feral with the need to change that plan and follow instincts that demanded I bring her here to this nest. Nests were meant for omegas, but I wanted to see Hartwell here. See whether she would bare her neck for me. How would she taste? What would her pink cunt look like? What sounds would she make as I locked us together on my knot?

10

VIOLA

t was a day to visit Olivia, so I was home and sadly blue devilled for I would not see the duke today.

I intended to spend the visit complimenting the duke. How could I not, knowing what kind of alpha, what kind of man he was? A good one, the best. Whose reasons for marrying were honourable. Whose reasons for not mating understandable, now that I knew him so well. I sat in the drawing room with the countess and struggled to pay attention to what she said, for my brain was full of my conversation with the Duke. If he meant what he said, that in marrying the countess he would save her from the fate she must face once her period of mourning ended. That in not mating her, he would be saving both from an unhappy... That she could find a mate if she wanted, but that he never intended to take one. Even if they weren't mated to one another... Could an alpha accept sharing their spouse with another? Could he truly do that? A man who required mastery in everything. I could not believe it, yet he had been in earnest. That firm mouth set in an unforgiving line. I swallowed at the memory and turned to face the widow in hopes of distracting my thoughts.

"Would you never consider marrying again?" I whispered. Our trysts, if one could call them that, were conducted in almost secrecy despite being so public. Her companion often interrupted when anyone spent more than a few moments in her close company. So our every conversation felt illicit; stolen moments as I tried to convince her that the duke would make the perfect husband.

Olivia, for that was how she desired I call her, now flushed prettily and shook her head. "Oh Miss Hartwell! Viola... You have no notion how... Awkward. I could not... The... The late Earl was most displeased with everything... I am..."

"Hush," I laid a hand on her arm to distract her since the other visitors had turned to look at us. I angled my body, the better to shield her from their eyes. I lowered my voice. "Olivia, do not think that all alphas are like that. I know one... I cannot say it here. There are too many ears."

For all that she had been so disastrously married, the omega before me clung to many of the romantic notions so typical of our dynamic. It was upon this that I sought to play and hopefully encourage her to think of finding a husband and save herself. If, when, she married the duke, she would have security. Given her agitation, it was the best I could hope for. She would give him an alpha heir. That is what he wanted.

"Sweet friend. Tell me, I implore you!" Came Olivia's hushed plea.

"If, and I say this as a hypothetical, a mere possibility of a romance, shall I say. But if an alpha had perchance seen you, fallen for you, and wanted to profess the feelings he must bury deep inside... Who knows what lengths he might go to... For certain I would, if I had fallen deeply in love, would do anything. The poets would write songs about the feats I would accomplish to win her affection. Remember the play? Twelfth Night? How Duke Orsino will go to any lengths to win Olivia? How Viola, disguised, woos Olivia in his name? Think, I am Viola in the flesh. And you Olivia. I am here to woo... You see? How romantic would that be?"

I winced. My words were painfully on the nose, but I believed I must make my case as explicitly as I dared. I had no such romantic notions, but if my plan were to succeed I must convince her that love, and love with an alpha, would be the only way to escape her current circumstances. From our (albeit brief) acquaintance, I felt secure in the knowledge that painting her as the figure of some great romantic story was the way to go. I did not understand it myself. How a woman so traumatised could cling to the stories of daring rescues.

"I have... I have always wanted someone like you," her bright eyes held mine. For the first time, I saw the girl she had been. Then it struck me, these tales of romance were what gave her hope that not all was lost.

"You deserve to find the alpha of your dreams," I told her, my voice thick with emotion. Such a fragile omega had earned a happy ending after the tragedies she had suffered. I now desired to find her a mate. One who would make those dreams into a reality more precious than any she could imagine. "A mate. You deserve a mate who loves you. You deserved to be wooed."

"Yes," she breathed. "Yes..."

"Miss Hartwell!" Caroline Wilson's sharp bark interrupted whatever Olivia had been about to say. "This note just arrived for you. I suppose you haunt our door enough..."

"Oh stop, Caro!" Olivia cried. "Viola is my dearest friend. Read your note, Viola. I am sure it is just your aunt begging you to come home before she forgets your face."

I turned it over and my stomach dipped. Though the seal was plain I recognised the odd hexagonal shape and the rich green of the wax. The duke was writing me a letter? Here? Without thought or discretion, I opened it up.

Hartwell-

Your presence is desired at mine this evening for dinner. I have things to discuss with my secretary.

-Orley

I looked up to see Olivia's face flushed. She looked like some romantic ideal, and when I compared myself to her there was a twinge of jealousy. I would never compete with one such as her. An alpha like the duke of Orley would never look at me when Olivia was in the room.

"You must leave me," she said with a sad smile.

"I'm sorry, my dear, but duty calls."

We rose together. "I—"

And with the hastiness of youth, she pressed her cheek to mine before running her nose along my neck. Scenting me! I realised with a start. No. Impossible. Omegas didn't scent mark each other. "I'll be back, Olivia. Don't give up. I will be back."

"If I could find an alpha as good as you..." she whispered into my ear. I blinked, her scent had spiked. It was cloying honeysuckle and sweet butter. I breathed through my mouth, trying to avoid taking too deep breaths. There was a reason that same-dynamic partnerships were so rare. Then why did Olivia's scent spike? I froze. What if she could smell lingering wisps of the duke on my skin? My hair perhaps? Or... I remembered my greatcoat. I had worn it over my cloak in the carriage on the journey from Weymouth Street. That coat smelt of Iris, which as her sister I would never notice but might catch the interest of another omega.

As I was being handed into the carriage, I heard my name being called. Caroline skipped down the steps.

"For some reason, my lady has a liking for you. I do not," she said.

"You've made that clear enough," I smiled. "Pray, if you dislike me so much, what business have you with me?"

"Here. She begs I give you this," she held out a twist of paper. I raised my gaze to the other woman in silent question.

"I did not read it!" She growled. "I've more love for her than that."

I nodded still confused why Olivia would feel the need to send me a note when I had only just left her side. "Thank you."

"Farewell," the alpha snarled, and I felt the full force of her hatred. I watched in stunned silence as she ran up the few stairs and into the house.

"Methinks that she is rather in love with the countess," my uncle's coachman chuckled. "She's as jealous as a fish wife."

"You shouldn't gossip or use such language," I said but did not truly mean it. I was grateful for the explanation, but it begged the question of why she might be jealous of me, another omega. Unless! My earlier fear that I carried an alpha's scent resurfaced. I raised my arm to my nose and sniffed. There was a faint trace of alpha on me, Iris's alpha smell from having her clothes in the carriage with me, perhaps that is what she had noticed? Unusual too, for an alpha's senses were not as sharp as an omega's. I shook my head, clearing it of all thoughts, and climbed into the carriage. The blinds were drawn, but I had grown used to at least beginning my transformation in near darkness. The first was to remove my gown and bundle it away. Then, removing my short stays until I was naked except for my thin chemise. Only then could I layer on two of Iris's shirts. For their scent was beginning to fade. I had written to Iris asking for more.

She'd responded she'd be in town soon and would bring more with her then.

When I felt that I was dressed enough to exit the carriage without drawing too much notice, I knocked, signalling to John Coachman that I was ready to be left in front of Orley House. I glanced out the window and saw I had time to read the note from Olivia. Her copperplate handwriting was wrinkled, but her words were clear:

You are all I have been able to think about since the moment I met you. My friend, you are the one good thing in my life.

I cursed. What madness was this? I was an omega. I was... I was not who she wanted. Hopeless Olivia was drawn to the traces of alpha that hung around me. Probably sensitive due to her isolation. Perhaps her heat was near. My cheeks flushed at the thought. Would that news reach the duke? Would he hear that and decide to act? To take matters into his own hands and press his suit. And what then? Did I have the right to stay by his side once he had a wife? I tried to imagine what it would be like to continue as his secretary while he married and rutted another omega through her heat. I could do it.

"Miss Hartwell," My head jerked up. The carriage had halted, and Horne, the duke's butler, held the door open for me. Since he knew I disguised myself as Viola, he had made it his business to ensure I could complete my transformation back into alpha, or so he thought. I thought he might see through me at first. That he might suspect I was an omega. But as the weeks went by I relaxed. Joked with him and Timms, His Grace's valet, about the necessity of returning to my natural self after playing omega with the countess. I wrapped myself in Iris' greatcoat and carried a bundle of men's clothes under my arms as I entered the hall and ran up the stairs to the bedchamber where I could change in peace. Today though, I could not find it in me to smile at his teasing wink. Instead, I gave a small nod and rushed to change. I was careless with my cravat and the way I rubbed lemon over my wrists and neck to remove hints of omega. I reached the landing before realising I had not anointed myself with the oils that most closely mimicked Iris's scent. It was always a risk, but one I was determined not to take. So I returned again to perfume myself. I looked into the mirror and was not surprised to see the frown and irritation reflected at me. I pressed my fingers to my temple and counted to one hundred in Latin, then Greek, before I was satisfied that I could keep my temper even and my passion under control. My anger had no target but myself.

"CALL ME SYON," HE SAID BARELY A MINUTE AFTER I entered the library, which had rapidly become my favourite room in the whole world. Inexplicably, his expression stern without the possibility of compromise. I winced at the all too familiar sensation of slick building between my thighs—his unforgiving alpha will tugged at my omega's conviction this alpha was what I needed. I blamed the fact I'd spent the morning garbed in my omega's clothes, sitting amongst my dynamic, and speaking with Olivia. Olivia, the omega he wanted to call wife. And now, when I felt exhausted and troubled by worries that I had brought upon myself, he was growling at me then smiling, in turn confusing me and softening me at once.

"I could not," I objected. "It would be—"

"When we are in private," he chuckled, his body relaxing when I argued—nonsensical alpha. "All this 'Your Grace' business becomes dull since you must always be calling my attention to this or to that phrasing of a letter."

"I do not mean to interrupt..."

"Hartwell, you do not mean to do much yet you are always doing."

"You don't take me seriously. And if I must call you Syon then you must call me... Keep calling me Hartwell. I like it more than my own name." I did not lie but wished the words back as soon as I'd given them voice. I damned myself for not thinking before speaking. But then while I longed to hear him speak my name, the sound of Hartwell made me weak because it made me feel like his equal—an unusual aphrodisiac. It was a nightmare in the making, and I desperately wanted to return to my nest and hide within its comforting warmth.

"Hartwell? Not Iris?"

"No one but you calls me Hartwell," I told him. Goddess, what was I thinking?

"Hartwell, then. Come here. I want you to explain precisely why I am now supporting voting rights for omegas in a bill concerned with Pitt's tax on powder for wigs... This is the third version of this speech that mentions an injustice and they change with each version... It is not your pet project of the Omega Property Rights Act. Explain yourself, Hartwell," he lingered on my name, stretching it out like a caress. I moved closer, hypnotised by the sound of my name on his lips. He might have called me Hartwell before, but never like this.

"Syon?" I tried the name out. How it felt like a supplication when it came from my lips. "Call me Hartwell like that and I promise to always behave... I will never slip things into your speeches without informing you first."

He startled and leant forward in his chair. I froze, realising he was sniffing. Had my scent spiked with my temper?

"You were at the countess's residence this morning," he stated. "You smell of omega."

"I— Just as you say. I was with the Countess this morning. As we agreed," I swallowed. I retreated to my small desk by the window. It would not prove to be a particularly sturdy defence against Syon if he chose to come after me, but it settled my scattered nerves to be close to the window. I opened it a crack and allowed the biting winter air to seep in. "You sent a letter to me there."

"I had not forgotten. But, in future, bathe before coming here. And close the damn window. Do you want to catch your death sitting in a draught? Or do you plan to kill me?"

"Oh. I should not change here then?" I asked, confused.

"Is that what you have been doing?" He sputtered. "And how have you been coming into my house and not been noticed in a woman's dress? Not to mention stinking of omega!"

I jumped at the bark that entered his voice.

"You find the smell offensive?"

He growled at me. "Answer the damn question."

"I remove my gown in the carriage, which goes around the square until I have it off. Then I wear a cloak and enter and change in one of the bedrooms."

He gaped at me. "And my servants are aware of this?"

"Your butler and valet."

He ran a hand over his face and stood. I watched him, curious if he were to go and summon his butler and demand an explanation. Instead, and to my horror, he stalked to where I sat. Syon loomed over me, his pupils dilated until his eyes were almost black, his scent so thick I felt dizzy. To say I was prepared for the full expression of alpha aggression would be risible. I fought every instinct to turn and offer him my neck.

"I do not desire for you to ever wear your sister's clothes

in my house. Do you understand me, Hartwell?" he spat my name out, but I could not understand his anger.

"Do not get so angry," I crooned trying to soothe his temper. "It seemed the most efficient way; otherwise I must return to Weymouth Street. By then, it is far too late in the day to come here."

"Then do not. Your day off shall be on whichever day you are to see the countess. All other days you are to be here and not smelling of *her*."

I bit down hard on the inside of my cheek. Irrationally, I wanted to argue with him that Viola, that I smelt just fine. But the haunting feeling his "her" was the countess sparked a fit of irrational jealousy. The thought he could smell her on me, despite how little time I'd had to pick up her scent, twisted my insides until I wanted to scream, primal and furious, that he preferred another's scent to mine.

But he is not yours, I screamed right back. *The alpha before you is no more yours to claim than it is possible to wish the sun and moon in the sky at the same time.*

"I will try—"

"No trying. You will obey me in all things," he barked. His alpha coming through so strongly that no alpha would have been able to stand up to it, especially in his own home where everything belonged to him—including me I realised. Whether he knew it or not, he owned my every thought in these past weeks. In retaliation, I sought to thwart him in matters as small as in how I mended his pens. He'd barred me from touching his pens a week ago, which was a shame because I loved to hear him curse when his pen sputtered. He returned the favour, aggravating me to the point I fantasied about strangling him in frustration over his alpha superiority. Then in the dark of my bed, forbidden thoughts crept into my imagination though I dared not put words to those too dangerous desires. Too often nights began with my face buried in my pillow, hands clutching the sheets, my core unsatisfied, and slick covered thighs pressing together—my body protesting at being denied.

"Now get back to work," he commanded. I took a deep breath, grateful the cracked window had thinned our scents.

I would master myself, I must master myself if I were to survive my time with Syon.

THE REST OF THE AFTERNOON WAS TENSE. THE AIR SO charged that when Horne came in to ask if we wished for refreshments, I gasped at the fresh air that came into the room. Syon—how had I come to think of him in such a personal way and so quickly?—refused to look up from where he sat squinting at the broadsheet Horne had brought, crisp from being ironed to ensure Syon's fingers didn't become stained from the ink. After snapping at him he'd be better for eating something, I ordered a light repast, and when it came I had to coax him to eat. He growled that I was fussy, and I growled right back that if he continued to be like this I would quit and he could sort out his own messes both in the managing of his affairs both in business and pleasure.

Our eyes held. Daggers drawn, and ready for a fight I was unsure either of us would emerge from unscathed.

"You are a scamp. I don't know why I put up with you," he said with such resigned humour that I snorted. He sounded like any beleaguered alpha forced to endure the nagging care of an omega. And here I was, neither an alpha nor his omega, yet falling into the part with such ease that I had to see the humour of it or I would find myself running from his presence as if the Devil himself were hot on my heels.

"Dine with me this evening," he smiled.

"What?"

"Dine with me; I already invited you to in my note. I desire your company. Besides..." he sighed, looking to the ceiling. "I should hear how your business with the countess goes."

"I can tell you that now," I said, somewhat bashful as I was not sure the propriety of my dining with him—though how a dinner could be more compromising than spending most days locked up with him, I did not know. "I believe my aunt will be expecting me."

He snorted and bent over the speech, crossing out a line with purpose. I growled. A smile tugged at his lips. "I promise she can do without you for one evening."

"Fine," I snapped. "But only if you agree to consider the unaltered speech."

"Convince me then," he said with challenge and lounged in his seat, crossing his arms over his broad chest.

"To begin with..."

We finished later than was our habit. And if Horne had not come to announce dinner was ready, we would have continued to argue the merits of omega rights until the sun had risen on a new day.

I had not seen much of Syon's London residence but was unsurprised to find that the dining room was dominated by a table I suspected could have entertained as many as eighty guests. He assured me only forty guests would fit about it but that he could fit near double that amount at Ayleigh.

"Do you entertain much?" I asked when the last of our excellent meal had been removed. I'd hardly noticed that there was no meat, for the food was delicious and filling. One day I would ask him why and when he had become a vegetarian and how he still managed to be so big and strong—an omega's curiosity would eventually be satisfied.

"No," he did not seem bothered by the fact. He'd turned his chair and stretched his long legs out before him, looking impossibly powerful and handsome. My core clenched and slick began to gather.

"Why? I can imagine you would have a great many dinners here. Political dinners, for instance..." I tried to distract myself by cracking more nuts than I could eat.

"There is no hostess, scamp!" He laughed and refilled my glass.

I had been drinking more than I ever had before but was enjoying the way the wine made me feel. A little reckless and far more intimate with Syon than I was sober.

"Come! You do not need a hostess to have your fellow alphas over!" I laughed.

"So says the daughter of the most famous omega of our times. Surely your sisters would raise their finely arched brows at your urging me to talk omega politics without one of you to keep us in line? Apologies, I meant one of your sisters."

I giggled into my glass. "My Grace, your Syon—"

"You are drunk!" He said with some surprise. "You aren't used to drinking... I shouldn't have poured you that last glass."

"Perhaps. But my point stands," I huffed.

"And what point was that? You've made many throughout our acquaintance." He smiled knowing my mind was foggy from drinking too much of his good port. I watched somewhat reluctantly as he took my empty glass away from me. But with my brain so fuzzy, I could feel just about my need to preen just a little in front of this virile alpha. Oh, how I wanted to be an omega like Olivia whom alphas could worship. Syon didn't even suspect I was an omega. My size, my behaviour... How could he? How could anyone?

I absently blinked at him trying to remember what we had been talking about. Ah. Politics. Alphas. Omegas. My favourite topics seemed so... Trivial perhaps? Why were we talking about serious things when we could be doing serious things.

"Firstly," I raised a finger. "Alphas are more than able to stand up for omegas. Second. Alphas are more of a mind to listen to other alphas. Therefore alphas talking to alphas without the supposed pressure of omegas..."

"Yes, Puss. I see your point."

"Good," I smirked, arms crossing under my breasts before my brow clouded in thought. "Did you call me Puss?" I asked, embarrassed by the endearment.

"You've claws but they cause no real damage. I've called you Puss many a time and you choose now to notice?" he laughed. "So you will come to a dinner I host and talk politics with my friends?"

"You don't have friends," I sobered instantly. It was not an accusation, though perhaps a man as proud as a duke would take it as such. More that, of a sudden, I realised his nights were almost solitary. His days too. Alphas spent their time at private clubs, but most days he was with me. His golden head bent over a letter, squinting a little. For a thought, his eyesight might be weaker than he would admit. If he was not with me, he was at Manton's—how I wished to go!—or with Jackson to box.

"You are my friend. But in general, you are correct. I am not friendly with those I am not familiar with," he said with equal gravity. "But in politics, you might call an alpha a friend over the table and curse him behind his back."

"You wouldn't do that," I said with confidence. "You would never pretend."

"Except with you. I am pretending in order to woo my future duchess. How exactly did you convince me? I must have been mad."

"Most likely," I grinned, but it was forced.

II

SYON

I never felt so alive as the moment that I looked across my dining table at Hartwell looking pleased as punch that she had convinced me to take part in her mad scheme.

"How's your progress with the countess?" The question seemed to sober her immediately.

"She is more interested in hearing a suit from an alpha," she frowned and ran a finger around the lip of the glass causing it to hum. "She... She has taken me into her confidence. I am unsure if it will be possible to... Perhaps she will see my deceit and willingly fall into the arms of another without much thought. Syon, and I ask this with a formality, do you think you can be gentle with her? Take her into your household and... She wishes to be a figure of romance."

"Yes, I can be gentle... Play with me." I realised I didn't wish to discuss my possible marriage to the countess. Not when it had her becoming so serious all of a sudden. I preferred playful violet eyes to sombre ones, but would she agree to my invitation? I closed my eyes to steady my nerves. Though why I should be nervous escaped me.

"Play? How would I play with you?" The violet eyes were somewhat unfocused. But her words caused me to focus on a pair of pouting lips. I had a very clear idea of how I wanted to play with her. How I wanted to play with that mouth. The image was enough that I shifted uncomfortably in my chair.

"Billiards," I said after clearing my throat.

Horne lit the candles, and I watched as the billiards room began to throw off the dark shadows. I rarely came here, having no one to play with, but the urge to keep her with me as long as possible had prompted me to insist we play. She'd admitted ignorance to the game, and instead of letting her off I only pressed harder.

"No, you are doing it wrong," I set my cue aside and moved behind her to better hold her body into the correct position. A mistake I realised as I folded my body over hers.

My hard cock, which I'd been working to forget, begged to grind against her.

"Is this necessary?" She looked over her shoulder. Every thought was arrested by the look in those violet eyes. "Is my form truly that bad?"

"Yes... You've the most unusual eyes I've ever beheld. What can I call you when it is just us," I smiled. It bothered me that she preferred being called Hartwell. "Tell me there is something you like more than Hartwell."

"No," she breathed, a faint blush staining her cheeks. "I like Hartwell more than anything... Too many treat me like a child because of my size. Iris Hartwell, the pocket alpha. All my older sisters were omegas. Iris and Viola could both have been alphas, both omegas. But in the end, it was one of each."

"Omega? You?" I huffed a laugh and rested my forehead against her dark curls. An omega? My body shook with laughter, bitter in the knowledge that she was an alpha. If she had been an omega, I would have said her manner was at times coy, flirtatious. No. She would never be like that. Every move, look, word proclaimed her unconscious of my carnal response. "Of course, that is it."

I licked my lips and searched for some topic that would change the tenor of our conversation.

"Did you know you could give me a glass of spoilt milk or meat gone off, and I would not be able to tell?" I asked her, knowing I shouldn't keep her trapped by my body. But instead of straightening, rejecting temptation, I shifted closer the better to feel her heat, catch the faint whiff of violets and vanilla.

"You can't smell?" she gasped. "But... Why?"

"I have no idea," I admitted, breathing in her scent, knowing my cock ached for her, for an alpha. I should not find her so distracting, I should consider the deviance of desiring another alpha. Instead, I wanted to conquer her more than if she'd been an omega. Conquer and claim. But my own damned honour prevented me from enacting what my cock and knot wanted: to fuck my secretary in all her holes. "Though I suspect my busted nose might have something to do with it. Until Viola, I have not been able to scent anything."

"Syon?" Hartwell asked. I liked the way she stretched the first syllable. No, to be fanciful, it was spoken like "sigh", rather than the Old Testament name for Jerusalem. She did not proclaim me Zion, but something far more illicit.

"Syon," I corrected.

"I know how to pronounce your name," she snapped and tried to straighten in my arms but it only pushed her into my body and aching cock. We both went rigid.

"Syon," there was a warning in her voice that I chose to ignore. A warning I refused to acknowledge.

"You are a beautiful, if impudent, woman, Puss. My body's reaction to your proximity is only natural. I'm not ashamed of it. Nothing improper..." Except nothing could be more improper... Unless she'd been an omega. Then I'd have compromised her and be obligated to marry her.

"Puss?" she huffed, still indignant at the endearment. But instead of moving away seemed to press back onto my cock, as if exploring what was between us and damn hard to miss because the "it" was damn hard. "Oh... I... I've never done anything like this. With an alpha," she whispered.

"Shall I show you?" I gave her no moment to protest and turned her, lifted her until she settled on the edge of the billiards table. Her violet eyes met mine. Our eye beams twisting and pressing forth any number of emotions, the principle of which was desire. "Have you touched yourself before?"

She smirked. "Of course I have. It isn't just men and omegas who take their pleasure into their own hands."

"Have you fucked?" I grinned. This time she blushed. My alpha crowed with pleasure. "You've never fucked. Been kissed?"

"By Sarah," she blushed again. I was shocked. I'd expected her to have a bit more experience than a single kiss. Even if she was young...A whiff of violets and vanilla wafted off of her, and I chased the scent, hunting down where it was thickest. Unsurprisingly, it was along her neck where, if she were an omega, her mating gland would be, though that was covered by her poorly tied cravat. It suddenly occurred to me that the twins might both smell of vanilla and violets. For Hartwell was not dressed in her sister's clothes. I told myself I wasn't going to kiss her. Our relationship was already too complicated. I drew back, prepared to put distance between us, when she turned her head just enough for our lips to brush in a delicately chaste kiss. Heavenly, and infuriatingly inadequate as far as my alpha was concerned. I pressed forward, pushing her thighs apart so that I could rub my aching cock against her hot centre. She gasped, and I deepened the kiss, taking advantage of that willing mouth. A wave of satisfaction that I was the first alpha to claim her like this washed over me. The heat between her legs increased and she began to rock into me, unconscious and so deliciously innocent. Then her fingers laced through my hair, a gentle tug pulling me in deeper. With stunning clarity, I realised I wanted her virginity, I would be the first to fuck her. The imperative to stick my thick cock into her cunt had my hands flexing over her hips. I'd rub her clit until she screamed and squeezed so tight on my knot that I would never stop coming inside of her... I jerked back.

"I..." My eyes flickered across her face. "I should not have..."

"Syon... Please, do not apologise," her hands clutched my coat, and her face buried into my chest. Her next words were muffled. "Oh, Goddess! But please do not apologise. As you said—"

"It is natural. It is nothing," I confirmed, tilting her face until our eyes met. She nodded, eyes bright, pupils dilated. Goddess, what had we been thinking?

"The wine? That... That lowered..." she trailed off.

But I had no such excuse. When I told her that, she cupped my face with her hand.

"I wanted it," she told me, her voice steady. "I wanted you to kiss me... Dammit, Syon. I kissed you first!"

I laughed. She had kissed me first. "We can forget it then?"

"Of course... I should probably go now."

I nodded. She needed to go, or I would do something rash. I would drag her to the duchess' nest and fuck her until her own scent was drowned out by my own.

≈

"I CANNOT BE A LEADING FIGURE IN POLITICS," I SNAPPED A few days after our aborted billiards game. I couldn't forget her heat or her kiss. But when she hadn't mentioned the interlude, had avoided looking at me for the last few days, and had only spoken when necessary, my pride determined it best to ignore the raging need to taste her again. All of her. "My position as a duke does not permit it. To think that I can stand and give this speech…"

"You should! I wrote this for you!" She waved it in my face, and I saw red. Hartwell knew I wasn't dismissing her work. She knew that. So her anger towards myself was a slap in the face, and one I would not tolerate. Perhaps I'd been too lenient with her, especially since the kiss. I growled and made to snatch the sheaf of papers from her, but she pulled away at the last moment

"Fine, I'll give it to Gale," Hartwell threatened, violet eyes flashing bright.

"She won't make it," I dismissed the notion.

"Not the Viscountess. Her son, Frederick is capable. He is standing at the next by-election. My uncle took me to a dinner with them the other night. I'll give it to him—"

"Frederick? Dinner? You think I will permit you to consort with that ass?" I snarled and grabbed her by the lapels of her coat. I shook her a little, which caused the pages to flutter to the ground, forgotten in the heat of the moment. "You will stay away from that alpha. Not because of his politics. They are liberal to be sure. No, you will keep out of his sphere because I will not have my secretary consorting with a known rake. Just because you like his politics does not make him fit for your company. And while we are discussing Mr Gale, keep Viola away from him as well. I won't have him sniffing around her like a bitch in heat." I spoke with sneering anger and could not have expected what happened next.

"Do not call Viola a bitch," she slapped me with surprising

force. When she realised what she'd done, those violet eyes went wide with fear. "Dear Goddess! Syon—"

"I like the fire, Hartwell." Because Goddess give me strength, but the fight in her made me hard. "But do not ever raise your hand to me like that again."

"You called Viola a bitch in heat," she hissed, her fury returned.

"I called *Gale* a bitch in heat."

"And don't insult omegas while you are at it!" she snarled.

"Never was there a greater idiot with an even greater intellect." There were times when I forgot my own strength. Now was not one of them. I wanted to remind this recalcitrant and alluring creature who the real alpha was. I pulled her across her desk until her face was pressed into the cool wood, her eyes level with my hard cock—Goddess help me, I was aroused by the thought of dominating her. With one hand I held her down. The other pushed her coat out of the way. I wanted as little between my temper and her willfulness as possible. My hand fell with a dull smack on a surprisingly luscious bottom that had her crying out more with surprise than any pain. There were too many layers of fabric between us for me to hurt her. Three more swift hits followed, and she struggled as each landed. Struggling more as I stepped close, my cock twitching in my breeches. I had never been so close to fucking an alpha—would her tie be as powerful as an omega's cunt? My body responded to her proximity in a way I could not have anticipated. I gave her a final spank that shoved her further up the desk, causing the contents of my desk to topple to the ground. I was on the point of pulling her breeches off, of fucking her when sanity returned with alarming abruptness.

"Get out," I snarled. "Fix your attitude before you return tomorrow."

"I have work to do." Her breath was heavy, but she did

not sound defeated. How she had the gall to continue to push baffled me. It drove my temper to new heights. I raised my hand to deliver a spanking she wouldn't forget when Horne called through the door.

"Your Grace, the tailor is here."

I swore. I didn't give a damn about my tailor, but I did need to get away from Vi.

"I want you gone within the hour," I told my brattish secretary. "Do not talk back. One hour."

I RAN PAXTON AND FORDOM TO GROUND IN A NEW GAMING hell owned by the darkly sinister alpha Oberon Drexler, who dressed in all black and was shadowed by a man known only as Puck, but called the Black Devil for his punishing left. They were as odd a pair as Paxton and Fordom. Though the former were rough when compared to my two... Friends, I decided. We had too many overlapping interests for them to be anything other than friends. The night was young, but the rooms were crowded, for Paxton had won his race between here and Newmarket in record time even with the roads less than ideal. He was being celebrated, though you would not know from the scowl on his face. When he saw me it cleared. He pushed through the crowd to my side. "We must talk."

"The Hartwells?" I guessed. "I've a question..."

He grunted and signalled to Fordom, who followed us into the quiet hall.

Up close the man looked like he'd been through the wars and then dragged backwards through a hedge rather than successfully beating the standing time for a race to Newmarket. "None of us can protect them forever. Mrs Hartwell's embassy to the French has failed. She and Beatrice are amongst the enemy, and Fordom is struggling to pry them away—both stubborn to the end—I wish to Our Goddess I knew where the vixen was so that I could box her ears and then drown her in the Channel. Now I'm hearing your Hartwell spends all her time with the Countess of Kellingham. As if she doesn't have enough to do with her time. Exert your power, Orley. You've more of it with the twins than we."

My secretary wooing the countess? I nearly told them the truth.

"I don't tell my secretary how to spend her time," I lied. "Besides, she's too young an alpha to be seriously sniffing after omegas."

"Alpha? Sniffing after omegas? Are you still going along with that ruse? Very well. Suit yourself. I wash my hands of all Hartwells and urge you to do the same. Unless you plan to take your little secretary in hand?"

I growled at the thought of taking my hand to Hartwell and spanking the insolence out of her. How I'd already done so and been interrupted before making the correct impression. But just as quickly thrust the image away in case my scent changed and the others perceived my... My interest in that depraved image. I looked between them. A truly odd pair to be sure, but then who was I to judge? I tossed and turned every night haunted by a patchwork dream of violet eyes and a scent of violets mixed with vanilla.

"Very well. I'll speak to Hartwell, see what she can do. Do you have any idea where I might find Iris?"

Paxton relaxed as if a weight had been lifted from his shoulders.

"You just took a weight off my shoulders. Viola... She is a brat. I'd rather not hang for strangling her. Better to get Iris to do something."

"Since when do you use their christian names?" Fordom laughed before taking snuff. He shook himself like a dog and then looked off into the distance. "Goddess save me from all omegas, especially those called Hartwell. I might jest on occasion but tangling with Beatrice was always purgatory."

"It is hell," his friend snapped.

"No, Pax. Purgatory. You are welcome to it, for I'll none."

"The two of you have issues," I said. "Tell me where I can find *Iris* Hartwell and explain to her how it's to be."

"Likely here," Paxton sighed. "It is why I wished to speak with you first."

I grunted and with a brief nod left them in the darkened passageway. Back in the well-lit rooms where the murmurs of conversation intermingled with shouts of laughter, I looked for my quarry. My hunt was in vain. Instead, I came upon Florey and a pack of his cronies rolling dice.

"Your grace, will you join us?" Viscountess Gale asked. She was a Whig by convenience, and I could see the taunt in her eyes. I found myself bristling.

"Another night, perhaps. Florey, I look for your niece. I don't suppose you know where I might find her?"

"Is she here?" Gale looked around, clearly curious about my secretary, which set my teeth on edge.

"Oh, leave the girl alone!" An ancient alpha protested. "She is having fun. Let the children play!"

"I believe she left a little while ago," Florey said. "But I cannot be sure."

"My thanks," I gave the table a bow and left them. However, when I reached the door I threw a glance over my shoulder. Florey was looking at me, his face pinched with worry. Perhaps he was aware of his niece's doings. But he had no need to be. I had every intention of leading Hartwell back to safe waters where I could keep an eye on her.

I left, hoping that she'd hung about... And I was in luck.

Hartwell laughed with an alpha male I'd never seen before. The pair had their arms linked and looked so at home in each other's company that I resented their obvious intimacy.

"Hartwell," I barked. She did not respond. "Iris Hartwell."

She turned towards me, and I saw the colour leave her face—a guilty conscience, no doubt. For a moment I did not recognise her as her face lacked its usual carefree smile.

"Excuse me, Your Grace," she bowed low. "May I introduce you to my friend, Mr Arthur Jones. Arthur, this is His Grace, the Duke of Orley."

"I must speak with you, Hartwell," my emotions were whirling, all because my Hartwell had a friend she'd never mentioned. I did not trust myself in front of the innocuous alpha with a weak chin.

"Arthur, go ahead to my uncle's. I will meet you there in a moment," she said. "Your Grace, shall we go inside?"

"No. The square will do."

We crossed the quiet street and into the square.

"You are wooing the Countess for yourself," I snapped. In truth, I did not care about that bit of gossip. I knew the truth. Rather I did not feel quite so comfortable with this version of my secretary—so much stiffer than I was used to. Bringing up the countess seemed as like to provoke her temper as anything. "Paxton brought me the news."

"Your Grace, 'tis a falsehood only a knave would spread! I would never, could never woo in secret. That you would think I could confounds me. Perhaps consider that Lord Paxton don't know what his business and what isn't," she said through gritted teeth. "If you know anything of me, you cannot believe that gossip. I, of all alphas, would never once seek to bring talk to an omega. My sisters are embroiled in enough scandal and pranks to turn a young alpha ancient. Have you thought, perhaps," and she looked around, lowering her voice even though none could hear us. "Perhaps if I were to wish to woo her, I would do so honestly? Like an alpha."

"Like an alpha? Do you seek to reprimand me, whelp?" I growled. "Must I remind you that you came up with this subterfuge?"

Her face blanked, and she gave a stiff nod. "You are right. I have no reason to tell you how to handle your affairs. My apologies."

"Now. That is not the only reason I should wring your neck. I hear from Paxton and Fordom that Viola is acting out."

"You are damn officious—" she choked off her words and flushed.

I growled at her. I wanted to grab the scruff of her neck and drag her to my study where I could demonstrate exactly how officious I could be. She should take it as a compliment that I clenched my fist and held my boiling passion in check.

"Iris? Uh... we shall be late if..." The innocuous Mr Jones gave an awkward cough. "Your Grace, I must be off. Viola is expecting us."

"She is Miss Hartwell to you," I growled, deep and threatening. No young alpha, especially one as pathetic as this Mr Jones or Hartwell who was in my employ, should be leaving the conversation first.

"You will stay at my pleasure," I barked, exerting all of my superior alpha will.

Hartwell twisted her neck in submission, but it did not give me the satisfaction it normally did. On every other occasion, that same movement would have me wanting to scent and bite. Now I just wanted to get rid of them both.

"You will be early tomorrow, girl," I told her, hoping she would respond as she was used to.

Instead, she unbent and briefly met my eyes before giving me a stiff bow and leaving with her friend. I stared after them. Confused and angry. The light was poor and perhaps that explained it. I had not realised how voluble Hartwell's eyes were. How eloquent and expressive.

~

HARTWELL ARRIVED LOOKING HARASSED, AND THOSE violet eyes shone with pent up emotion. From the moment she entered the library, I was alive to her every movement, every breath. I wanted nothing more than to lecture her in a way I could not do in public.

"Your Grace," she began in a rush. "Syon. Yesterday evening. I was... You must understand!"

I waited for her to continue.

"Mr Jones... I was wrong to speak to you as I did. I regret how we parted." There was a slightly deferential tilt to her head, which lacked the outright submission from the night before. A pair of sparkling eyes glanced up at me with hopeful rather than forced submission. Something inside of me gave way. Here was my Hartwell, my secretary, and the constant thorn in my side.

"Hartwell..." I sighed. "You are a nightmare. As for the countess—"

"I'm not wooing her for myself!" She burst out, taking a hasty step towards me, a hand outstretched as if to physically restrain the direction of my words.

"I—" I paused. I had been about to tell her I did not care if she courted the countess or not. I hadn't last night. But now? Now I wanted to snap and tell her that she was too young to be courting anyone, let alone a countess who was older than her.

"So, Miss *Iris* Hartwell is not wooing Lady Clare, the Countess of Kellingham" I teased.

"I promise. And Viola isn't either," she rushed on with a faint attempt at humour. I hadn't thought that but was amused she wanted to tell me her omega sister wasn't courting an omega. Then blushing, she continued. "Viola... Viola likes an alpha."

"Viola likes an alpha? And isn't presented? Tell me it ain't that Jones fellow, I'd expect her taste better than that bull calf! But perhaps in picking such an unremarkable alpha..." I ground my teeth. This was madness. What did it matter to me who violets and vanilla married? "Your twin seems destined to create as many waves as your eldest sister."

"Viola? Waves! No. I think she is coming to realise she would rather work behind the scenes. The power behind the throne." A sheepish grin peeked through.

"She will struggle to find a mate who allows it," I pointed out. "I do not mean that unkindly. But no alpha wants to be manipulated. No one does."

She visibly deflated. "Not even Arthur Jones?"

"You must be mad! Fit for Bedlam." I couldn't imagine Viola with such a weak chinned, inconsequential alpha. "No."

"Yes. She thought to marry him. If she has a husband who takes her politics seriously, perhaps..."

I growled. The idea of her with another had not occurred to me. But with that uninspiring alpha? A man with no presence?

"How could she shine married to one such as him?" I asked, unable to hold back the faint snarl.

"I don't know!"

"He has a weak chin!" I snapped.

"You, Syon, are a horrible snob. What does a chin, or a nose for that matter, have to do with anything? I have not told you this before but, if I did not have direct contact with your servants and did not see the respect your tenants have for you, I would thoroughly dislike you," she huffed.

This was my secretary. It must be out of some desire to

impress her friend that had caused her to behave so oddly the night before.

"Yes, you'd hate me, brat," I grinned. "Bad politics and all."

"Ooo, you make me mad! Agreeing with me! Fine, I wouldn't *hate* you but I'd think you terribly stuffy and backwards. In fact, you ain't all bad and your politics are improving... Though perhaps..."

"Manipulating me, Hartwell?"

"I do love when you call me that. But I am educating you, Syon," she winked at me. Loved when I called her Hartwell? Was she flirting? Perhaps she would... Never. No matter her dynamic, it was a mistake to think about fucking my own secretary. She walked to her desk as if she hadn't seen how hard I'd become. It happened occasionally. Out of nowhere, a purely innocent word or look would come my way and I would find my cock stiff and straining against my breeches while my swelling knot beat in time with my heart. How she could miss it, I did not know. Perhaps she ignored it but then why? For when it happened her scent flared as well. And I would know. For still I could smell nothing but violets and vanilla when she was near me. Logically, I knew it was my mind playing tricks, but I refused to give up the illusion. Hartwell and that scent were one and the same to me.

12

VIOLA

By the grace of our Goddess, Syon had not noticed the difference between the real Iris and myself. Any number of reasons came to mind. It had been dark, Syon had been angry, or perhaps something as simple as my disguise being effective. Most likely because he had no sense of smell. Still, like a pathetic omega, I fretted. I hardly knew what had happened between him and Iris. My foolish twin had brushed the incident aside and said only she had told the duke she was not wooing the countess.

The next few days signalled a return to my new normal. Nothing so easy as the first weeks with Syon. That comfort had long gone after the kiss. How could I look at him and not think about the kiss? Dream about his taste and the way he felt between my legs. Dammit. I'd never believed in heaven until that moment—only a fool wouldn't dream of heaven once they'd experienced it. Instead, I couldn't concentrate and I had an itch along my mate gland into which I rubbed peppermint oil. I crushed the seeds of Queen Anne's Lace for tea until my aunt discovered and grew agitated that I might take too much and trigger my heat. I had never heard that it could increase fertility and nearly stopped drinking my tea altogether. Instead, she ordered her doctor to procure Wild Fernweed.

"It is an old wives treatment but far more effective. Your Papa... He was the one who used to find it for me before I was married. He always looked out for me as if he were an alpha instead of an omega."

It was the nicest thing she had ever said about my father. Once again I wondered at the strangeness of my uncle and aunt mating when they seemed so incompatible. She was young, I realised. Certainly not in her forties for she had been much younger than my father. While my uncle would have been older than my father if he had still been alive.

"Why do you look at me like that?" she huffed.

"Do you mind it?" I asked. "Being mated and married. To need to follow an alpha's needs. To have your world..."

"Do you think I am unhappy? La, niece! You mistake things. How could I be unhappy?" but her laugh telegraphed her bitterness. "I have everything an omega is meant to have. A husband. A mate. *What more could I want?*"

Children, the word popped into my head but I caught it before it slipped out. Every omega desired children. An alpha might desire them—especially an alpha child—to inherit, but omegas had a need for children. I knew it myself. So easy to smile distractedly when little ones skipped about in the Park with their nannies attempting to manage their excitement. A desire I had only considered natural. Never had I thought about the possibility of never having them. The image of the house on Weymouth Street when I left... Quiet. No voices, not even those of my aunt and uncle. Unless they happened to run into each other on the stairs or were forced to go to some social gathering together. What of her heats? I wondered if they were happy then or if it was yet another duty as mates that they felt the need to fulfil.

I REMEMBERED THE CONVERSATION THE NEXT MORNING AS I sat in the library staring at Syon's golden head bent over some letter or other. He was squinting. Not for the first time, I wondered if his eyesight was as poor as his sense of smell. My tongue grew thick in my mouth as I sought the words to ask him... Ask him for reassurance that when he married the countess he would not mind if she could not have children. Whether he would cast her aside. She had not produced for the late Earl.

"Looking severe, Hartwell," he tutted me when at last he looked up. "Why so serious? Is there ink on my face?"

I was in no mood for teasing and shook my head.

"I..." I faltered, for I could not ask the question. "Perhaps it is indigestion. May I go?"

A frown drew his brows low. I'd never given it any thought to his eyebrows being darker than his hair. Now, I fixated on them in hopes of distracting myself. But Syon could not leave well enough alone. He crossed to where I sat. It was the closest we had been since the night I had kissed him. No, he'd spanked me, but I'd not enjoyed that at all no matter that I'd flushed all over. I watched, entranced, as he reached out and placed the back of his hand to my brow. "You are not hot. No fever."

"I said indigestion, not that I felt feverish," I mumbled.

"Of course," he withdrew his hand so quickly it was as if he had been burned. "I can have Horne bring you something."

"A walk might do me well."

"Go then. I'll see you tomorrow," he returned to his chair and fixed his eyes on whatever he was reading.

"Syon. I am sorry. I did not mean... I think," I tugged at my cravat in hopes that it would loosen the noose which tightened by the day. "I am not used to spending so much time in the city. I am not used to so many people."

"Then we should go into the country. Retire to Ayleigh for a few days. I admit I too miss the country. You must think me a hermit. I hardly spend any time in my clubs."

"Perhaps you should visit Ayleigh," I said in a soft voice. "But I cannot go to the country. I must think of my sister and your suit with the countess. The bill for omega property rights. Your interests in town..."

"Damn my suit. Hartwell, you are not thinking clearly. Come to Ayleigh with me. Rest for a few days. Ride, shoot. Whatever takes your fancy, I'll provide for it."

My refusal sparked an argument punctuated with stretches of hostile silence. But the sum of it: he would not let me leave the house if I did not agree to spend at least a week at Ayleigh with him. The stalemate was brought to an abrupt end when Horne intervened with the information that Syon had agreed to attend a card party that evening in Richmond and should Horne call for His Grace's carriage. I tidied my desk with unnecessary vigour. "I am glad Your Grace has decided to go out more."

"It is a card party... It is all politics and no matter."

"Politics do matter! What do you think I have been striving to do these last weeks but demonstrate how very much politics matters," my chest heaved as I drew in deep breaths. His scent, his alpha scent inflamed me. My temper heightened and my need to... I did not know. There was no need beyond him standing by my side, at my side. To do what? I slammed my fist into the wall then shook it out. "Dammit."

"Claws in, Puss. What's put you out? You've been unruly of late and not just in refusing my invitation."

My cheeks grew hot when Syon called me Puss, and it made my breasts feel heavy and my pussy ache with need.

"I will see you tomorrow," I almost shouted as if raising my voice would prevent an alpha from arguing with me.

I rushed from his presence. Angry, confused. Part of my soul demanding I return, go to my knees, and beg his forgiveness. Then again, I wanted to rip him apart for being so high handed, for making me want him to take me in hand, to master me. I was never so needy outside of my heats.

WHEN I REACHED BOND STREET, I FROZE. PAXTON STOOD on the corner with a gentleman I did not know. I hesitated a moment too long. Paxton looked up, saw me, and signalled for me to go to him. I had dreaded seeing him again.

"Young Hartwell. This is Colonel Fordom," he motioned to the other alpha, who doffed his hat but made no move to leave. I'd thought Paxton's silvery handsomeness broody but this Colonel Fordom hinted at dark secrets, dark thoughts, and dark passions. Yet I experienced a ghostly familiarity, long ago memories paired with hazy recollections that I should know him... Inexplicably he smelt like Bea. I pushed away the thought. There were no military men in our circle of acquaintance and the only Fordoms I knew were in Edinburgh, a family of beta printmakers. I could not imagine these two alphas tempered each other but rather urged one another towards greater heights of depravity.

"Good day, Sirs," I bowed and attempted to move on.

"Viola. Stop," he snapped.

I froze. How could he know who I was? I had been so careful. For sure, he had not known me the first time we met at the club, but since then had he met the real Iris? Because for all of our similar colouring, up close there was one very obvious difference. My twin had dark brown eyes. Damn Iris, when had she met Paxton? Had she met him that same fateful night she'd spoken to Syon? What a mess. I made up my mind to have Iris only come up to town if summoned. Damn alphas and their freedoms.

"You have no right to use that name," I hissed. "And I have no problem in calling you out for speaking of my *sister* like that."

"Dammit. Stop!" His alpha bark made me wince but did not have the power over me as an alpha's bark might have had before I began working for Syon. I'd built some immunity to them. "You think I want to be entangled in another public scandal with your family? Enough that I have to deal with your shrewish sister—"

"Leave the fair Beatrice out of this, Pax," Fordom admonished. "You know you don't mean it."

"Enough. Both of you. Viola, consider the dangers of your foolhardy prank. If Orley, if he finds out what you are doing..."

"You have no right to that name. Nor do I know why you believe I am my omega sister," I spat. "I know what I am doing. I am his secretary—"

"We do not live in a forgiving society. I know you to be a sensible and clever young woman. Risibly young for this farce." He hissed his next words, "*You are an omega.* You are Viola Hartwell. But, I won't have... Your sister hates me enough, but if she knew what you were doing and that I did nothing to stop it?"

I blanched, then flushed with anger. "You think... You presume to care for my reputation?"

"It seems no one else in your family will, child," Fordom interrupted before Paxton could respond. "While I do not know your story, if I were you, I would pull out. Just tell Orley you are going home to Hertfordshire or back to Oxford."

"You have no right," I snapped. I would have loved to scream but could not afford to bring more attention to us.

"You'd be surprised what rights I have," Fordom said with a grim smile.

"You've no notion..." Paxton growled on top of his friend's words.

I looked back and forth between the two alphas and wondered why I had not heard about them from my sister before. Hard as I tried, these two men brought forward no memories. Yet their every action, their every word spoke of an intimacy with Beatrice that surprised me. She spoke her mind freely and if she did not like these gentlemen, surely she would have warned me of them when I came to town. Instead, I had a near violent run-in with Paxton the first time I met him.

"You could ruin me... I promise to... I promise not to be too reckless. That is what I told Iris," I bit my lip and gave them the same look that I'd used on my Mama on far too many occasions for her to have been fooled every time. But the two alphas before me seemed convinced that it would do something to hold back my more wild schemes... If only they knew.

"I shall keep an eye on you, Viola. As if I were your brother, since it appears your alpha relatives are incapable of doing so themselves," Paxton glared.

"He'll keep an eye, I'll keep two. Take care, Miss Viola Hartwell," Fordom flicked my cheek. "Come Pax. I believe you promised me a quiet afternoon, yet so far you've only caused the lovely Miss Hartwell..."

He drew Paxton away. I watched them longer than I should have, glad they were not my alphas. I preferred Syon's quiet teasing and flashes of dominance compared to Paxton's intensity and the quiet mockery in Fordom's eyes.

~

THE FOLLOWING SATURDAY, I WAS ONCE AGAIN VISITING with Olivia. The more I came to know her, the more I grew to admire the very qualities I had so rejected in the early days of our acquaintance. Her book learning was not great, but from lack of opportunity rather than application—her father and mother hadn't the resources to give her beyond the basics of education. In its place was a natural ability to play whatever instrument came her way and a beautiful singing voice. There were many days when I found myself longing to listen her to play and sing, for they soothed ruffled nerves and these were the moments when she blossomed. I liked seeing her happy. Today was one such day. I sat next to her, turning the pages of some new piece of music she had received that morning.

"Without your company these past weeks, I do not know how I would have managed," Olivia confided when she'd finished and we'd returned to her favourite sofa by the fire. "The weather has been so grey…"

I took her little hand in mine and squeezed it. "Soon it will be Spring and then Summer. You will get to see flowers…"

"No, my dear friend… You *are* my friend, you know. My dear friend, I need you to know that I have no expectations to enjoy… You are so sheltered from society. You remind me of myself when I first married. Though I confess there are times when you seem to have seen more of the world than I. You must understand that without the expectation of a husband I shall be dependent on the charity of Caroline's family. She has my interests at heart, I know. But her father is not so kind, and I do not think he will desire another mouth to feed."

I bit my tongue at the mention of Caroline.

"What if there were a marriage?" I asked instead. "What

if... Oh, I don't know. Someone like the Duke of Orley were to propose? You have heard me say that my sister, Iris, is his secretary. And I have never heard—"

"The duke! He is a... The late earl liked him. And I..." she swallowed nervously. "I do not think I could love someone like him."

"But Olivia, if you require a husband, and I swear on the honour of my father, on all that I hold dear. The duke is a good man. He is a man of honour. He would never force himself on you. Please, please believe me. I know no ill of him. He is the best of alphas!"

"Have you met him?" She asked.

I absently traced the bracelet she wore on her wrist. "If I say I have, then know that if... There are alphas in the world who would lie down in the mud rather than allow your foot to touch the ground. Think on it, Olivia. If you could have your most perfect life what would it be?"

"I'd rather hear yours first..."

I frowned. Her bracelet was very pretty, and I was so enamoured of it that it took me a moment before I answered. "I would want... I would want to marry, to mate with someone I could always be myself with. To always give an honest answer. Even if we lived the simplest life, I would be happy with the person who—"

"That is how I feel."

I looked up to see her face so close to mine that I could feel her breath on my cheek. Her scent had thickened with the strength of her emotion. "Olivia, I should probably—"

"Don't leave me," she begged. "I was just going to tell you what I dream of. A quiet life. Away from the city. I am so shy around strangers. I want warm arms to sleep in at the end of the day. To rest my head against a pillow-like breast..."

She trailed off at the humph from her ever present chaperone. I'd seen her sneer at Olivia, at me, but there was no way to be rid of her.

"Do you take issue with what we are speaking of, madam?" I asked.

"You omegas are so full of yourselves. Your perfect little dreams lack any understanding of the realities of the world. You have been put on this earth to temper alphas nothing more. An omega is worth the price of their holes. If that cannot—"

"Enough!" I roared. "How dare you speak so? Do you think that there is no equality..."

"I am a beta. I am not ruled by those urges," she sneered. "The urges turn you into snivelling beasts. Rather be born a beta than an omega. The basest and lowest of all dynamics. We'd be better off without any of you."

I did not notice myself moving but I felt the moment that my palm connected with her cheek. The crone recoiled with a scream as if I had stabbed her.

"You are a creature that deserves a muzzle like the bitch you are," the beta screamed so loud I winced. "Do you think you will get away with this, you dirty whore!"

"That is enough!" Came a deep bark from the door. It was Caroline, looking every inch the powerful alpha in her dark suit. "You are no longer needed. Leave this instant. Your things will be—"

"You cannot. I was hired by your father, the vicar, not you."

"And I will tell him exactly what you said. And do not expect a reference. Out!" the alpha shouted.

"I shall take this up with the relevant authorities. Alphas always bowing and scraping to the delicate omega needs. Betas are the oppressed! We shall overthrow you here as we have in France! There will be revolution and alpha and omega heads will roll."

"I do not care what dynamic you are," Caroline said with deadly calm. "I do not care what dynamic these ladies are. You are discourteous. To your employer, to her guest. Leave now while my temper is..." I marvelled that Caroline allowed the bitter woman to leave without throwing her out. Syon, I knew, would have thrown her out. Perhaps as a woman, she had a kind of control that a male alpha might lack.

"I'm leaving, you bitch!" She shoved me so that I tripped over my skirts and fell hard to the ground.

The door bounced on its hinges but that was the only noise until a tremulous sob broke the silence.

Olivia sat on the sofa, her hands clutching her skirts and tears streaming from eyes that were scrunched closed. Caroline moved first, falling to her knees at Olivia's feet. But she hesitated to touch the crying omega, and I knew why. It would be a gross overstepping of alpha authority. No matter her instincts to soothe and protect, she was held back by the courtesy that she was not Olivia's alpha. Caroline looked to me, begging for assistance. I struggled to my feet and sat next to Olivia, a hand on her back and a gentle kiss on the wet cheek.

"Has she done anything to you, said anything that made you uncomfortable before tonight?"

The small cry and the hands going to cover her face told us enough. Olivia's companion had been... I did not know what.

"That bitch," Caroline hissed.

Olivia flinched in my arms. "Olivia, you are fine. We shall find someone else... Someone kind."

I looked up at Caroline. I had no authority to say as much but in that moment I would have said, would have done everything to protect the fragile creature in my arms.

"Let her take you to bed, Olivia," Caroline pleaded. "Let her help you."

Olivia safely in bed, I rejoined Caroline in the drawing room.

"You could move in," was the first thing she said. "You could be her companion."

"I thought you hated me."

"I hate to see her unhappy. I hate knowing that my estate is so far beneath hers that there will never be a chance for—"

"I understand."

Caroline's gaze sharpened. "Perhaps you do... If only I had known what she was suffering!"

"The beta has been here since before the Earl's death," I said calmly. I was better at handling alphas now. "There is nothing you could have done without her exposing herself."

"Was Olivia... Was she physically..."

"No. There is no sign that Olivia was harmed in any physical way," I assured her. I did not reveal how thin the omega had been as her maid as I had helped her into her nightgown. She'd looked skeletal underneath her clothes. I had been surprised to see she wore a wig and that her hair was thin and cut short to her head. I could not reveal that to Caroline, I could not imagine that Olivia would want me to. "Perhaps you should be the one to move in. I know that she would feel safer with someone here. You could be that someone."

The alpha sagged against the back of the small settee. Her head tilted back until she was staring up at the ceiling. "I sometimes envy betas," she said as softly as if confessing some sin.

"I never would have thought that," I said confused at the change of conversation.

"I envy them," she continued as if I hadn't spoken. "I read your mother's book. Your father's too. I know the kind of omegas and alphas there are in your family. There is cruelty within every dynamic. I've seen it. Over and over again. You've been raised differently. Above the fray. I envy you too.

I wanted to join the cavalry. My commission was bought. But when Lord Clare died, Olivia needed me, so I stayed. But I... Goodnight Viola. I think... I hope we can be friends."

I LEFT THE HOUSE WITH MY MIND SO FULL THAT I STUMBLED as I stepped onto the street.

"Syon," I whispered, needing my friend, and moved on instinct. By the time I'd arrived at his door, I'd been running. My blood pumping through my veins, my breath coming in short pants. I patted my cloak and drew forth the latchkey I'd been given by Horne. I headed straight to the library where I knew I'd find him. I just needed to see him, though I did not understand why.

"What racket... Hartwell? What is this?" he asked when I stormed into the library.

I pushed past him. "It is late. I am sorry."

"Where have you been, pup? You smell... You are dressed as Viola!"

"I'm sorry," I waved a hand as if to dispel the scent. "I needed... It isn't my story to tell."

I could see a frown on his face. Concern. The last thing I wanted. "Would you like a drink?"

It did not take long for me to get drunk. I refilled my glass liberally and soon lay sprawled in a chair in front of the fire that burnt in the library.

"What were you doing up?" I asked.

"Thinking. I am allowed to do that." He sat stiff in his chair, though I couldn't understand why. Or why he was taking such shallow breaths.

"Of course you are. I do not want to think," I admitted. "Thinking... Hurts here." I slapped a hand over my heart. I wanted to wipe the image of Olivia's gaunt figure from my

153

mind. What had she suffered? What had happened to her before the earl had died? I felt powerless to help her when the abuse had been body and mind. What could I do? What could Syon do? Would he do anything?

"The wine you have been drinking blurs your mind. Stop... Hartwell, stop."

"You have no say of my actions." I snapped and picked up the bottle to drink from the source.

He growled and stalked towards me. "Give me the bottle."

"You do not own me," I slurred then drained the bottle to prove my shallow point.

"Hartwell, you will do as I command," he barked. I jumped up, clumsy on wine drunk legs. He steadied me with a hand on my shoulder. I looked up, craning my neck. For the first time, I felt small. Our sizes had never concerned me. Yet here I was, a tall omega, and I was a dwarf compared to him. If I was a real omega—if I was dainty like Olivia—then he would never have been duped.

"I am unnatural," I murmured. "I am unnatural and every time I am with you I realise how unnatural I am. I want to be a proper omega."

The hand on my shoulder tightened painfully and a whimper escaped my lips. "What did you say?" He growled.

My eyes felt heavy and they closed of their own will. "It does not matter. I am foxed, the drink has taken hold. Pay me no mind. Words will not change things no matter... No matter that I wish I was an omega like—"

My mouth was stopped by warm lips. Lips that were firm yet did not press.

"Goddess, but I love..."

My eyes closed and everything faded to black.

∾

I WOKE UP THE NEXT MORNING FULLY CLOTHED IN THE bedroom I regularly used. My mouth was full of cotton and my head felt like an anvil being pounded by a hammer. I tried to remember how I'd got here, but other than the disaster with Olivia I could not think of how I ended up in one of Syon's beds and fully clothed, except someone had loosened my dress.

But my head throbbed too much to think on it, so I rolled over and went back to sleep.

13

SYON

She had said she wanted to be an omega. It made no sense, yet was so right that I could not keep any thought in my head that did not turn naturally towards the way the words had tumbled from her lips, and then to how I had kissed her for fear of hearing more. Kissed her and then voiced the feeling buried so deep I could still deny it. Yet her secret deserved an equally weighty confession. More words that might drive me down a path from which, once I stepped on, I would not be able to return. There would be no retreat if I followed down the road Hartwell seemed to want to tread. When she'd woken with a splitting headache that made her surly and incapable of doing her work, I sent her home with instructions to stay at home tomorrow as well. Grateful for the distance between us. She clearly did not remember what she'd said (what I'd said), let alone the kiss, or how I'd carried her to the duchess' bedroom, loosened her gown, and forced myself away lest I strip her naked to see exactly the shape of her breasts and colour of her nipples.

≈

Two nights later, my table was filled with the brightest political minds—including, I flattered myself, my secretary. Florey and his cronies puffed with pride as they introduced Hartwell to their political rivals. And, despite her obvious youth, she was welcomed with open arms. It was not often that one so young was so knowledgeable or so ready to speak her mind.

"I've not much of a head for wine," Hartwell confided. Her face already flushed and her words more deliberate. I kept an eye on her for fear she'd confess her desire to be an omega. That admission was for my ears alone.

"Well, there is no harm in that amongst the omegas, but alphas must know how to hold their drink," someone chided.

"A greenhorn can be foxed on a sip of good canary, there is no shame in that," the Prime Minister, William Pitt the Younger, chuckled, looking far more lively than I had ever seen him. I'd placed him at the far end of the table for fear that some political arguments with my secretary would not end well for my young friend. But, despite the difference in their politics, Hartwell and Pitt were chatting amiably about rhetoric. I indicated for Florey to get in between his niece and the Prime Minister. I disliked the way they were looking at each other. As if they were sharing secrets. Her secrets belonged to me.

"Your protegé will cut us out at the next election," James Lowther observed through his looking glass. "We must ensure Pitt secures a decent majority in the next by-election."

"What? Must you always be bringing your people in through those boroughs you keep in your pocket?" Paxton sneered. "She will best any you pick..."

"Why my dear Paxton. I thought you and the pup were

not friends?" the slippery toad's smile had Paxton's upper lip curling.

"Lowther, watch your tongue or that one will demonstrate her bloodthirsty side. I do not think she has plans to run anytime soon. Far too young," Paxton smirked. "Ah, you do not believe me? She has been near to challenging half the town for even allowing one of the fair Hartwell omegas' names to be mentioned."

"Makes the blood heat to think of them," a bluff beta chuckled. I managed to hold a growl back and a glance at Paxton showed the same. He bared his neck in submission. "Not like that, my lords! I meant if they were alphas, or even betas, they would set the world alight. Ain't that so, Florey?"

The uncle to the omegas in question merely smiled. "I believe they will, but because of their dynamic—not despite it."

Lowther snorted and made some excuse to leave our little group, but it was with some consternation that I watched him cross to where Pitt and Hartwell sat.

"Leave her, Your Grace," Florey chuckled. "She throws her heart over the fence no matter."

Paxton's frown deepened as he watched the tete-a-tete that had just been interrupted by the slippery Lowther.

"Excuse me, but I will go and prevent a duel," Paxton gave a stiff bow and broke away. He strode towards the group with a purpose I had yet to see from him. Paxton bent closer to Hartwell, whispering something into her ear that caused my secretary to blanch. At Paxton's insistence, Hartwell trotted after him like a dutiful puppy. I found myself circling through my guests until I was close enough to the open door to catch something of their conversation.

"... Beatrice would..." Hartwell's voice was stiff but hushed such that I missed what she had to say about her sister.

"Viola is the one I wish to speak to," Paxton said. He

sounded on edge. "Or will I have to go to Weymouth Street to meet her?"

"Viola..."

I held my breath. Was Paxton interested in Viola? And why? Beatrice seemed to fill his every thought, no matter the circumstances. "I do not think that Beatrice—"

"A word more about any one of my sisters and I shall call you out," Hartwell snapped. "Their names should not cross your lips. If you must speak of them, Miss Hartwell shall be the only thing I shall find acceptable. Do you hear me, *Lord* Paxton?"

I grinned at how the scamp had sneered Paxton's title as if it were a slur.

"Why, you brat!" Paxton snapped.

That was my cue. I pushed open the door and stared both down. Neither seemed embarrassed, but I could not hold back a soft growl when I saw how close they were. "I think this tete a tete is finished," I told them. "Paxton, stop crowding my secretary. Hartwell, stop challenging your betters."

Both alphas bristled at my words, but this was my house and my word was law. I might not have Paxton's height, but I had strength on my side.

My firecracker secretary gave me a stiff nod and strode back into the bright room, the picture of offended dignity. Any other time, I might have smiled at the ruffled feathers. Perhaps even sought to ruffle them further before soothing the bruised ego. But I was in no humour for levity.

"Paxton, what are you doing? Harassing my secretary? She is a whelp not worth..."

"You're a fool, Orley. You really have no idea what you've done? Gotten yourself entangled with that family. Madness. Bad enough that Beatrice is in Paris when we are at war with

France. Now Viola must run mad. If you had any sense of propriety—"

"Propriety? Rich, coming from you!" I snapped. "She's a child. Leave her be."

"You don't know, do you?" Paxton pulled a face of disgust. "Dammit, man. I put this firmly at Beatrice's door. If it weren't for her stunts last summer, Viola would be safely mated off to some sensible scholar or rising politician— perhaps one on the other side of this door. And Iris would have her nose in a book, rather than sneaking about town."

"Leave," I growled, a deep possessiveness of the twins reverberating through my chest. "I'll not have you acting nursemaid to those who aren't your responsibility. I'll watch over my own secretary."

"Orley, I'll go. But let me warn you. That family. They've no care for anyone but their damned ideals. If you don't fall into line, they turn vicious. Watch your back."

"And stay away from Viola," I snapped.

Paxton laughed. "Viola is a rebellious little brat with no one to rein in her flights of fancy. Not her alpha twin. Not her sisters or mother. My only interest is to keep her out of trouble. But if you think you can manage her," and he tilted his head with a bitter smile. "Perhaps it would do you good to tangle with one of the Miss Hartwells. Teach you a lesson in humility."

"Even Beatrice? Should I woo her?" I couldn't follow his conversation but the taunt was out of my mouth before I could stop it.

Paxton stepped forward, barely keeping himself under control. "If you were... Beatrice is the thorn in my side. Not yours. Never yours. She shall never belong to—" He growled in frustration. "Let us say I am drunk. My mind muddled... The omegas in that family are a sickness you never want to be cured of. I just hope you don't catch it."

"WHY WAS PAXTON SO DESPERATE TO TALK TO YOU LAST night?" were the first words I spoke when Hartwell entered the library the following day. The evening had passed smoothly after Paxton had left, but my eyes kept tracking back to her dark head bent close to another's, deep in conversation. That Paxton had chosen to corner my secretary puzzled and vexed my alpha. That possessiveness had kept me tossing the few hours I had tried to sleep. I was bleary-eyed and irritable. I snapped at Timms and was dissatisfied... I knew what was bothering me. My secretary.

"Some trifle—" she waved a hand. The easy dismissal caused a growl to reverberate deep in my throat.

"Since when do you consider your sisters' honour trifling? I overheard some of your conversation. Do not bite my head off. I was concerned. He is a rake, and dangerous. Do not snarl like that. Let me finish. If he is putting any pressure on you, on your sisters, you will tell me. I will ensure—"

"My conversation is none of your concern, Your Grace," she said through gritted teeth. "My sisters are not your concern."

"Paxton seems to be very interested in both—"

"Dammit, Syon. What does it matter what someone like Paxton thinks?" she shouted. "He is a rake..."

"What did you say?" I could not contain my fury. This whelp had the temerity to raise her voice at me, and in my own house? When I was showing understandable concern for her beloved sister? For Viola. But it wasn't just that. She was refusing my help. And *that* I would not allow. "Did you try to alpha me in my own home?"

That stubborn jaw tensed, but she did not deny it.

"Follow me," I growled. My alpha would be satisfied. I must dominate, exert my obvious superiority. Put this pup in her place—beneath me. The image caused my cock to give a twinge of anticipation. There was a moment before I heard her steps struggling to catch up with my longer stride. We arrived at the gallery, its long walls covered with paintings of long-dead Orleys and their mates. I had converted it to act as a place to practice fencing when I'd been a young man. The furniture was sparse and shoved against the walls. I strode down its length to where at the far end were a collection of blades I kept for my personal use. I found my breath coming out in harsh pants. Something basal had riled my temper, and it was on this girl I intended to take it out. She claimed to be so good with a rapier that she would take on any alpha, and she just a stripling.

"Choose," I snapped as I stripped off my jacket and began to roll up my sleeves, carefully tucking away the lace cuffs.

"What are you doing?" she asked. I spun around to find her standing before me still dressed and making no move to take a sword from the many I kept.

"Prepare to cross swords. Any number of times I have heard you brag that you could take on any alpha. Come on! Test your metal against me."

"I will not," she replied ever so calmly, but I knew all her expressions by now that I could see the tension around her eyes telling me she was not as composed as she would wish me to believe.

"What? Do you insult me?" I stalked towards her. My behaviour went against my every principle. Yet I could not stand another moment with this child standing before me so aloof and cool while I lost control.

"Pick up a blade," I bit out.

"You'll regret this," she said but removed her jacket with a grimace. She wore a suit of plain mustard velvet, which suited her. With every hair in place, with every smooth motion, I wanted to force her to break her unnatural calm and become as feral as I feared I was turning.

"You shall regret drinking too deep last night," I snapped.

I slashed my blade through the air, satisfied with the way it cut through the still silence. But greater was my pleasure to watch as she picked up her own weapon and tested its weight. This was no coward. Not my secretary. Not my Hartwell. Mine, and no one else's.

"Are you determined to do this?"

"On your guard, whelp."

It was clear from the first that the young alpha was a genius with a blade. She glided and parried with ease that bordered on beautiful. But what she had in style she lacked in strength. The length of her arm put her at a severe disadvantage, which I was not afraid to press. Soon she was on the defensive, backing down the length of the gallery, her nimble feet keeping her forever just out of my reach. A good reminder of how elusive I found her at times.

"Fight! Stand and fight!" I snarled.

"This is madness!" she snapped. Her breaths were coming in shorter pants. There was something though in the air, a faint whiff of heaven, that had me press on and on. Violets and vanilla tickled my senses. It was madness, but until I could get everything that represented this entrancing and infuriating woman out of my system, I would be forever caught in a spell of the memory of Hartwell in that dress, smelling like of her omega sister. How I had wanted to rip Paxton's arms from his body when I'd seen their little encounter last night! I could not get it out of my head that there was something private between them. Hartwell's private moments belonged to me. She was my secretary. She was mine to order about as I chose. Mine to fight. Mine to reprimand, to forgive, to care for.

"Syon. Stop."

My vision cleared at her shout. I saw the advantage and pressed on, relishing the way her shirt was slowly becoming drenched with sweat. She leapt forward and with a flash of her wrist she broke through my guard, and the buttoned point of her blade touched my side.

"Touch. Again," I said. We took our positions. I started with a rush and lurched forward, returning the favour, only my mark was her heart.

"Touch," she batted my blade away. "To what end, my lord? Why are you doing this?"

"En garde!"

"This is madness, stop!"

I growled deep in my throat and leapt forward. She had not expected my sudden movement and tumbled, landing on her back. I stood over her, primitive joy singing through my body to see her laid before me, defeated.

"I've stopped," I panted and made no move to hide the triumphant grin that spread across my face. Taking in deep lungfuls of air I caught again that same scent I had become obsessed with weeks ago.

"Would you want to kill me?" she asked from where she lay on the floor, propped up on her elbows, a frown marring her pretty face. Her head fell back and for the first time, I saw the slender column of her throat bared in true submission. She then rolled to her feet and stood before me, using her sleeve to wipe away the sweat that dripped down her brow. Again, sweet violets and vanilla wafted toward me.

"Where were you this morning?"

She froze. I'd never seen a person stand so still before.

"I overslept, Your Grace," she snapped. "My head aches from your good wine. Why must we do this now? Wooing is a long business. What is that the reason you choose to challenge me? Because I can't win your omega for you fast enough? What demon must you exorcise this morning?"

I stopped myself from speaking. The countess? I had not thought of her, or my plan to marry her, in days. What did I want with an omega I'd never met? Had never even seen.

"You smell of omega," I walked into her space, coming closer until she was pressed to the wall and I could lean down to the crook of her neck and inhale that intoxicating scent. "Like you did that day in the dress."

"Viola," she gulped. I was close enough to see the faint beat of her pulse. I ached with need as well but one I could never act upon. Shatter this precious relationship? I would not risk it. "I should go and wash... If that is alright with you..."

The image of the two of us bathing together flashed across my vision, and I took an unsteady step back.

"Yes," I managed to get out the single word. Yes, I had said but to what? The madness of seeing her naked or the fact she wanted to get rid of her scent. "Go. Have one of the servants draw two baths, one for each of us."

She nodded and fled the room, leaving her jacket behind. I sighed. I was no servant to be picking up after her, but it gave me some strange pleasure to bring the cloth to my nose and smell. Only there was nothing of alpha in the rich fabric. Just Viola's heady scent—but beneath it something purely belonging to a pair of fine violet eyes that I knew as well as my own. I reached down and grabbed my cock, ran the heel of my hand down to where my knot pulsed. It seemed that it could not go down no matter what I did. Every moment an agony for someone I could not have.

14
VIOLA

I pushed out the door to find Horne and Timms standing to the side. I frowned at them. "If it had been His Grace finding you listening at keyholes..."

I let the reality of their indiscretion hang in the air. Syon would have roared at them if he'd been the one to discover servants, no matter their place in his household, listening in.

"We were concerned for your well being," Horne's dignity wrapped about him. "A bath—"

"*Baths*," I emphasised, afraid they'd only heat enough water for one. An irrational fear, but my nerves were stretched thin and the last thing I wanted was even a sliver of confusion to creep into the minds of servants. Ones I must trust. "A bath for His Grace and one for myself."

"At once. I shall see to it myself," Timms bowed and turned. There would be a chaos of whispers and questions amongst the staff. How could there not be? It was barely noon. The night after the first dinner Syon had hosted in years. And directly following a screaming match between us. They probably wondered why I wasn't being tossed out the street—alphas had been known to do more for less. Or why a doctor had not been called to care for my wounds. I rubbed my arms at the thought of fighting off a sawbones. Then the question of preparing two baths. Surely that would cause as much comment for such a luxury. But better than if one bath had been ordered and we had shared it.

I found my way to the bedroom I'd used for the past few weeks and shook my head at the familiarity of it all. The unfashionably heavy fabrics hanging about the bed. The even older furniture. It was hard to believe that the house had been designed and built only thirty years before. I turned and caught my reflection in the mirror. My hair curled wildly about my flushed face. My eyes though... Fear. It must be fear, for to contemplate any other emotion would be admitting too much. I could claim to be afraid of Syon when he raged. I should be afraid of him. But instead, his temper pricked me. I wanted... I wanted him to prove that he was the alpha for me. "The," not "an". The definite article, not the indefinite article, for he was the only one that mattered. The one whose dominance I craved. My alpha. Not some other omega, who would quake and hide from him. But for me! I who had faced him, fenced with him. The omega who didn't cower or tremble with fear. No. I would not do that. I had been taught better. I became lost in my thoughts for what seemed like hours. People passed on the street, carriages came and went, and my thoughts revolved ever deeper and yet unsatisfactorily around the problem of Syon. Syon, the man and alpha, rather than the duke. The one who had saved me from my tête-à-tête with Lord Paxton. The one who barked at me this morning. I pressed the heels of my hands to my temples and cursed all men and alphas. But the person I cursed longest and most fluently was myself.

"And that is the truth of it," I muttered. "You love him."

"Your bath is ready, Miss," Timms said. "If you need anything, do not hesitate to call."

I gave an absent nod and waited for him to leave before reaching for my ruined cravat. I discarded each piece of clothing onto the bed until I stood naked. Stripped of every material protection. I was too tired in my body and soul to worry about the recklessness of my current nudity. Too reckless to care when my hand brushed against the dark curls covering my sex. Too reckless as I slipped my fingers between the folds and found the gathered slick. I felt no humiliation at my arousal. Syon had worked me over whilst we had battled and then scented me, giving over his aggression in favour of a different kind of dominance. One I should not have desired, but with every passing day, I wondered what it would be like. Not to hide my dynamic but to stand before him like this. Perhaps not so naked. But certainly as myself, as an omega.

Impossible. He would never forgive me. He'd proved today that even the smallest challenge to his alpha would result in irrational retribution. Swords before words. He'd never hear me out if the truth were discovered.

The bath's steam scented with lavender and rose filled my lungs with an altogether less intoxicating smell. With each inhalation, I relaxed. I washed my body but soon I focused less on becoming clean and more on the pleasure I could draw with each pass of hands over skin. My nipples tightened, and I closed my fingers around one, giving it a hard pinch while the other pressed down on the little bud between my thighs. My breath caught as the need humming through my body began to harmonise with my practised touches. I had touched myself before—how else could I get through a heat unattended by an alpha?—but never had I had someone to imagine playing with my body. Now all I could picture was

Syon looming over me, his body hard and hot. The outline of his cock, pressing against his breeches. When I'd been on my back, it had drawn my gaze like a lodestone. I'd wanted to see his knot which his tight breeches could not hide. Whoever he wanted—Olivia, or possibly even Viola—I could take that look in his eyes and turn it into fantasy. My slender omega fingers would never be enough but I did my best. Scratching and pinching my nipples, rubbing at the little button of heaven between my slick folds. Even in the bath, I knew I'd produced more the slick than in any previous heat.

"Syon!" I gasped as I imagined his hands taking the place of mine. I did not think he would be rough. No, not Syon. His fingers would work hard and steady, focused on driving me towards a cliff of bliss before yanking the reins and keeping me hanging on the precipice. He would torture me like that for hours. My breath came in short pants at the thought of him in the bath with me. Leaning against the solid plains of muscle rather than the tub. Caged in his arms, his giant cock pressing into my back. Bigger than any dildo I had used during heats. And the knot at his base beginning to swell until it plugged me. I might only have anatomical drawings and the erotic etchings Beatrice had given me as a gift after my first heat, but my imagination ran wild. The knot would grow, and as his fingers edged my orgasm I would reach behind and massage the base. If he teased me, gave me no relief, I would have him suffer the same. We would go on like that until he lost all patience and would spin me around. I would be facing him, my breasts against his chest. My eyes flew open staring blindly at the ceiling as I worked my fingers faster between my legs. Abandoning my breasts, I shoved two fingers into my slit. Pressing deep but never as good as the real thing—my instinctual knowledge that I needed a knot to truly satisfy me. I forced a third finger, but still it was not enough. In my fantasy, Syon worked me, tested my opening on his knot which he wanted, needed to shove deep into my tight, slick sex. Testing, stretching me until a sudden thrust, and we were tied together.

I bit my lip as my orgasm crashed upon me, my back arching sharply as my walls grasped for a fullness that wasn't there. An unfamiliar drowsiness came upon me. Normally I would be dissatisfied, fretting over the unknown feeling of an alpha's knot. I knew the difference though— the fantasy my mind had concocted had a face, it had a name. My body recognised that an alpha was responsible for my slick. Tears pricked my eyes in frustration.

After dressing, I stood at the head of the stairs, on the point of fleeing, but my resolve cracked, shattered. I closed my eyes and turned around to hunt him down. Everything demanded that I see Syon before I left. He could not force his knot into me, but I could look at him, even if just for a moment. I followed his scent to his bedroom, a place I'd never been to before. He'd not closed the door, and I used that excuse to push my way in. His back was to me, and he was naked as the day he was born. I'd never seen a naked man. To say I became enthralled by the powerful muscles that covered every line of his body would be an understatement. I longed to run my hands and tongue along every inch of his sweaty skin, taste him, feel his weight, knowing I could not break free on my own.

"I think that she is opening to the notion of a husband," I told Syon's back.

"You will leave for the afternoon."

"Syon," I stepped into the room but stopped when he spun to look at me. His eyes were black with arousal and his mate stain like an oak leaf stood out on his sharply muscled abdomen. I swallowed at the sight, unsure where I should focus my gaze. He had his stiff cock in one hand and jerked it up his length, rubbing his thumb over the flared head, spreading the pearl precum before running it down to where his knot had begun to swell. I gulped at the sheer size of it. After what I had done in the bath, my need had grown to a fever pitch. The unmistakable sensation of slick gathering between my thighs at his heightened scent. My omega desires clamoured for more, and my hands (I knew) still carried the faint whiff of my own arousal. A part of me wanted to raise my hands to his nose, taunt him with that smell and expose my sham. But then I also felt a thrill of the deception. It was an ugly thought, but something about his nose blindness made this little meeting almost a figure of our joint imaginations.

"Foolish Puss... know your destiny then. Come here. Kneel at my feet, Hartwell," he ordered—a purring, seductive command more powerful than if he'd barked at me.

I teetered on the point of refusing him, but my baser needs carried me closer until I knelt at his feet. Up close, the smell of him was even more heady and addictive. His expression did not change, but he began to jack his cock with harsher strokes, using more of the liquid that seeped from the tip to ease his way. His movements hypnotised me. I did not know how long I knelt at his feet like a supplicant. I dared not touch for fear the spell would break. I watched entranced when he directed his cock at me and with a series of grunts painted my face with his seed. I felt it warm on my skin; so much more of it than I thought possible.

With deliberate movements, Syon used his cock to smear my face with his spend. Rubbing it on my lips, my cheeks. And I? I nearly fainted with lust for the scent was overpowering. Only a hand on his powerful thigh kept me upright. I craved it. I wanted it, but as much as that I needed him to mark me with his scent like this. People must know that he'd claimed me like this.

"Lick," he commanded, bringing his fingers to my lips. Goddess, the taste! Unlike anything I'd tasted before. Almost like the taste of my own slick but stronger, salty and smooth.

"All of it," he said and used his fingers to gather what I had missed and feed it to me. When he was satisfied, he turned and picked up a damp cloth, which he used to tenderly clean my face. I wanted to complain he should leave it—I *wanted* to smell like him—, but this moment was his, I knew that. Whatever my desire, he needed this.

"You should leave now," his voice was tight, forcibly controlled as he gripped his unsatisfied knot.

I stood, moved away, fully aware of the dangers of staying a moment longer. "I'll be back tomorrow then."

"Puss... Hartwell," Syon closed his eyes and took a deep breath. Then he met my violet eyes with his dark ones but it was as if we spoke different languages for I could not understand what he was trying to convey without words. He huffed out a breath. "You need to know—"

"You don't need to explain," I stuttered and struggled to my feet. "Natural. We agreed. After the kiss... We agreed."

Then, like a courtier, I backed out of the room unwilling to miss a moment of his heated gaze. On reaching the head of the stairs and began to descend, my hand gripping the bannister and carefully placing each foot in front of the other. My chest fluttered at the sound of something above me. Would he storm down and drag me into his arms in hope of finding an omega's scent still lingering on my skin? Would I give in? Would I push him away? Did I possess the requisite strength to deny him? Between each too loud heartbeat, my ears strained for the sound of that familiar step. Was that itch the weight of his gaze on me? Could I turn around and run back up to confess everything to him? And what were my feelings and thoughts, versus those of my omega dynamic responding to the nearness of an alpha? At the bottom of the steps, Horne stepped forward with my overcoat and tricorn hat in hand. He froze when I was close enough for him to smell me. How could he not? Syon's scent coated me like a warm blanket, comforting and... I felt safe knowing that the world could smell him on me.

"He is in a mood. He's not used to so many guests. Don't take it to heart," Horne told me as he helped me into my greatcoat. "Take care of yourself, for it is cold out. I wish you would permit me to order a chair or carriage for you."

I hummed in understanding. "No need, Horne. The walk will do me good. Make sure he remembers to eat."

"Of course. You take such care of him."

I froze, dread building that I was suspected of being other than what I appeared. Very slowly, I turned to look at the old servant. His face was completely impassive, and I cursed at the skill of long-serving servants to keep their thoughts so close.

"Perhaps that says more of the care he..."

"No need to come to blows," he put up hands to forestall my protest. "Merely that before you came, His Grace rejected any fussing. You have made our job much easier. We hope you will be around for as long as—"

"I leave at the end of this parliamentary session," I cut him off. "If not before. When he marries..."

"I hope that is not true. That you will change your mind."

The words were spoken with such kindness that I ground my teeth and resisted giving him my best alpha growl. "I am not some changeable omega."

"Which is why you are so good for him," Horne assured me and opened the front door. I paused for one long moment. "So like the dowager duchess."

"You are lucky he would hunt me down and rip me to shreds for quitting over something you said. But I might risk it if you continue."

His smile was enigmatic. "I was butler to His Grace's grandmother. My loyalty lies with her and now with His Grace."

Frustrated beyond measure, I made it to the pavement and was grateful for my decision to walk rather than take a chair or wait for a carriage. A carriage would have me surrounded by Syon's scent, while fresh air might blow it away. If only my worries were so easily dispersed.

TURNING ONTO WEYMOUTH STREET, I REALISED I WAS NOT prepared to face my aunt or uncle, should they be home or wanted to see me. My aunt had taken to bed recently, complaining of some nervous disposition, and my uncle was spending more of his time at his clubs than before. Instead, I crossed the street and knocked on Mrs Markham's door, giving a silent prayer she would be home. Her butler opened the door and when questioned, admitted me with a squinting observation that I seemed to have lost my coat. I cursed. Until then I'd not realised I'd left my mustard velvet at Orley House. The butler led me up the stairs to a brightly lit drawing room far more fashionable and richly furnished than what I'd expect for a widow living in this part of town. He was a great, if ancient, alpha, and I was surprised to find an alpha working as a servant. When I questioned her, she laughed.

"Dixon? Oh, he isn't my butler even if he pretends to be. He was a colleague of my late husband's and a widower. When I decided to rent this house rather than stay in Hampstead, he said he would come too. To protect me! I think he is bored and wanted to feel useful. Alphas do not always have it easy, my dear. Their instincts to protect what they deem is theirs is... I think difficult might be too gentle a word. May I say you look very fetching in your men's garb... But flushed... Are you unwell, child?"

"I'm well... I just..." I stopped myself before committing some indiscretion. I realised her daughter was not present. "And where is Hero today?"

"I've sent her to school... It is not easy being a beta heiress."

"Heiress? I'd not known. You... You were married and mated, yet your child is a beta?"

"Yes. Shall we begin your portrait?" She raised an eyebrow, challenging me for I'd yet to visit her home and sit for her. Syon had taken all my time, which I did not regret for a second.

I watched the enigmatic omega work out of the corner of my eye. She had refused to let me see her work no matter my pleading, but I enjoyed our afternoons together when she came to visit my aunt or I met her at the countess'. I still did not wholly trust her. Her ever pointed questions about my relationship with Syon. But of all my acquaintances in London, I liked her best. We were friends of sorts. Both intelligent and independently minded. Though she chose to use those smarts to portray a frivolous society matron. And I? I masqueraded as an alpha. We talked of art and society. She told me stories of her youth and the scandals she had learnt when her sitters shared tidbits of gossip. Our conversations did not give me the same kind of joy as those with Syon. Still, I enjoyed being able to talk freely about my ideas with an omega.

"Tell me. How is your alpha?"

"He is not my alpha. He is my employer." I flushed. She

would be able to scent him on me, and I prayed she could not guess why his scent was particularly strong.

"I think it is more than that. I heard you were at a very select political dinner last night. Surrounded by alphas and very few friends of yours or your uncle's."

I huffed in annoyance. I did not want to discuss my own life when I could make such little sense of it.

"It was... Very instructive." I shifted in the chair. My memories of the night. The conversation, the food, the comforting presence of Syon as he watched me share my ideas. I'd even caught him smiling into his glass after I'd cursed at Pitt for plans to prevent omegas from being permitted to travel on their own. A thought occurred to me. "You are like my uncle. Always conceiving that I have feelings for the duke. I entered his service to gain support for the Omega Property Rights Act. To push politics, not passion."

"You enjoyed it! I've never seen... your scent is so sweet. And politics are your passion," she teased. "Don't worry. Your response to him is natural."

"I had not noticed... Being so close, physically I mean, does it cause the body to react? Or is... I am so sheltered," I sighed. "I know I respond *physically* to him. But that is nature. I cannot conceive why I am telling you this..."

"Let us take a break. Some tea, perhaps?"

"No. I can sit a bit longer."

"Well, I would like a break."

She called for tea and it arrived, brought by the intimidating Dixon. After we were left alone, Mrs Markham turned to me and cocked her head to the side. "Do you think Dixon and I are immune to each other?"

"Yes," I said without hesitation.

"Why?"

"You were both mated to other people."

"Then you are wrong. A mate bond is a wonderful thing

and the loss is—I cannot put it into words. But an alpha or omega can mate more than once. I am sure you know the Lords and Lady Cross? They are three alphas and an omega. And the duke's grandparents had a pack."

"But they never took lovers after their mates died."

"La, child! What did your Mama teach you?"

"That she could not consider a mate after my father died. There were interested omegas. Or rather, their families. Some younger than Beatrice... My age! Mama rejected all of them."

"And sometimes that is the case. But... Omegas in particular have needs. A heat does not quiet until we are advanced in years, and while an alpha's knot might continue to swell—"

"You speak very plainly."

"Faith, but the world has grown prudish. You are raised so sheltered it is almost remarkable you know what goes on between a man and woman."

I wondered how red my cheeks were, if my scent was spiking as I remembered what I had been doing with Syon early that day. I stood abruptly and strode across to the canvas but stopped short of seeing how she had captured me. I did not want to be confronted by image. Not yet at least.

"I know what happens!" I snapped. "Beatrice knew an alpha when she was younger. I remember it was when we were still in Scotland. It was why she never accepted any of the alphas who proposed to her. Even though she is... To look at, she is a perfect omega. But her disappointments set her against alphas..."

"I'm surprised you know of that. You must have been quite young."

"I listened from the landing. Our house was not very large," I smiled at the memory. I'd been ten. "I think my parents wanted to protect us from that. And..."

"I'm aware of what your parents did in the past. They created a rather ignorant omega daughter."

"Ignorant to think I could pull this masquerade off," I sighed.

"Oh, child! You are... You have not been caught. You are under his nose every day—quite literally. I think he must have the worst nose in London."

"I take suppressants and... He lost his sense of smell after a fight that broke his nose."

She howled with laughter. Joyous and carefree, continuing until she wiped tears from her cheeks. "You might not want to reveal that. Alphas are proud—but it is a good sign he trusts you."

Her smile broke through my brown study like the sun through clouds.

"As likely, he could never expect someone to conceive of such a mad scheme. Alphas lack the subtlety of omegas. They need..."

"To be taken care of," I sighed. "Bea takes care of Mama, who'd forget to eat if she wasn't reminded Hippolyta keeps company that makes alphas nervous. Why do we have to be the ones caring for them? Our abilities are greater than that of a helpmate."

"Sweet child. Do you think alphas so great? Imagine being run mad at the thought of your mate in danger. The struggle to let go and let them explore the world? Your Mama is a rare alpha. And you should find one as civilised. You could do worse than the duke."

"I thought you wished him to marry Lady Clare?"

"And he would run roughshod over her. She is a gentle soul and would not stand up to him. That is not to say all mates or marriages must have that kind of spark. Many omegas would be better paired with a gentle beta. Rather, I think of you, my dear. What are your ambitions and how are they best served?"

"Very well, a mate who saw me as an equal. Who took me

seriously. That is my ambition. And... And one who loved me as I am."

Her eyes twinkled, though she forbore to say anything. Try as I might, I could not summon the face which belonged to Iris's friend. He'd dined with us when Iris had been in town, but I could not remember him beyond his name—Arthur Johnson, or was it Andrew Jones? I'd considered marrying him, what a fool to think an alpha as innocuous as him would be enough for me. Syon was correct. He had a weak chin.

I sat with Mrs Markham for the next hour and contemplated the tangle I had found myself in. How dangerously careless my actions were. I should quit my position as Syon's secretary. I should quit and never look back, never wonder. The rational part of me fought against the fear. It pointed out that my disguise had been successful except that Mrs Markham had seen through it. Paxton had met the real Iris and noted the difference, but like Mrs Markham, he seemed determined to keep my secret. And those were persons who knew my family, who knew me. All others did not question my dynamic. There were no glances that sought to see past the presentation. It was only when I was with Syon, alone and tired, that I feared being caught. When I relaxed and my defences were lowered.

I blushed. Those were not the only times.

I also felt on the verge of being caught any time his scent heightened and my body responded. The longer I spent with him and the more sensitive I became to his moods, the more readily my body betrayed me.

I shook my head to clear my thoughts. My plan could not be said to have reached the halfway point. There would be many more days spent with Syon before the bill went to a vote.

He must marry Olivia. My heart rebelled at the thought,

but it was the only way to save her. There were other alphas, but she needed rescuing and Syon was the only one I trusted to treat her with the respect and care she deserved. I thought of Caroline, of how she pined for Olivia, of how she would not be able to pay Olivia's omega price.

"Viola? Go home, child, and rest," Mrs Markham touched my shoulder. I nodded and trooped across the street.

As I climbed the stairs to my room, I heard voices—my aunt and uncle's caught in a fiery argument. Despite their chilly relationship, I had yet to hear them fight. I crept closer until my ear was pressed to the drawing room door.

"Yes, you would use her," my aunt sneered. "Anything for Charles's children. Anything to get ahead in your career. You should have married him. But Christina proposed first. I know that is why you married me. I know that you never loved me or wanted me beyond my proximity to Charles."

"Maria—"

"Do not call me that. You are a coward. You offered me security. A roof over my head. Promised to respect my needs and desires. Then you forced a mate bond on me." Her voice was thin, harsh, and so full of anguish. "You took away my choice! You took it away and then you abandoned me when I did not give you children. But did you ever think that it was *you* who did not give *me* children?"

"I am... I cannot express how..." My uncle's voice dropped, and I could not hear what more he had to say.

I sagged against the door frame, the little pieces of the puzzle falling into place. My uncle, in love with my father? My uncle... It made its own kind of sense. His steady correspondence but my father's sporadic responses. How he had asked for his letters to be returned on Papa's death. Mama's cold response that she had burnt them. How my aunt had conceded to my stay in London only when Mama had been forced to leave for France.

My heart pounded in my chest, and my hand crept up into my mouth. Only then I smelt the faint smell of Syon's release. I muffled a moan and escaped to my room to fuck those fingers into my cunt. For a moment, I forgot that not all couples received the blessings my parents had.

15

SYON

I rolled onto my back and took a firm hold of my knot which was swelling almost painfully. A rough jerk at my hard cock was a kind of punishment for not recalling the dream that had caused me to grow increasingly frustrated each morning for the last few weeks. I closed my eyes for a moment and breathed in deep through my nose trying to draw in the scent that haunted my days. Yet it was dangerous to touch myself, for then I imagined violet eyes. To conflate Viola and Hartwell—even if she wanted to be an omega—was dangerous.

I stroked up and ran a thumb across the head, smearing the precum and stroking down with a hard stroke trying to mimic the tight grip of an omega's quim as I thrust deep inside Hartwell. Omega or not, I knew she'd be tight around my cock and knot. I'd fuck the insolent challenge out of her... I groaned. The reality of what I imagined more effective than a swim in a cold lake. An alpha? That did not cool the ardour. But the knowledge that in indulging these fantasies, allowing them to rule my passions would only bring pain. I would not take a wife and mate another. No matter how much my heart called to Hartwell, the likelihood of two alphas having children was low, and oddly those children were almost always betas.

I rolled off the bed, tossed a dressing gown on, and strode to the window, looking out across the square. The countess's house mocked me. I could almost remember her face seen across a ballroom when they'd been newlyweds. But the harder I focused on fair hair and pale eyes, the more I conjured dark curls and violet eyes. My hand shook as I lifted the lid of a plain box on the table by my bed and removed a lace handkerchief I'd found dropped by her desk. I brought the delicate fabric to my nose and caught the first whiff of violet eyes—I could not put a name to that scent without pushing myself beyond the limits of a civilised alpha. A near feral growl reverberated through my chest as my cock stiffened once again.

Without thought I reached down and pumped steadily, precum easing my way. Again that smell with a sweet underlying hint of Viola's vanilla and violets. The combination brought forth the flush of my impending orgasm. I gritted my teeth hoping to prolong the moment and switched hands so that the one holding the delicate fabric fisted my cock. The other gripped the swelling knot. My balls drew up before my orgasm pulsed through me, the handkerchief catching my spend. It was a poor imitation of where I wanted to plant my seed but better than letting it completely go to waste. At least I had now marked something that belonged to... Viola. Or was it Hartwell, who had taken Viola's scent... I did not care. It would have to be enough because I would never let myself take what I so desperately needed—my knot lodged deep, my mark fresh on her neck. And after yesterday? I wasn't certain I was alpha enough to resist the temptation Hartwell offered. I'd see her on her knees again.

Torture indeed, especially when I knew Hartwell would

be arriving within an hour. Yet I could not feel disgusted with myself or the feral alpha lurking beneath the surface. I was soothed by the knowledge that in some small way I had marked what was mine. Enough that I was able to spend the day with Hartwell with only the now constant need to fuck my secretary.

~

HARTWELL STOOD IN FRONT OF ME, HER FACE FLUSHED. I grinned. If I wanted she would go to her knees again. Only this time I would fuck that perfectly insolent mouth.

"Viola has been called to Kellingham House... I must change here... Your Grace?" She licked her lips, and my gaze fixed on how tempting her plump bottom lip looked. I blinked, her words breaking through my thoughts which increasingly trended towards depraved fantasy when she was near. "I, uh, I need to change here. I am supposed to attend a concert as Viola tonight. I had not thought... Mrs Markham sent a message around... She wanted us to join her for dinner beforehand as she will be my chaperone."

"What?" I glared at the eyes that haunted my dreams. It was one thing to fantasise, another to have that dream presented on a silver platter. "You didn't tell me this before."

"I didn't know how. I... Viola was invited this morning. I planned on going home to dress..."

"When did that change?" I gripped the desk to hold myself still. I had forbid her to dress as Viola in my house. Even the memory of her in a dress sent my pulse racing. I longed, needed to see the vision of Viola in my house. Her scent filled the room. And with it came the memory of when she had expressed her wish to be an omega.

"When it became clear there was too much to do!" She

growled. "We still have to go over your speech before the lords. The business of being your secretary must come before my social engagements."

"And you have your things here?" I interrupted.

"I sent for them, yes. I can just use a guest room. You don't have to see or smell Viola."

I swallowed at the sudden image of a naked Hartwell in my house and knew if I had to suffer that knowledge I might as well complete the torture by having her change behind the screen as she had done before. My voice was understandably hoarse when I told her. "You will change behind the screen as before while I practice my speech."

"Is that wise?" Her voice was soft. "We've... We've done things."

We had not once spoken of what happened after the duel. How I had fucked my hand until I'd ejaculated on her face. All the while hoping to stuff Hartwell with my cock and knot in her every available warm and wet opening.

"I think I am more than capable of controlling myself," the lie slipped off my tongue.

"I'll ask Timms to bring it through then," she said softly.

"What?" I snapped. When had my secretary commandeered my valet?

"I needed to have the wrinkles released from the gown. Our Goddess, Syon, do you expect me to appear in public in a creased gown?"

"Puss, I couldn't care less how you appeared, I want to know why you are instructing my servants." All too often Hartwell made some move on the board that pulled me up short. I'd gone from wanting to fuck my cock into her mouth to annoyance that she had command of my servants. I smiled at the turn about. I couldn't even be angry with her about it.

"I am your employee. You pay me a wage as you Timms or your footman or charwoman. I can speak to them..."

I stood for a moment in shock. I had never considered my relationship with her in the terms she used. "You are not a servant."

Hartwell chuckled. "As it pleases, Your Grace."

I growled but without any heat. If she chose to needle me, then I would indulge her as I was coming to realise I indulged her in all things. "Fine. Order my servants as if they were your own. See if I care."

"As you wish," she swooped into an exaggerated bow. The bell was rung, and there was a flurry of excitement that brought in both Horne and Timms to arrange the screen, place candles, and finally with great decorum a gown. I tried to avoid the parade of ceremony that passed by my desk. It disrupted my work and gave me ample time to build the anticipation of what was to come. For though my secretary held my interest, the unknown Viola caught me up in a swirl of desire. The gown being the *pièce de résistance* of lavender satin gave off the intoxicating scent of violets and vanilla. A fragrant manifestation of the power of omegas over alphas.

At last, it seemed to be time. By some invisible summons, Hartwell put down her quill and tidied her desk as if she were not about to transform into her twin. I sat back in an armchair and watched as Timms helped her shrug off the well-fitting coat. With a careless wave, she sent him away and disappeared behind the screen.

"Why not recite your speech," came a muffled voice.

I gritted my teeth at the youthful alpha ordering me in my own house. "It is too dark. Tell me instead about this sister of yours, who allows you to steal her dresses and masquerade in her place."

"Viola does not like the masquerade."

"Oh? And you?"

"I understand why I am doing it. And if all goes well, then the deception is justifiable. Do you think I can pull it off?"

"I believe you capable of anything, but I do not believe you would play me false in this. You would not manipulate or lie to me. I know you, Hartwell," I chuckled. "If you were to pull the wool over my eyes, however? I'd hide you for the insolence."

The silence stretched on except for the sound of silk on skin and with each passing heartbeat, my desire rose like the tide. My unspeakable need to know what was happening on the other side.

I stood and walked towards the screen but stopped abruptly. Because the mirror above the fireplace caught the reflection of a naked back dipping low but not low enough for my liking. Yet I dared not step closer lest I lose my increasingly tenuous control. Instead, I studied her as best I could in the flickering light. More lightly muscled than I'd expected after crossing swords with her. I watched entranced as she dropped a chemise over her head covering her nudity but not removing the temptation. I had seen women tempt as they removed their clothes, but watching her dress was almost more alluring. As each piece of clothing was added, my arousal became more insistent against my breaches. Closing my eyes, I took a deep breath and held it for a count of ten, letting it out slowly, then drawing it in again. I nearly gasped at how strong my own scent was (that I could even notice it) and how it mingled with Viola's. The smell of lust filled the room. I dared to look into the mirror again, to see if perhaps she had noticed. But she was an alpha, her sense of smell not nearly as strong as an omega's. Perhaps she would feel a little more aggressive, perhaps she would bristle, thinking I lusted for her sister. I almost wished she would challenge me. I would gladly cross swords with her again. My temper was in check this time, and I knew I would hold back to better see her gracefully dance with a rapier in hand.

Hartwell stepped around the screen with her focus on smoothing her skirts and fussing with a bracelet on a slim wrist.

"Viola," I breathed in awe. I had yet to meet the omega, but if what Hartwell said was true, they looked remarkably alike. Enough to be mistaken for one another. The pull towards this facsimile of an omega almost proved too great. Dark hair was threaded through with ribbon in a feminine fashion and easy to accomplish without the aid of a maid. The low cut gown revealed breasts fuller than Hartwell's.

"How did you achieve," and I gestured helplessly at the swell of the gown. The fashions of the day displayed breasts to perfection, and seeing her now, I wondered if I could persuade her to give up men's clothing for evening gowns. A temptation too far.

Her face heated, and she mimicked my movements around the illusion of breasts. "I... They are mine. I bind them, normally."

"Ah," I said, attempting to force a casualness into my voice which I did not feel. I wanted to hold the vision in front of me. Press our bodies close together, inhale that intoxicating combination until I lost all rational thought. But I would not. I might be an alpha, but I was no stripling or feral savage. I was a peer of the realm. A civilised creature who could overcome this reckless obsession.

"Did you...?" I bit back a curse. Hartwell had challenged Paxton for speaking of her sisters, and here I was asking about her breasts. "Forgive me. They are beautiful."

"I... I should call you out for that. But after the other day, I would surely acquit myself ill. Just respect that I cannot answer that question—"

"For you wouldn't know. Faith. If you did call me out I

would let you pink me. I cannot imagine what overcame me," I groaned and ran a hand over my face desperate to wipe what had just transpired from both our memories. Yet while I wished my words unsaid, I now must imagine what those breasts must look like, feel like. A cursory glance, an assumption that those were the picture of reality, and I was tortured by the thought of what colour those nipples might be. I focused on breathing through my mouth to lessen the impact of Viola's scent, which was quickly filling the room now that she had moved closer. And closer still until if I had wanted, I could have reached out to run a finger down that graceful neck down further still to then trace the swell of her breasts.

"Could you help me with this? The clasp is tricky, and I cannot seem to make it work. Syon?"

I blinked, startled from the spell she'd wrapped me in. "Help you? Of course. Come here."

She huffed a laugh but came forward, her silk skirts shushing on the carpet. But my desire would not be silenced. The necklace was an intricate piece of enamelled panels, pearl, ruby, and gold twisted as intricate knots.

"My father gave it to my mother," she said without prompting. "Then she passed it on to me. It is more correctly a collar."

"I've never seen the like." But I was looking at her, not the necklace. How could a necklace compare with the greatest of god's creations? A collar, though. They were out of fashion, but at one point alphas and male omegas had given them to their mates. A declaration of intent before a wedding formalised the pairing.

"Turn," I growled. I wanted to collar Hartwell. I wanted it almost as much as I wanted to feel her cunt squeezing my knot.

A shy smile was all I saw before she turned.

"Here," she held the ends of the collar to me. I took it, careful not to allow our fingers to touch.

"Lift your hair," I commanded.

Delicate hands gathered dark curls allowing me to fiddle with the clasp. In the soft light, it was tricky, but perhaps I allowed myself longer than necessary to secure the clasp. Finished, I rested my hands on white shoulders, giving them a comforting squeeze, and brushed along where an omega's mate gland would be. When she tried to turn back around, I held her. Like a marionette, my hand drew up along the graceful curve on her neck until I wrapped it around the slender throat. I stayed there. A gentle pressure to ground us both, or so I hoped. Instead, I could feel a rapid pulse. My thumb caressed where a mating bite would go. The current fashion was to expose the neck, some even went so far as to put a bit of rouge to enhance the scaring. How perfect my mark would be. How good that alphas like Gale and Pitt would back away knowing I owned all of Hartwell.

"My mouth," Hartwell whispered into the silence. If I hadn't had my finger on the racing pulse, I would have been fooled into thinking that she had commented on the weather. "Last time I did not touch you. But... I wanted to use my mouth."

I groaned. This could not be happening to me. It had been its own kind of torture when Hartwell had knelt before me, perfectly obedient as I sprayed that beautiful innocence with my seed, had rubbed my essence over that face and into that her wet mouth. How would those hands feel about my cock? And now she wanted to put her mouth on my aching cock? I could imagine with ease because I saw her pink lips almost every day.

"Do you want to kill me?" I asked.

"A little death," came the husky reply.

"A little death," I agreed. "I can't let you—"

My tormentor just turned and gracefully dropped to her knees before me. I looked down briefly but only saw a head of dark curls and billowing silk skirts.

"I've never done this before," the confession was an aphrodisiac. Mine, mine, mine to train. To show how best to suck my cock. I'd train my Hartwell up.

"Take it out," I ordered.

Delicate hands reached up, fumbling with the fastenings. I groaned as those same hands pulled me free, as they held my knot, and fingers teased along the length. I heard a soft rustle of silk and then had to feel the heat of a body against my legs. Lips brushing up my cock from base to the flared head.

"Put it in your mouth and suck," I groaned and closed my eyes, hoping that by blocking out the image it would lessen the intensity of feeling a willing mouth sucking on my cock. It was too much, I realised. This would change everything. There was no way I could ever give her up after this. I'd have her go down on me every day... I went to grab her head, to stop her from taking us further down this road. My hands threaded through the curls, prepared to jerk away.

"Please do not ruin my hair," the words blew against the head of my cock. "Let me..."

"We have to st—" The words were cut off with the first feeling of Hartwell's mouth around me. The heat, that wicked tongue doing wicked things. I knew, I *knew* that she was innocent without her telling me. That made my alpha purr. That made me want to halt this madness.

"Little one," I purred. "Look at me."

Her eyes sparkled up at me, my cock stretching her lips. Those eyes though, they were not as violet as usual, for they were black with desire. This wasn't some nameless, faceless creature giving me pleasure, but my secretary, my very particular Hartwell who wanted to fellate me in my library. Another alpha might care about dynamic, might be repulsed by the thought of an alpha sucking his cock, but I had never cared about the trappings. But Hartwell! That forever perfect combination of omega scent, feminine appearance, and the aggressive fire one would never find in an omega overwhelmed me. Never before, never again would there be someone more perfect than my secretary. She was my undoing. So I demanded eye contact as I slowly began to thrust in and out of that perfect mouth. I would not go too deep. She had never done this before. Nor would I be gentle.

My orgasm built slowly until suddenly, I felt my balls tighten and my knot throb. I grabbed my knot squeezing it with all my alpha strength. Though my hand paled in comparison to an omega's hot cunt or ass when it was leaking slick and desperate to clamp down on a good hard knot, but her mouth might be as good. Her tongue worked. She sucked me deep, forcing more of my cock into her throat until she gagged and tears streamed down her cheeks and her lips brushed my hand.

When it came, my orgasm was like a wave breaking on the shore. I shot my cum down her throat, and she could not swallow all of it so that it began to leak from her mouth. I pulled free, still erect allowing the last shots of cum to land on her chest. I ran a hand through my hair, breathing hard as I looked down on a dazed Hartwell, whose eyes were cloudy with desire.

"Hartwell... Here, let me." I fished my handkerchief out of my pocket and carefully dabbed at her breasts to remove my cum. It went against everything I wanted, but it had to be done. Because now more than ever, I wanted to spread her out on the desk. Taste her, fuck her. No, *that* had to be done. Now. This instant. "I need to taste you."

"No," she grabbed my hand. "I must... I must go. I'll never forget... Goddess, I must go! I'll be late."

I watched confused as she stumbled to her feet and fled the library. The rejection filled me. Impossible. I was the dominant alpha. She would never reject me. Still, I felt empty as I tucked myself back into my breeches and slumped into my chair. Dazed and confused about what the future held for us now... As master and servant. As a pair whose relationship was closer than friends.

"YOU SEEK TO MARRY THE COUNTESS?" FORDOM ASKED, HIS face showing his genuine surprise. He arrived an hour after the vision of Viola had left and demanded to know if he could hide out here, drink my wine, and play a game of chess rather than attend some party or other. I'd relented, for he knew the Hartwells and I had questions for him. Questions I wanted to avoid asking but needed the answers as much as I needed my next breath. But instead of providing me with an opening, he had spoken of other things. That is, until now, when he had decided to remind me of my plan to marry. "May I ask why?"

"You may not," I growled. "Whom I marry is my concern alone."

"And surely the omega's as well. But does your secretary know your intent?"

I frowned across at the alpha who lounged in the chair. A long leg extended, the buckle on his shoe glinting in the firelight.

"Why'd you ask?"

"I come from a gathering where I happened to see the countess and Miss Viola Hartwell. They are often in each other's company, much to Caroline's annoyance."

"What has that to do with anything?" I held my temper in check. He was speaking of my Hartwell, and I did not like it.

"Oh, nothing. Viola is a most beautiful omega," he

scratched his chin and a smirk twisted his face. "She will be presented soon, and, I expect, will cause a few ripples."

"Why? There is no fortune there," I snapped and wanted to tell him the truth. It was Hartwell he'd seen, but I could not reveal it. Dammit. Viola was not some society prize. When she mated, it would be for something other than her social standing.

"Perhaps not, but those violet eyes. And that quickness of thought and conversation. Besides, of all the sisters, she is the most... Shall I say innocent?"

I growled. I had not seen those eyes or mouth but I knew another, and that is the one that flashed before my eyes—one in lavender silk with my cum on her face.

"Faith, what have... Unless it is not the countess but Viola who has caught your attention? Viola, my own goddess." Though he did not sound surprised as he raised his glass of wine to his lips. "Well, if the wind blows in that direction..."

"And how would I know Miss Hartwell when I have not met her?"

"Has Hartwell not sung her praises? Paxton is not here so I feel safe to say that Beatrice is the fairest of the sisters. Hippolyta is beautiful but wild. Viola, however. Now she is a hidden gem. By far the most dangerous to an alpha's peace of mind. Though I have a feeling you would not want some sit at home omega. Surely not after that dinner you threw the other night? My understanding is that you gathered the brightest political minds? Paxton came away grumbling that Hartwell is going to push you into a leadership position—"

"What?" I barked out a laugh at the absurdity of the thought. "My little secretary, bullying me to do something?"

Jack gave a Gallic shrug, his smirk still plastered on his face. "Paxton's history with that family is not as long as mine. Beatrice and I grew up together. Though she'd rather swallow broken glass than speak to me—never mind that. But I'm sure that if Beatrice looked in Pax's direction he would explode with frustration."

"Why not just mate and marry her? Or you could share her. I hear you've done it before."

"Why not indeed? And why not just take Viola for yourself? She is far more politically minded than any other and would make an excellent political hostess. And beautiful."

"I've yet to meet the lady. And I'm no politician." It was a poor excuse when I knew her scent lingered everywhere in the library. At least he would be ignorant and just take the scent to belong to some other omega.

"Oh? Her scent..." he frowned. "I could swear..."

I gritted my teeth, anger swirling about as I considered why Fordom would know Viola's scent. He, who by his own admission was persona non grata at the Hartwell residence. Viola, not yet presented. Viola, carefully watched and protected from alphas. Viola, who was not the one sitting with the countess but safe at home and aware of her sister's masquerade. Viola, whose name had tumbled from my lips this morning as I'd fucked my hand. The name I'd nearly called out as I came in Hartwell's mouth.

"As for politics? Orley, your dinner the other night was considered enlivening, to put it mildly."

"Well, then you and Beatrice?" I tried to change the conversation.

"I'm more likely to marry a shrew than my lady disdain," as he took snuff. "She would not have me again."

Again? I wondered what he could mean by that.

"You and Paxton protest too much, methinks."

"Yes, it is a romance only Shakespearia could do justice. I knew Beatrice as a girl and when I say that to tangle with her a second time would be the death of me, I do not lie. But Orley, in all seriousness. Do not take into your head to ignore your instincts. While mine have, on occasion, led me astray, they do not do so for all alphas. I am man and alpha enough to admit I stumbled in my handling of Beatrice... But she and I were young. She was far too young. We both live. Do not make my mistake, though. Claim your Hartwell. Or cut yourself free before you are burnt."

16

VIOLA

I felt hot and shivery at once.

"Syon, please," I cried out, uncertain what I was asking for but needing to be released from this spiral of uncontrolled anticipation. My core clenched, begging to be filled. My head begged that he would release me and release me... Sat back in my chair, amused at the flowers growing out of Syon's ears. My heart wanted both. The sound of a symphony filtered into the throne room, I wished to escape the vines binding my wrists and see what kind of alpha he truly was. Would he try to master me? Would he use some new way to express his will? The cool breeze of my mother's garden soothed my heated flesh. For until now, he had not physically imposed his desires on me. Always it had been a word or look. These new interactions filled me with electric anticipation. Musical violets bloomed with spontaneous galloping force, and Syon held me, coaxed each desperate, sobbing moan of pleasure from me...

A whimper escaped as I rubbed my slick covered thighs together. What had I been dreaming of? I could not remember anything of it, but my fingers went immediately to my sex and began trying to find some relief by sticking three fingers into my cunt at once. There was a moment of resistance at the sudden intrusion that had me gasping, but I relished the bite for it was the closest I would get to the abrupt fullness that a knot would provide.

After my disturbing, deliciously erotic dream, I sent a note round to Syon informing him I'd not be able to join him today. He would understand. I'd gone too far last night in the library and could not face him. In truth, I was not afraid of his reaction but my own, convinced that should I see him, be in his presence, I would want to do more than suck on his cock until he came on my tongue. I wanted to taste him again, know that his scent mingled with mine. Go as far as I dared, before pulling away at the last moment to maintain my disguise. I felt sick at my deception, but unable to quiet my omega instincts which cried out for Syon with alarming need.

My needs, however, must be put aside. There was one whose need, albeit a different kind, was greater than my own. As sick as I felt at the thought of him with another omega, better that than risk the Countess being abandoned to the streets. From Caroline, I knew that her father the vicar resented that he would be responsible for Olivia's board and upkeep. It should have been her parents, who'd been paid ten thousand pounds for her, but they'd disappeared after the wedding. I'd pledged to help her and from what I could see, Syon offered her the best future.

You could reveal the truth about your dynamic. You could have him for yourself. The insidious thoughts crept in—not so easily dismissed these days. Syon would hate me if he learnt the truth. Hadn't he expressed his disgust at being manipulated the day before? Or at least that he would punish me for deceiving him. And what punishment greater than to send me away?

～

THAT EVENING, A NOTE WAS DELIVERED TO MY UNCLE'S—Olivia, begging for my presence. Caroline was out, and Olivia was alone and desperate to speak with me. I too needed to speak with her, and in private, for my thoughts were akimbo, warring like a kite caught in a storm. I needed to press on with Syon's suit. Our recent conversations had won me a point: Olivia wanted to marry again and an alpha. The sticking point for her was which alpha. I dressed quickly as Iris for it would be easier to travel so late as an alpha, but did not bother to bind my breasts or wipe away my scent counting on my twin's clothes to do most of the work.

Tonight I would propose in Syon's name. My role would be done, and reluctantly, for I could not imagine them happily married. But I had made a promise. Eventually, I would find a way to go back to the life I was intended to lead. To be sure, it was not the one I longed for, but the past months had caused me heartache. I did not want to continue with this farce. Better to end the charade before I was in too deep. An obvious lie—how much deeper could I fall? I wished to tell Paxton and Fordom that they had been correct. That I could not continue my masquerade any longer. I would once again tame myself, grow out of my childish pranks. I could not ignore my dynamic any longer. I did not want to. Being with Syon almost every day had taught me how dangerously appealing an alpha could be to an omega.

My thoughts were a gorgon's knot. I chuckled. The last thing I wanted was to cut through a knot. Not when I was dreaming of an alpha's one. That kind of knot... I froze. My thoughts too frequently were turning in that direction. Perhaps my aunt was correct, and my heat would come unexpectedly after I had tried so hard to suppress it. No, I might resign myself to an omega's life but I would not let myself be ruled by passions. That would only prove to alphas that they were correct: omegas were weak and unable to think beyond their sexual desires.

$\approx$

THE BUTLER OPENED THE DOOR AND IN A HUSHED WHISPER told me I could find her ladyship in the drawing room. I took the stairs two at a time, in a rush to propose in Syon's name before my resolution left me.

The door was ajar, and I slipped in, closing it, and turning the key, locking us in the drawing room. It was lit by a fire and a few candles but otherwise it was hauntingly dark, or perhaps seductively so. A place to receive a lover, rather than a friend.

"Olivia," I called to the little omega, who curled kitten-like in her chair. In the time that I had known her, her looks had improved. She no longer looked on the verge of tears. She had put on weight, a pleasing thing for an alpha since omegas with curves would weather a heat better than one all skin and bones. And a strong heat meant she was more likely to catch.

Her head shot up, and she scrambled towards me. When she was within arms reach, I dropped my cloak.

She fell back, a fluttering hand touching her breast. "Oh," came the soft voice. "I wanted... Viola?"

I hated what I was about to do but it needed to be done... I could think of no other way. I must play a part of an aggressive alpha... I must pretend to be Iris, I must propose in Syon's name. I could only hope that I'd laid the groundwork, that she was receptive to marrying again, and that Syon would come across as an alpha who wanted to marry her enough that he would do anything to win her heart.

"Not Viola, never Viola. Sweet lady, I have committed a fraud," That at least was the truth. "I am Iris Hartwell. I came dressed as my sister, dishonourable wretch that I am, to woo you. Not for myself but in the name of the Duke of Orley, who wishes to marry you. Knowing your sad tale, he wants to marry you. He wants to save you from a miserable future. Make you his duchess. Please lady, forgive my presumption. He is wild with... I am so sorry... I conceived of this deception to help him."

Her eyes were wide, shining in the firelight. I thought her silence would end in a scream, expose me. She rushed towards me and grasped my hands in hers.

"Let me see you, come to the fire and let me see you," there was a longing in her voice.

"Please, my lady..."

"Call me Olivia as you have before," her hand drifted to my face as if not believing what she saw. "I will not know what to do if you call me anything but Olivia. Please, tell me... Your name is Iris. You are Viola's twin. You are..."

"I am Iris. Viola's twin." The lie was too ingrained in my mind, but to give voice to it in front of her made me uneasy.

"Viola's twin, an alpha. I knew it! I love you," her voice trembled. I stood frozen before her, unable to know what to say. This must be some mistake, a joke. What could I do? To reveal my true identity, to say that I was Viola, an omega, and not my alpha twin as I had confirmed with my last breath? "I love you, Iris or Viola—it does not matter. Please, say something."

"My lady... I do not know what to say, or why you think I am... His Grace... It would be... It is impossible for me to respond. And solely inappropriate under the circumstances. The duke! The *duke* is the one who desires to marry you. He wants to save you. He can protect you. As his duchess, you will want for nothing. He is good and kind... He is the best man I've ever met. I would not trust you, dear friend, to him if I did not believe with all my being that he would take care of you."

"But you are here!" she cried. "You came because you loved me! I knew. I knew almost from the start that I loved you. And then it was no great mystery to discover you were not Viola. There was always something about you, a scent that tickled me to my core— I was slick for you. I knew you were an alpha!"

"I told you my meaning," I interrupted her and tried to draw back. "I come as an emissary for the duke."

"Oh, I hate the mention of him! He is an alpha. A man. How can he be any different from other alphas? I won't believe it. You came for yourself. Deny our friendship... You cannot."

"How could I? We are friends, but I am his secretary... I might be an alpha, but..." I reluctantly maintained the lie. But this lovestruck woman made me feel like a fool. Caught in a trap of my own making, and one I did not know how to escape. I crossed to the window and looked out. A single candle shone in the window of Syon's library. All my thoughts were with him, and I cursed myself for coming here when, if I had my wits about me, I would be tucked into my own bed. Or I'd come dressed as myself. Fool, for wearing Iris' clothing tonight, but it was safer to wander the streets as an alpha in men's clothing than as an omega in skirts.

"True meeting of hearts. True mates! We have spent many hours in conversation. Are you to tell me that was a lie? You are the one who gives me hope. You give me kindness. Not the duke. I do not care for him. I do not know him. I love you."

"Olivia, you do not love me. Not truly," I drew her to a chair by the fire and not so gently pushed her into it. Her scent flared, and I perceived my mistake. No omega would use force as I had. I cursed myself but pressed on hoping my words would get through to her. "You, perhaps, love the romance of an alpha coming here in secret to woo you. But this is no novel written for omega's fantasy. Love does not happen upon you suddenly—"

"But I am not saying it did! From the first, I knew I could trust you. Love grew with each passing day."

"You mean my sister." Though I was not sure I meant my sister or me. What a muddle. Syon was correct. I made things too complicated.

"No, you! I would know your eyes anywhere. I swear upon all. It was, it is you I love! Please. Take me from this prison and make me yours!"

For all her ardour, the little omega had stayed in her seat by the fire. I wondered if an alpha would be crossing to her, taking her up in their arms, and... What, I could not know. Growl at her? Purr for her? Kiss her? I tried to think what I would want in such a moment. I would have crossed to him. I knew. I would have crossed to Syon and forced him to look at me. Because his resolve was great, and he would not want to give in. That was not his way. He was civilised. *He is also feral*, my traitorous heart reminded me. *When you fought with him, when you changed behind the screen and he sat there. When you tasted him and wanted more. Then there was something dangerous lurking in his eyes*. He would not care if I was man or woman, alpha or omega—no, I was wrong. His desires were as confused as Olivia's because they did not know the truth.

I wanted to flee to Syon, put my arms about him, and beg him to hear my tale. To forgive me or not, I did not care. All I knew was that this charade must come to a conclusion.

"I am sorry, Olivia. I am not what you want. Give me a day and I shall prove to you that you deserve better than this shadow puppet you've known these past weeks."

Like a coward, I ran from her and did not stop running until I'd arrived at Weymouth Street. I stood in front of the house and was violently sick, but the acidic taste was nothing compared to my own heart's bitter anguish at all I had done to two whose friendship and happiness I valued more than my own. When had it all gone so wrong?

~

I WROTE TO IRIS THE NEXT MORNING BEGGING HER TO return. I would not be able to unmask myself without her presence. She would strip my mask free. And, like Beatrice, I would become yet another scandalous omega by the name Hartwell. It was necessary. I could not do this for a moment longer.

The letter sent, I sat at the small table in the drawing room, unable to form coherent thoughts. My stay in London was over. But as yet, I had no notion of how to see through to the end of the game without sacrificing the queen, without sacrificing my own dreams and happiness. It would be worth it though, I had to convince myself of that. Syon and Olivia, together or apart—they'd know the truth and be better off without me.

"His Grace, the Duke of Orley," Roberts called.

"The Duke?" I gasped, sounding quite stupid. I stood, causing my chair to clatter to the ground.

"Yes, Miss Viola."

"I..."

Roberts was thrust aside, and Syon walked in as if it were his own home. He was dressed for riding and clutched a crop in his hand. His hair was in disarray as if he'd run his hands through his golden locks. It only emphasised the frown which crossed his face on seeing me alone. With a curt word, he dismissed Roberts. I bit my lip. This duke would see nothing amiss in his high handed manner. Roberts, however, waited until I told him to order some tea.

"Your Grace," I curtsied. "I am afraid you find me alone.

My aunt has gone out and my uncle is not here. If you wish to leave a note..."

"Your sister? Not home? Good," he asked but did not move any further into the room. "My manners. You are Miss Viola Hartwell."

He came forward to grab my hand in his, staring at it as if it were a disagreeable letter from his steward. He dropped it abruptly without shaking it or—heaven protect me—kissing it, leaving me bereft of his touch. His manners were odd. I had never seen him display any nervousness. But today he gripped his crop and tapped it against his thigh. My mind went straight to the day he had spanked me, and I felt my core tense with need. He could not scent me, I reminded myself. If there was slick, he'd not notice it. I closed my eyes, breathed in and released both to find him watching me keenly.

"Is this a bad time?" Syon asked. "I had hoped..."

"My aunt is not at home. I said that already..." I swallowed unsure how I felt about the propriety of speaking with him without a chaperone. I did not fear for my virtue, but I was alive to the very real possibility that if ever I were to be caught in my deception it would be now when he could see no difference between me and my facsimile. Or if someone else came in and perceived this to be a compromising situation. I could end up married to him. Married and unmated. Could I accept that? Knowing he might find a mate? Knowing what we had done together while he thought I was Iris? I tugged at the collar of my dress.

"We will keep the door open then."

I gave the barest nod and invited him to sit. He declined and strode to the window, looking out onto the street, still beating his crop against his thigh. The room was so quiet that one could hear the clock tick. I glanced at it and watched as the time crept on. Five minutes and the hour chimed.

"I have made a decision," he said. "But, I wanted to see you first. You are close with your twin, are you not?"

"If you mean Iris, I am, your Grace."

His eyes flashed. "Call me Syon."

"It would be improper," I hedged and faced the fire for fear I might give something if I could see him.

"More improper than coming into this room with me?"

"I did not come! You came!"

Roberts returned with the tea tray. We waited again until he had left. I could look anywhere in the room so long as it was not him, and so jumped when I sensed fingers hovering over my shoulder. How I knew that I could not say—except, perhaps my body was attuned to his that even blind and deaf I'd find him in a crowded room. He came nearer until I felt his breath on my neck. He was scenting me. My breasts felt heavy and hot within the confines of my gown. Instinct told me to lean back. Allow this alpha to surround me with his rich aroma. To bare my neck, to entice, to invite him to mark me as his.

"I won't touch you," his voice was rich and dark against the shell of my ear. It echoed through me. More seductive for withholding his touch than if he had knotted me. There was a rasp that caused my heart to catch mid beat.

"Your virtue is safe with me," he purred. "Always. I would never do anything to dishonour one of the Hartwell sisters, you most of all."

I nearly groaned in frustration. I wanted to scream out that I was his Hartwell. I was the secretary he had been with almost daily since January. I had tasted his cum, touched myself almost every night, burying my face into my pillow to muffle my voice as I called out his name. But to tell him risked everything. No, I could not bear to see his face when he learnt my lies. He would not just cut me in his rage but he would probably destroy all of my sister's ambitions too. I shook my head to dispel the unjust thoughts. He would not be so cruel as that. He would not... I let out a shuddering breath.

"Have I upset you?" his whisper sent a shiver through me, and I noticed my scent spike with anxiety.

"Upset me, Your Grace?"

"I do not mean to discomfit you... You scent..." he trailed off. How... How could he notice the change in my scent when he couldn't smell spoilt milk?

"Why are you here?" my voice broke on the question. He'd been pleased to learn I was alone, but why?

"Your sister is wrong."

"Often," my laugh was bitter. Full of disgust for my actions, and Iris's own folly for talking with Syon. "She is... principled, and it can lead her to pig-headedness."

"At times."

"Is there a reason you called?" I asked again, for I had not received an answer and the longer I spent in Syon's company, the greater the risk I would expose myself. Cloves and alpha musk filled my senses. Already I knew the alpha part of him was not indifferent to my omega. But it was not me, the women, he sent heated glances to but my omega. Our dynamics were drawn together. That was all. I could not hope for more. I relaxed when I felt him move away. Only to find him standing in front of me, hands thrust into the pockets of his greatcoat. His brows drawn together in a frown that I longed to smooth away. I hated when he was like this—shut off and frowning—for I could not tell his thoughts when he grew so restlessly quiet. I dreaded what made him so introspective.

"She is wrong to think I shall forgive her not coming to me this morning—never mind that. I had much to think about yesterday. Tell her I will do my own courting from now. And she does not need to come by tomorrow. She is no longer my secretary. I plan to go into the country for a few weeks. She refused my invitation to come with me," He glanced down at his gloves. I had not noticed he'd removed them. "She should go back to Oxford. Finish her degree. Or if that is not to her liking, then take the Grand Tour. I won't have the time for her once I am married."

Tears pricked my eyes. Did he know what he did to me? Shattering my heart. I floundered for an appropriate response. One that would not reveal how effectively he had destroyed my every chance for happiness. I could, I told myself. I could continue at his side as his friend and secretary. He didn't know my lie but still pushed me away as if I meant nothing to him. But to be repudiated without doing anything wrong near killed me. I wanted to beg. I'd been on my knees before him more than once. Had those times been a lie? Had he used me as I had told him to? Had... Had I meant nothing to him beyond a hand and mouth to fuck because there had been an omega's scent nearby? A natural response.

"Iris will finish her degree, I believe." Before he could speak again I rushed on. "Can I offer you tea?"

"Thank you."

But he would say so since I was already pouring.

My heart stopped when our fingers brushed.

"How did you know how I took my tea," he asked.

"I... I was not paying attention," which was true enough. I knew how he liked his tea. Had known for weeks and would have needed to think about it as much as I would need to remember to breathe. I expected him to sit, but he moved to the fireplace and proceeded to stare at me.

"Your eyes are very like hers. I've never seen anything like. And now I think perhaps you are... I will be brief. I must let your sister go. I cannot have her..." He put his cup on the mantle and crossed to the door, closing it and locking it. My heartbeat as fast as a rabbit's. "I cannot have her in my life when I am married, when I am wed. Then I must... It would be... Do you see? I would be... I wouldn't be able to have her near if I was married to another... She will understand my meaning."

"You've said that already," my voice sounded choked. "Why must you say it again and again? Why must you do this to me?"

"Do you think I am happy about this?" he snapped.

I did. I didn't. How could I see when I only wanted to jump up and smooth that frown away with a quip. Tell him there was no need to marry when he had me. Omega, woman. All the traits he so desired in a bride. It would hurt, but I would forgo a mate bond if it meant being by his side. Yet I could not tell him. Never. The words of love and devotion would never be spoken.

"Jack Fordom said you were a dangerous omega. I believe it now more than ever," Syon continued. "I have insulted you. I beg your pardon. I see you, and she comes to mind. I forget myself," he growled. I fought the desire to purr, to soothe the monster that prowled behind his facade. As long as I had known him, I had never seen him so at odds with himself. "You are close to her. I need you to tell her... Soften the blow. With her, I have no control. You must make her understand. To woo in my own name. I never should have agreed to this prank of hers."

"What do you mean by that? I—" The realisation that Iris might have been more indiscreet than she knew drew forth a frown. I had certainly not said anything like that. "I cannot believe that Fordom would bring me up with you."

"Well, he did. Last night. I will speak to you with gloves off. If I prick you... I mix my metaphors. Words are not my friends when I am in your presence," the pause pregnant with meaning. He growled and took a step towards me until he stood over me. Instinct had me look up his impressive figure until our eyes met. His gaze heated and confused. Dear Goddess help me. "If I prick you, forgive me. Forgive me my sins, Viola. Though I must set you both at a distance... Tell me... If the world was yours, but the person you loved was out of reach, how would you tell them that you loved them but you must leave them? When you had yet to hold them but knew by the way they moved and smelt that they were the only one for you and you for them? But still, you must set them aside for reasons, principles impossible to ignore. Tell me, Viola, please tell me."

If I had been an alpha in truth, I would have wanted to order him from my sight. He ran hot one minute, cold the next. But I had cursed myself to hear his half confessions with the ears of Viola. And like Viola, unknown to him an hour before, I must answer him.

"If our positions..." I turned my head, but his gaze made my cheeks blaze hot. How could I be asked to answer this backwards declaration? I could understand why, in theory. He must have an alpha heir, which needed an omega and woman. This was the stuff of romantic tragedies. A bitter thought, since until this moment I had taken myself to be the heroine of a farce. "I don't know..."

"And what would you say, Viola? Not Iris. I ask you, Viola and omega. Would you tell me to go after what my heart wants? Or must I do my duty? I came here knowing what I must do but am now more confused than ever."

Too terrified to speak, I stood that I might escape the familiar yet unknown alpha. What would I be able to say? I wanted him to follow his heart so long as that heart led to me. But I was an omega he had just met. He did not know me from Eve. The most he knew was my scent, but what did that matter to a man with no intention of finding a mate? A strangled cry escaped me. I couldn't.

"I don't know. Yes. Follow your heart—"

Syon growled and grabbed my hand, squeezing it tight, and pulling me closer. "I knew it. I should have... I should have never told you I would leave. I should not have put you through that, Hartwell. Come with me..."

"No," I panted and tugged at his firm grip. He had discovered me. By accident, to be sure. But he knew. Some primal part of him knew.

Syon dropped my hand as if burnt.

"Damn, I am a cad. A bastard. I beg your pardon, for in the heat of the moment I mistook you—" he growled, deep and low, but caught my hand in his again. If possible, it seemed he might draw me near, and my body leant towards him. The unmistakable feeling of slick between my thighs. Dammit, but he would discover me...

"Syon!" I whined. "This is not..."

"Viola," He started when my scent reached him. And I? I stumbled back, landing in an undignified puddle of shame on the floor. He moved like lightning, picking me up, clutching me close even as his words pushed me away. "I leave you now. I must clear my head... You understand. Of course, you do. I'll be at Ayleigh... That's in Oxfordshire."

A kind of energy like the nervous excitement of riding a young horse towards a fence raced through me. Knowing that you would throw your heart over and make the jump and continue to gallop on to the next field. But not knowing if the horse could take it, or would throw you to the ground. My heart pounded like the horse's hooves and I was not focused on the rapidly disappearing ground between us but on the field beyond. I'd already thrown my heart over, I'd already committed to my actions, and there would be no going back. I didn't think about the consequences, I'd accept them. I had to. Because I felt his cock pressed hard against his breeches. I needed to hold that hard length in my hand, weigh it, measure it against my palm, my arm for it was certainly longer than my hand. I'd tasted but I'd not yet explored. Dear Goddess, what was I thinking? Why was I so desperate to humiliate myself like this? Some fever in the brain.

He spun away from me. Putting space between us, moving towards the door, leaving me forever.

But tripping, like the prisoner towards the gallows, my feet, 'gainst my will, dragged me towards him. His growl warned me off. Instead, it worked on me as a siren's call beckoning me closer. Perhaps we could somehow convince our fevered brains that this was just bodies. I had to convince myself it was just bodies. That I was merely a tool for him to use.

"Syon... You... You need to tell me to stop."

I rested my head against his broad, powerful back, breathed in the smell of him, raw and alpha. His body shuddered with each breath and two large hands gripped my wrists when I wrapped my arms around his waist.

"You don't have to do this," he said.

"I know. Just..." I took a stammering breath. I needed this to be something we both wanted too much to ignore. "Just use my hands. Imagine. They... You need relief."

"Yes," his whispered plea broke my heart.

Blindly, I struggled with the fastenings. Blindly, I reached for him. Blindly, I felt how his hot length sprang free and bobbed in the cool air.

I grasped it at the root, just above the swollen knot.

"I need to see," I told his back, my nose tracing up his spine. "Tell me you want this."

"I do," he growled but did not let me go. He would not let me see him. I stepped into his back, pressing him into my embrace until there was no way he could escape me. Of course, he was stronger, perfectly capable of setting me aside —but he didn't. I had never felt more powerful or more pathetic. This alpha, so impressive and so very much at my mercy but who did not want me as I wanted him. He might be hard, but that was my omega scent and nothing more. What I wanted from him was far harder to give—his mate mark. My breath came hot and fast on his back as my hands gripped his cock and gave it sure strokes up and down while squeezing his knot.

As he came in my hand, he spoke my name like a prayer. "Viola."

We stood there for an unknown amount of time. He wiped my hands with a handkerchief and stepped away from me. I wanted to stop him. My omega rebelled at the thought of his seed going to waste when I could spread it on my skin or better still lick and suck it from my fingers. I turned my head away, embarrassed. Afraid he would see the tears falling down my face. That he would think I was disgusting, an untouched omega helping to his orgasm. I needed to tell him now. After what had happened, I had to tell him.

"Syon, it is me... I am," my head jerked up at the sound of the door slamming.

He had already left, even as I was about to confess.

Viola fell silent and, like one possessed, went to the window to watch the clouds come in. It is like to rain, she thought.

17

SYON

I gasped, pulling in deep lungfuls of crisp winter air that was not saturated by Viola's enthralling scent of violets and vanilla, the hypnotic way her violet-eyed stare cut through me. Her eyes had looked so vulnerable but also near black with desire. And her slick. Goddess! her slick. Then how she'd wanted to...How she had! My balls ached, and my cock hard again. The urge to return and give her what we both wanted... Except would she want me to fuck her mouth, quim, or ass? I wanted to give her my knot in all three. How could I have left her when she smelt needy and ready for an alpha's knot? It was cruel to her, and torture for me.

Viola Hartwell. I looked up to the drawing room window and saw her looking up at the clouds. An unattainable ideal for any alpha. And for me a temptation I had rejected.

She was more than I could have hoped for. More than I could have longed for. She put me in danger more than her twin. For Viola, I was feral. I could grasp control of myself with Hartwell. She was an alpha. In Viola were all my ideals and requirements in a wife—and ones I'd not realised I wanted. But she had one quality I could not discount: Viola tempted me into taking her as my mate. The way she had so gently bared her neck for me, and I'd been on the brink of mate-marking her there. Unlike with the countess, I lacked the control to rut Viola and not mark her then and there. Her scent so strong I knew that even though she wasn't in her heat the mark would have taken. Then where would I be? In a marriage with a mate and no guarantee I wouldn't turn as jealous as my father had. Jealous to the point of challenging alphas if they dared look on my mate? I would not hate her as my father had hated my mother. But Viola deserved a mate of her choosing rather than a feral alpha. I owed Hartwell that much if I married her sister. Worse still, it didn't change my feelings for either of them. Could I take them both? I was hard from the fantasy of the twins in the duchess' nest— easily the most erotic things I'd ever imagined. Twin perfections. Who would refuse that?

And yet the passionless marriage to the countess put me on edge. If I subjected myself to such a connection, would I then become my grandparents, who were married in name but mated to others? I'd not give up Hartwell. I could not. Amongst the peerage, packs were acceptable when the parentage of the heirs could not be questioned. Hartwell was a woman. She could give me children, alpha children... Except not. Alpha-alpha pairs were barren more often than not. And if my wife were to take a mate? If I married Viola in order to keep a facsimile of my secretary near, what would I do if Viola mated another? If I mated her twin? The thought of Viola near another alpha nearly had me returning to her and claiming her, ruining her on my knot, holding her close until someone discovered us and saw exactly how an alpha claimed an omega. It would be a rape and I would never do that.

No solution came to mind. None that would solve my problems and keep others safe.

"No good can come of this."

What I had done with Viola was a betrayal of my relation-ship with my secretary, my Hartwell, but I could not regret it. I must do the honourable thing. I needed to marry the count-ess. Save her. There would be others for the Hartwell twins. An omega for Iris. An alpha for Viola. I'd give them up despite what Viola had said. I knew if our situations were reversed, she would do the right thing. Save the countess.

I PASSED A RESTLESS AND FRUSTRATING NIGHT. NO MATTER the number of times I jerked my stone hard cock or squeezed the life out of my knot, I returned again and again to a state of perpetual arousal that only an omega's, only Viola's slick coated cunt could provide. I was near to a rut and no easy lie could change how I fixated on violets and vanilla. I had to find some relief and flirted with the idea of kidnapping Viola. I could just keep her in the duchess' nest. I didn't need to touch her, fuck her. Just knowing she was there... Building a nest... That was a lie. I could not have her or Hartwell near with me without my near feral alpha taking over. Violet eyes were the only thing that might provide relief. Violet eyes looking up at me as lips over my cock, which I would thrust deep into a hot and willing mouth. Or violet eyes dilated in ecstasy as my knot stretched a hot and slick hole. Or violet eyes half shuttered with the bliss of too many orgasms.

As dawn approached I came to my conclusion. I could not marry the countess. I could not deny myself and my needs. Let another save the countess. It was arrogant of me to think other alphas wouldn't be interested.

I held off for two days before I headed to Weymouth Street and demanded of Florey where my secretary was.

"Kellingham House," was the unwelcome reply, but at least it was across the square from my own residence, from the duchess's nest. It would suffice. "The countess is receiving alphas. My niece and mate..."

But I was off before he could finish.

The countess' butler tried to forestall me when I arrived, but I pushed past and stormed the drawing room.

The widowed omega sat on an elegant little sofa in an equally elegant room. She could have fit into my pocket, the perfect representation of an omega. But I could not look away from where Hartwell stood by the window talking with a woman I did not recognise.

"Countess," I bowed to my hostess.

Then I turned to my quarry, who looked pale as the tucker that spilt from a gown of cornflower blue, which set off her eyes to perfection. I knew it was Hartwell and not Viola from the little frown and disapproving shake of her head. So different from Viola's omega instincts when I'd been with her the other day. I did not think I had beheld anything as perfect as my secretary being irritated with me. I grinned because I realised two incontrovertible facts: Hartwell was my best friend, and I was wildly, madly, deeply in love with her.

"I would talk to you before I leave. Now," I said. Not quite a bark but I would not permit her to thwart me.

She hesitated for a moment, looked at her companion before following me out the door. A fortunate thing, for if there had been a hint of reluctance, the feral alpha inside of me would have pounced and dragged my prey from the room. Once within reach, I grabbed a slim wrist and pulled us into the nearest room, a library, the curtains thrown back to reveal a room that looked like it had not seen a soul in many months. What more proof did I need that the countess was not for me? The abandoned chamber was more than adequate for my purpose. A lair for me to press my case, and make it known I would have mine. But *civility*. I clung to my control, despite the fight put up by my alpha to claim, even in another's house, what belonged to me. For now, we were alone. I must depend on every expectation of polite behaviour to hold me back. I could not scare her—if Hartwell could ever be scared. Another grin played with my lips as her frown deepened.

"I am taking you now. Hartwell, you are mine," I spoke plainly so she would not misunderstand my meaning.

"Your Grace, you are mistaken. I belong to no one." Her voice might tremble but the chin and eyes were all proud defiance. "I'm Viola," she hissed.

"I know exactly who you are. You are mine."

"Fool! You are blinded by an omega's scent," violet eyes flashed. I knew who those eyes belonged to because they were the eyes of the one I loved. This creature before me could stop my world with a smile or a spark of temper. She had demonstrated a knowledge of politics I wanted to nurture and encourage. I wanted to see this incredible woman before me grow and flourish. Yet, I could not allow myself to get closer. Whatever scandal might come, I could allow it to fall on my broad shoulders. But the thought of it touching my dear beloved—for that is what the owner of those violet eyes was to me—to allow even a breath of scandal to harm this perfect formation of body, mind, and heart was a knife through my chest. I could bear it, though. I had the power and the will to clear the path. But first I would have her in the duchess' nest. Alpha or omega I would rut Hartwell in her nest as my mate and wife deserved.

"No scent could hide you from me," I purred. "I would know it is you by looking in your eyes. Those flashing orbs which sent forth our souls to combine... See Hartwell, I turn poet for you. You enthral me."

Those startling eyes shuttered, hiding whatever emotions were coiled and pleading to get free. The delicate throat rose and fell as she swallowed down some words before looking back into my eyes. Violet eyes, so slightly dilated that I knew we both rode the rising, tumultuous passion. Her actions had already proved as much. Yet there was sad resignation in them. My heart pulsed as if it had been dealt a blow it would never recover from.

"Did you speak with Viola?" I asked, suddenly afraid the twins had revealed all to each other. "So much has changed since then. I should have come to you sooner. The very moment I knew my mind..."

"What is't you want, Your Grace? Did you not tell Viola you must marry the countess. What need to speak with me except to tell me to leave and never see you again?" Her nostrils flared, and I relished how her violet eyes dilated when she realised exactly how aroused I was.

"Whatever was said to Viola about you, about the countess—ignore. I will have you. You are mine. Understood?" I growled.

"I..." she began. That delicate flush I'd become so painfully aware of in the past weeks swept from fair cheeks to what was exposed of her chest. "You cannot want me... Not forever."

"Oh, but I do," I would not permit dissent. I was an alpha and I would have what was mine. "You might be too young for me. Eighteen. But it won't stop me."

"I shall turn twenty this year, my lord," she choked out the interruption. "Why would you think I am seventeen!"

"Truly?" I chuckled, amused and distracted by the way Hartwell would interrupt me with such suppressed outrage. This was why she was so much more mine than any other. This challenging, amazing creature belonged to me, body, mind, and soul.

"I would not lie to you about my age when the information is readily available. Ask... You cannot mean what you said. You cannot. That you would know me like... I cannot believe you. You are... There are omegas... You are responding to Viola's scent—"

I would not let her continue like this. I had spent weeks, days, and nights with her. Everything in my being told me to rut and mate Hartwell. But to force myself on her, in the house of the omega I'd asked her to woo in my name! I was infamous enough for telling her of my passion in such an abrupt manner. To go further would be intolerable. The worst possible insult to her. Still, the things we'd done. The kiss. The way that mouth had licked up my spend. How she'd taken me into her mouth...

"Not your sister. I can count on a single hand the number of times I have been in her presence. Once, once I have been in her company and that two days ago. I am wild for you, Hartwell. Do you understand me? I was wrong to tell Viola I would not see you again. I have been tormented these past days. But it is no struggle to put duty aside when you are by my side."

A sound caught in her throat.

"Viola smells delicious, but when I see her, I am not seeing her but gazing upon you in my mind. Wishing it was you I was with."

Dark lashes fluttered closed contrasting to the porcelain skin.

"Please stop, Your Grace... Syon, can you not see what you do to me?" she begged. I saw tears gather and with reckless instinct bent my head so I could kiss them away. A whimper escaped. I rested my forehead on hers and breathed in deep. There it was, beneath the heady scent of violets and vanilla, the thing that made her mine. Mine irrevocably and for all time. "Please."

This time she spoke "please" as a supplication I could not ignore.

My lips travelled along her brow, across cheeks that were faintly seasoned with salty tears I wished away with all my heart. I hesitated. To kiss? Not to kiss? I did not wish to take more than was freely given. While I felt trapped with heady need and indecision, lips reached up and brushed mine.

The kiss was chaste but did not stay so for long, for once I had tasted, I was a man starved for more. My hands, so carefully held to my side, sprang up to pull my dear beloved into my embrace. The alpha in me rode me hard, urging me to press forward, gain entrance to this temple of temptation. Despite how my body ached from arousal, how my cock pressed hot and hard against my breaches, I held back. This moment, too precious to ruin by rushing us. There would be years of frenzied fucking, but only one first time. I would tease it out as long as possible. It didn't stop the growl from echoing in my chest to feel her retreat and step away from me until once again we were at a respectable distance.

"I cannot do this." She sounded physically pained. "Syon... Please. Take the choice from me."

The plea was all I needed, and I backed us until she was pressed against the wall and I could fit myself firmly against her body, grinding my erection against too many layers of skirts. Hands clutched my arms as we renewed the kiss, more fervent this time. I demanded entry to her hot wet mouth that tasted too right. I did not believe I could taste anything else again but find it lacking. At first tentative, she became bolder. Soon the kiss turned wild as we battled for dominance. She would never back down or show fear even after the briefest of hesitations. Around us, our scents built and heightened, until I knew of nothing but my alpha need and that precious violets and vanilla paired like a fine wine. A scent I desired to lick from every inch of her skin.

I trailed kisses across her neck until I found where her scent was strongest. Her mating gland was normally covered by her poorly tied cravats, but in a gown, it was exposed. A mating gland. Of course, my Hartwell would go beyond the bounds of nature and possess something that should only be found on an omega. I dared to bite, not hard enough to break the skin and bind us forever together, but the desperate moan nearly broke my resolve. My hands wandered to the cinched waist and along the lithe back, down again to cup the perfect orbs of her bottom, so much fuller than I could imagine. I pulled her tight against me, regretting the fabric keeping us apart. And with each caress, the most intoxicating sounds tumbled forth. Half expressed thoughts and mumbled words as we rode this mad passion together.

"I need to be inside you," I growled into the mating gland. "I shall go mad if I cannot have you."

"Wait!" small hands pushed at me, forcing me back. Only surprise allowed her to succeed. "We cannot. Not here. What madness has overcome... You will never forgive me. What was I thinking? Your Grace—"

"Syon. You will call me Syon," I murmured into her mating gland, running my teeth along the thin skin. The sweet toxin within would flare hot when I bit and infect me with her very essence. In return, she'd be left with a scar to proclaim to all that she was mine. So damned perfect that she could be all in one.

"Syon. Please. You are tipping into rut. I can smell it. We cannot. Not here... The consequences."

"Damn the consequences," I reached to pull up the skirts I so desperately wanted to burn. My fingers barely touched a thigh covered in a silk stocking when she gripped my wrist. I could have forced it. Broken free of her hold but...

"Stop," Hartwell begged. "We cannot. Please."

Then I noticed how bitter and distressed her scent had become. No alpha, however lost in their instincts, could let their mate—my future mate, because as yet there was no mating bite for me to lick and worry with my teeth until we truly were mindless—be in distress like this. Soon, though. Soon, she would be mine.

"Please. I must... I must tell you—"

Whatever she wished to tell me was cut off by the knocking on the door. "My apologies, there is someone here for Miss Hartwell..."

We froze. Some beta servant had come upon us. Broken through the spell of lust that held us both enthralled.

"I shall be out in a moment," Hartwell's voice was harsh.

I looked down. Her dark hair was mauled making her look ravished. I wanted her to be ravished. Fucked deep into the duchess's nest. We could be there in moments. But I must shut up that feral instinct for I should not force my mate when she was so distressed. I could wait a few more moments as the end was a foregone conclusion.

"There is a mirror. Your hair," I motioned to the coiffure I was certain she would not be able to fix without a maid. I wanted to pull it apart, let it fall against bare skin so that everyone knew what we'd been doing.

"Who helps you with your hair?" I could not help but ask. It was an attempt to fill the pregnant silence and distract me from air heavy with the scent of slick. Slick? I pushed the thought away, my mind must be playing tricks on me. I watched with wonder as deft fingers smoothed the hair.

"No one. Styles have altered so there isn't much to do. My curls are impossible to manage anyway. Do not look at me like that, Syon," she snapped. Our eyes met in the mirror. Mine burned with passion. Hers showed little of her thoughts, but the slight crease between her brows was eloquent. She was thinking hard. "We cannot do this again. Not like this. Syon, you know I speak the truth. To... To continue as we have is madness. It will ruin us both. And I... I am nothing, but there is so much for you to lose. And I could not let that... I..."

"You are all I have to lose," I growled. "You think that everything is so complex. You would complicate the natural act of breathing if you put your mind to it. The fact remains, I am an alpha. A strong, powerful one. One who can exert control over his instincts. For if I wished, I could take you now. You know that is within my power. Yet I exert restraint. Hold myself back as a sign of my respect, my regard. But make no mistake, you are mine. For as strong as I might be, even the smallest look from you makes me weak".

She groaned. I grinned. There was a special kind of torture in knowing her well enough to recognise when she knew I'd won an argument. It made me love her more.

"I do not *think* it is simple! I *know*, better than you, how complicated..." she spun about and in her anger took a step and then another closer to me until she could prod my chest with a finger. The fierceness in her look so enchanted me when contrasted to her much smaller size. "Stop looking at me like that."

"I will look at you how I choose," I clasped the hand poking my chest and held it above my heart.

"Let me go, Syon. Let me go. Leave for Ayleigh just as you planned. You say I am too young, very well. But leave now. Forget me. I will endeavour to do the same. You will regret this. Perhaps not at once, but once your ardour cooled? Marry Olivia. She will make you a good duchess. Give you alpha children and not complicate your life."

"Have you not been listening to what I have said? However you are, you are mine. Damn the dukedom. Why should I care for its future?"

A whine escaped her and without meaning to, I reached up to place a comforting hand about her throat. The racing pulse smoothed out, and I breathed a sigh of relief. She might reject me with words, but her body responded to mine perfectly. Just like it had every other time I chose to touch her as an alpha would touch his mate.

"I will let you go this time on one condition," I purred.

She nodded.

"If I ever wish to see you again, you will permit it."

"I—"

"Do not deny me this," I tightened my grip and felt her pulse flare.

"Syon, I would not deny you anything that is in my power to give you," she purred and stroked her hand over mine, which relaxed, mollified by her words. "But no one, not alpha, beta, or omega, can promise the—"

"You deny me now?" I growled.

"Because I must. Anything else... It would dishonour you and me. I must go."

"Say your goodbyes, then return to me."

She gave a defiant shake of her head and slipped back into the hall. I followed my Hartwell, who sought to rebel against me. I would permit her to return to the drawing room without interference.

Then we would go to the duchess' nest.

Then I would speak to her mother.

Then she would be mine in the eyes of the law.

18
VIOLA

"You are mine," Syon smiled. He anticipated victory and it made his eyes bright, nearly mirrored gold. His feral alpha manifested behind the civilised facade. I growled, knowing how close he was to a rut, and there would be no rational thought if he went there. "You will not deny me again. Go. Say your goodbyes."

"You don't understand!" I snapped aggressively. My gown felt too hot, and I rubbed at my mating gland which itched more than usual.

"Understand you are mine. The sooner you accept this, the better," his smile nearly killed me, for my heart was breaking.

I shook my head. Anger thrummed in my veins. My thoughts came as an illogical jumble of sexual desire and annoyance that it was the omega who was keeping a clear, logical head, while the alpha went off into a sexual frenzy. I struggled with my hot and cold response to Syon. For the first time, I lost all sense of my argument and allowed my unruly feelings to lead me. "I am not. You are... I cannot believe this. You see me as an object to be collected as you would collect

Olivia. Do you intend to marry and breed me? Or will you find some other poor woman to be your broodmare? No. No. I cannot... Let me go," I leant forward and grabbed the handle to the drawing room. An iron grip prevented my escape. I needed to break free. I'd do anything to have him let me go for both our sakes.

"If you leave this house without me, I will run you down and never let you out of my sight again. I will physically bind you to me," he snarled. Looking into his eyes, I could see them turning feral, the light reflecting over and over until his eyes glowed mirrored-gold like a predator stalking its prey at night. With every breath, with every inhalation of my own rising scent, the baser instincts of his dynamic began to rule him. If I did not get away, he would tip straight into a feral rut—blind to anything but mating and marking. My heart broke for him. It broke to see him so lost to the part of him that he'd despised in his father. That he hoped to prevent by never mating. I understood now. On a basic, animal level I understood what he wanted to avoid.

"You don't want to do this, Syon. You don't want to hurt me," I purred. "Just wait here..."

"Hartwell," he growled, but there was a moan of deep and confused need. My damn slick was doing this to him. My own selfish desire to have him for myself. Not as a facsimile of Iris, but as Viola Hartwell. I desired his knot, his bond. All the things I could not have. I wanted to scream but instead, I spoke softly, soothingly. The wildness in him met with my tenderness, my omega power to calm her mate. I dared to think of him as such even if only for the moment.

"You have to let me go, Syon." I ran a hand through his hair, the golden locks as soft as slick. I cupped his cheek with my free hand and with a ghost-like touch drew him close until our lips brushed.

"You are Syon," I whispered into our kiss. "You are not

going to hurt me. You will control this. You can. You are the best of alphas. The best I've ever known."

My kiss seemed to work, for he released my wrist, and I pushed into the drawing room, closing the door behind me. I could feel my heartbeat in my core which clenched around nothing. Had I kissed Syon? Had I agreed to go back to him? My Goddess, I needed to tell him what I'd done. Before he found out in some other way, I needed to tell him.

I looked up to find Olivia looking at me with concern. We'd come to an uneasy understanding. She was confused and hurt, but I didn't think she hated me. Rather, we were both embarrassed and unable to explain the breach in our friendship without revealing the cause.

"My dear Viola... You look... Are you alright? Who was that?"

"I... I think... I need a moment," I assured her. Just a moment and then I would be back with Syon. "He... He is Syon. The duke of Orley, I mean."

"Oh!" she gasped. "Some tea, perhaps?"

I floated towards the sofa where Olivia sat and reached for her hand, craving my friend's touch.

"You—" she took a sharp breath.

My eyes went round. I reeked of slick and alpha. She dropped the teacup and pulled me down. Her lips crashed into mine, her kiss was too sweet and soft compared to Syon's masterful kisses.

"Stop!" I wriggled away from her as she pawed at my clothes. I didn't want to hurt her but I needed to get free. "Stop!"

"You—" her eyes were blown black with desire.

I scrambled back and righted myself. Caroline growled, barely controlling herself. My aunt held her back. If Caroline had been a dog, her hackles would have risen. Knowing she must recognise that some alpha—that Syon!—had been groping at me. I scrambled for the door. Syon would be on the other side. But that seemed the lesser evil when compared to the chaos of Olivia's needy howls and Caroline barking to be let free.

I ran straight into Iris's arms. She was white as a sheet, for just behind her stood Syon.

"Iris," I cried, throwing my arms around my twin. The masquerade was finished, I was exposed. In this time of need, my twin was here.

"I missed you, Vi," she hugged me close.

"What is the meaning of this?" Syon snarled, crowding us back into the drawing room. The terrible anger in his face made me shudder with genuine fear.

"I came to see my sister, who I heard was visiting with the Countess of Kellingham," my alpha twin said as if she'd not walked into the lion's den.

Olivia moaned as Iris and I stood next to each other.

"I'll be, but the resemblance is uncanny," Caroline gasped. She stepped forward, her brow wrinkled in confusion. "Tis' most perplexing. But how am I to know which is which?"

Syon's growl grew, thankfully masking my own frustrated rumble.

"Very easy," my aunt said. "My sister-in-law had twins, twin girls. Iris is an alpha. Viola, an omega. As you see before you, Viola's eyes are violet—my brother was feeling particularly romantic the day they were born. The difference is as clear as day, though otherwise they look remarkably similar."

"And which are you?" Caroline asked Iris.

"I am Iris. If you wish to know my credentials, I am sure my aunt would be most happy to supply them."

Silence reigned.

"This is my sister," Iris looked around the room, catching

each person's eye before shooting me a reassuring grin. "Sister. Omega. Her name is Viola."

Syon reacted as if he had been slapped. I tried to move to him, to explain. This was not how I had planned the deception to be revealed. I needed to get him away. Explain in private because his eyes were no longer mirrored gold. They were deadly angry.

"She is not the alpha you are looking for, Your Grace," Iris smirked. I wanted to slap her for daring to provoke the dangerous alpha duke. "Neither am I but for now, I will settle for her freedom from this farce. Come, Viola."

I'd never seen her so alpha before, but it would not protect her from Syon, whose growl was near loud enough to shatter the windows.

"Prove it," Caroline said through clenched teeth, causing my head to whip towards her. I wanted to scream. She was intelligent enough... Could it be that impossible to tell the difference when we stood next to each other?

"Syon," I pleaded. "Syon, say something."

"Very well," Iris spoke right over me. "I shall demonstrate without a shadow of a doubt that I am an alpha."

She shrugged out of her jacket, handing it to me along with her waistcoat and cravat, and only then did she begin to strip off her shirt.

"Iris!" I hissed, horrified by what she was about to do. Everyone watched her with eager eyes now that my sister was halfway nude, her chest bared to the cold air. Her breasts were smaller than mine but it was the port coloured mate stain between her breasts that marked her as an alpha. All the while my eyes were on Syon. Syon at his most closed off and unreadable. Syon whom I could not reach.

"Satisfied? You can check the alpha registry to confirm where my mate stain is," Iris told the room. "Should Viola also stip down to prove she does not have a mate stain? Or shall I show you my alpha tie? "

She reached for the fastenings of her breeches. I squeezed my eyes closed, not desiring to see the tie of muscle at the opening of her sex that would prove she was a female alpha. Olivia gasped and her too sweet scent spiked.

"Iris! Put your clothes on!" my aunt snapped. "You've caused enough trouble already."

"Hartwell, follow me," Syon barked.

"Viola, you don't need to go with him," Iris stood in front of me.

Over her shoulder, I saw that Syon's face was a thundercloud, and didn't doubt he'd burn the place to the ground if I didn't follow him.

"I must. I must go with him."

Our eyes met. Clashed, and everything that had happened came rushing back. Slick gathered between my thighs and a soft whine escaped my lips. He searched my face for something and whatever it was satisfied him. With a vice-like grip on my upper arm, he dragged me down the stairs. I almost tripped on my skirts, but he held me up. I would have cried out because he was leaving bruises, but I was too afraid that his temper would fracture even more.

"My cloak!" I protested as he shouted instruction at his coachman and crowded me into his coach. It smelt of him, and I moaned. In anticipation, in fear. Anticipation fled when he wrapped a hand around my throat just tight enough to remind me that the beast could crush me if it so chose.

"Let me explain," I tried.

"Explain?" he snarled. His eyes were all mirrored gold. The civilised alpha was gone. In his place was a feral beast who acted on instinct and would resist all reason. "Confess, more like. You betrayed us, our friendship. You betrayed your principles. For what? A joke?"

"No. Not like that."

"You played this prank. To what end? Did Olivia know? Were you laughing at me? Is the whole world laughing at me? Tell me, Viola," he sneered my name, and tears leaked from my eyes. If he had shouted it would have been a million times more bearable than his sneering anger.

"No. Let me go. Let me explain. You will never forgive yourself if you hurt me. We will hate each other... Syon. Don't do this."

"Why?" he roared. "Why did you come to me?"

"The votes," I whimpered. His hand around my throat went slack. "I needed your votes for the bill. I approached you as Iris because I knew you would never hear me out if I came as an omega, as myself. But I stayed as your secretary because I loved the work. I've never been happier before than when I'm arguing..."

"You lied about who you were. Every day for weeks... Or doesn't that bother you? All to get a few measly votes? All of it was a lie. Everything we said and did together was a lie."

"Syon, no! Other than my name and dynamic everything was true. I did not lie about who I was. I am sorry... Whatever you want, I'll do it." I'd never meant anything more in my life. So long as he did not look at me like that. So long as I knew he would smile again, even if I would never see him again. I wanted to do whatever I could to make things right.

"You were mine," he shouted, then more quietly. "You were my truth. But you have shattered that beyond repair."

"No," I begged. "I am still your Hartwell, your secretary. Before you said it didn't matter who I was. Has that changed? I haven't changed..."

"It didn't matter. When I thought you were honest with me, nothing would have mattered but having you under me and at my side," he said with cruel calm. He released me, and I crumpled on the floor of the carriage.

"I tried to tell you," I sobbed. "I wanted to tell you. But each time... I knew it would be like this, that you would hate me. And I couldn't have you hating me."

"Commiserations. I hate you."

It was worse than if he'd thrown me out the moving carriage, worse than being hit, worse than being ordered from his sight.

"Syon," I knelt, reaching for him, but knowing any chances I had at mending this were long gone.

"Never speak that name again," he barked, causing me to flinch away from him. His face blanked and those deadly eyes met mine. "Never come within my sight. Never make a connection with another alpha. Because only then will you begin to understand how I feel... Never... No. I can never allow another alpha to touch you."

"What?" I did not understand his meaning.

He dragged me into his lap, his hand once again bracketing my throat. He forced my head to the side to expose my mating gland. I began to struggle when I felt his teeth against the fragile skin. He was going to mate mark me against my will. It wouldn't be a true mate bond because I wasn't in heat nor was he in rut, but it might leave a scar. Marking me irrevocably as his.

"Please don't," I whispered. "This isn't you."

"Viola," he groaned and held me tight, his bite relaxing until he was kissing the unbroken skin. He sat back, looking at me in silence, his face closed off. The carriage rocked to a halt. Then he leant forward and pressed a chaste yet punishing kiss on my lips. "You are mine. You will never be with another alpha. I cannot allow it. That does not change. But I will never mate you."

"Syon..."

The carriage door opened and he pushed me out into the waiting arms of a footman.

"Do not repudiate me in this fashion!" I cried out, not caring who heard.

"Take her inside," he said and closed the door.

"No!" I screamed. Inside my omega raged as her alpha left us in the arms of some beta. She was feral and feverish with anger. I felt someone pick me up and carry me inside but before the door closed, my vision clouded and my world went black.

～

I CAME TO WITH MRS MARKHAM AND MY AUNT HOVERING over me with a burnt feather and smelling salts.

"He'll come around," Mrs Markham tried to reassure me.

"Viola? Child..." My aunt took my face in her hands and kissed my forehead. It was the kindest gesture she'd ever bestowed, and a pathetic sob broke free. "Tell me... My Goddess! What happened in the carriage? We were convinced he'd taken you to Orley House."

The story came out haltingly as I stumbled over what I could say and what was better left unsaid, but knowing the older omegas would know how to interpret the gaps in my story.

"You'll make an admirable duchess," Mrs Markham said with an encouraging smile. "I will give your portrait to your—"

"Please," I begged. My skin itched hot and uncomfortable. My core empty and aching. "My dear aunt, Mrs Markham. Please do not speak of him. It is over. He thinks the worst of me. I was some golem, created by my hubris. My blind belief that I could..."

"Could be equal to any alpha? And aren't you? If what you say is correct, you have an alpha who loves you regardless of your dynamic. Surely that is an accomplishment?"

"A farce. If he cared, would he not be here?" I wailed bitterly. "If he loved me as he says... He never even said he loved me! Just that I was his like some object. No, you weren't there. Didn't see his face. His words," I could not tell them he'd nearly forced a mate mark on me. That had not been him, but something ugly that had possessed my alpha. He'd stopped when I'd told him to. He knew it was wrong and he'd stopped. Part of me wished he had bitten me. That way I would always have something of him with me.

"If you overset his plans, damaged his pride... Surely he must be granted some chance to evaluate his feelings?"

"He... He knows his feelings. He loved the fake Iris," I cried. "He doesn't want me. He hates me."

My aunt, however, did not seem to care. "Stop being so theatrical. That is Polly's game. Your blood is still hot from being with an alpha in such, ah, heated circumstances. Child, you are feverish. Best go to bed, my dear, and rest. You cannot expect a man as proud as Orley to just stride through the door after this. Are you certain he will not return?"

"Certain," I mumbled into the handkerchief before blowing my nose. "I'm ugly."

"Yes. With all those tears you look quite hideous."

These teasing words did their work, for a small smile tugged at my lips. With a little more gentle coaxing, they decided that I would stay in bed for the rest of the day. I did not have the strength to argue and accepted the arm of a housemaid to half carry me up to my bedchamber.

I stripped my clothes off, throwing them on my bed, and grateful for the cold air on my flushed skin. Then saw for the first time something I should have noticed weeks ago. I was nesting. It was not a small nest either, but one built high with a deep hollow in the middle of it to sleep in.

"Oh, Miss Viola, yes. You've been nesting. We have just been bringing you fresh—" the maid smiled at me.

"For how long?" I asked.

"Oh, two weeks. Maybe three."

"Thank you." I was not thankful. Nesting? Impossible, for my heat was not due for months.

She bobbed a curtsy and left me staring at the intricately layered fabrics and pillows. Throughout I could see hints of colour. I shifted closer and bent to sniff the clothing I had placed. All of it held a trace of Syon, and in the middle was my lavender gown that held his scent and my slick. I climbed in, too exhausted to consider the consequences of what building a nest signified, and pulled the fragrant clothes and blankets over me. Buried in my nest, I inhaled the familiar cloves and musk that belonged to my mate. Mate... The word had slick pouring from me. Hoping that it would tempt him to return, even while I knew he was miles away.

The tears came next. Not the same grief I'd felt on my father's death but loss so profound I could not breathe. No one was responsible for my devastated heart by my own hubris, my arrogance.

The next day, my body ached and my aunt came to tell me that my uncle wished to speak with me. She refused to let me out of my bed, and the conference was awkwardly held as he stood at the door and I huddled in my nest.

"You will end this charade," my uncle pressed his alpha will on me.

I did not bother to reply. I, more than any, knew that everything was over.

"What? You won't fight me?"

I bit down on my lip to stop the tears that threatened to fall.

"Leave, Richard," my aunt pushed him aside. "Viola? My dear? Your mating gland is swollen. Are you expecting your heat? No! Well, you are about to go into heat. Don't worry, child..."

She sent for a maid who returned with a tray of barley water and broth. Then it was a matter of bringing even more nesting materials and forcing me to eat small meals so that I could keep my strength up for the heat I had not expected.

It was the worst heat of my life. I keened and howled, unable to find the relief I needed. At one point a serving girl entered carrying a parcel of shirts that I ripped from her arms. I brought them to my face and found my body relax, soothed by the smell of my alpha mate. The one who should be my mate. They soon became lost amongst the linens of my nest as I writhed in agony at my loss.

My hands were inadequate to the task, and I used the large wooden dildo I had brought with me from home. In my past heats, it had helped with my need for a stretch but now I whimpered knowing that somewhere slept the alpha who would be able to stretch me more, better than some toy. But I knew that only Syon's knot would soothe my omega needs.

On the third day, my heat broke. I lay in my nest weak and delirious, stinking of sweat and slick and sex. My aunt sat with me, bringing tea loaded with sugar in the mornings and bitter beer in the evening. It took some time before I was strong enough to leave my bed for a bath, and as I soaked in the steaming water, my muscles began to loosen as did my control of my emotions. I could not speak my anguish but I could cry, so I did.

"It was not a proper heat," my aunt said with a sideways glance at Mrs Markham, who had come at her request.

"What?" I asked. "I think it was real enough."

"You had a false heat, which is why it was so... Difficult and short. Only three days?"

"False heat? I've never heard of that," I pressed a hand to my still feverish forehead.

"Lord save me from omegas who are raised only by

alphas!" My aunt threw her hands in the air. "My dear niece, did you get no instruction on your heat?"

I tried to remember. "I read books and of course I have had a heat a year since I was sixteen. My father died barely a month after my first heat."

The two older omegas looked at each other.

"But your sisters never spoke to you about a false heat? Flash heats?" Mrs Markham sat forward in her chair. She pressed her lips together and took a breath as if preparing to petition the king. "A flash heat happens on the cusp of your first heat with the alpha you mean to mate. It is to ensure the alpha will stay by you until the real heat comes. You would have had a real heat if your alpha had remained close, but now your body is in limbo waiting for him to return. You will be weak and irritable until an alpha can help you through your heat."

"A mate heat?" I asked. "That is a fairytale. True mates are a fairytale."

"Oh, that is true enough, but if an alpha and omega have been exposed to each other for a very long time, bonds are formed. For both of them. Especially if they have been spending months together on a daily basis. The alpha's bite is merely the final culmination. If... if you have been exposed to an alpha... Known his seed."

I blushed remember all that had happened between us.

"That duke!" My aunt spat. "I knew it was a mistake to let you spend so much time around that alpha. I warned your uncle. But no. Alphas must always be correct. He said you seemed to handle it just fine. Fool."

I found a distressed laugh bubble to the surface.

"I suppose your uncle will need to approach him..."

"No! Please. We do not know if it is a false heat. Perhaps it was just... it is my first not at home. It was an unfamiliar nest. No. I cannot... He hates me!"

"Hush, child," Mrs Markham purred. "Sleep."

MY DAYS WERE A STRANGE BLUR OF SLEEPING, FUCKING myself to unsatisfying climaxes with a rotation of dildos. When I was lucid, there were snatches of conversation that I tried to pay attention to.

"If you do not come to terms with the duke—" my aunt looked grim.

"How... how can I..." my voice so quiet it was a marvel she heard me.

"If you cannot come to terms with him, we must find you an alpha, a mate. As quickly as possible, otherwise your heat could be set off..."

"I am sure it is not so urgent," Mrs Markham tried to soothe my aunt's agitation.

"I do not want her... to be compromised as she might be... for we do not know who might have seen her... Best to find her a safe haven quick. The doctor is worried."

"My dear..."

"We will have her take a strong dose of suppressants so that she doesn't start a riot. Viscountess Gale has an alpha son. It would be a good marriage and mating for her. He is interested in politics, well-travelled."

"And the duke?" Mrs Markham asked.

"He hasn't returned..."

I muffled my tears in the shirts that no longer carried his scent.

AT LAST, I FELT LIKE MYSELF AGAIN. INSIDE MY HEAD WAS A jumble of thoughts. Still, I forced myself from my nest to the small desk. Someone had tidied it, but I easily found paper and pen and ink. My letter to him was incoherent, but I did my best to explain the whole story. From the moment I had arrived in London last August all the way through my false heat. I addressed it to him, hoping that when it arrived in Ayleigh he would read it and perhaps understand.

19

SYON

A few moments after leaving Viola at the house on Weymouth Street.

I had nearly committed a rape. Not of her body but her soul. I'd nearly, in my fury, bitten her mating gland. No matter that it would not take since she was not in heat. Thank Goddess, she had broken through the feral anger and pulled me back into myself. I might eventually move past her deception, but I would never have forgiven myself if I'd mated her against her will. And Goddess, but the fact she was an omega made it all the more baffling that I'd been able to hold back at all. She'd felt so good in my arms, smelt so good, and I hated her for it.

Except it was not hate.

She claimed I'd repudiated her, but the knife cut both ways.

～

VIOLA. NOT AN ALPHA BUT *VIOLA*! A WOMAN, AN OMEGA, who I'd spent an afternoon with and... Almost, I realised, almost I had known. The afternoon in her aunt's drawing room, something about that enchanting omega called to me. I'd known her yet not known her. I had. More fool me for not recognising one I professed to love. I'd spent months with her and never known. What kind of alpha did that make me? A pathetic one. To think I'd have discovered the ruse if I'd given into my instincts after our duel and rutted her in the duchess's nest.

"Viola..." Her name as sweet as her scent came easily even as the fury at the deception bubbled to the surface. Did I want to rip her head off or rip off her gown? Both. Both were darkly appealing. I could punish her in the most intimate way possible. Bring her to the brink of sexual bliss over and over again and then leave her begging and confused for more.

Could I? Her scent would spike, her slick would gather, and what alpha could refuse that?

Viola of violets and vanilla. The owner of the first scent I'd experienced in nearly a decade.

But why? Why had the foolish, headstrong omega taken such a risk? No matter what I had said to her, I did not hate her. My pride was in tatters. But that was between us. Her twin stripping had been for Lady Clare who, it seemed, had fallen in love with Viola, thinking her to be an alpha. I'd found myself in the centre of a farce, but at least in the eyes of the public, not a subject for ridicule. I'd hazard the guess that only Viola and her sister knew the whole truth—Goddess how similar they looked. As they'd stood next to each other, I recognised Iris from the night she'd been with her friend. Damn. I wanted to drag Viola to the duchess's nest and punish her. Show exactly how an alpha dealt with recalcitrant omegas.

First, to Ayleigh to cool my temper. Then I'd return, and we would talk.

I jumped from the carriage and barked at Horne to have everything made ready to leave London for a couple of weeks. I'd stay at Ayleigh, shoot, prepare the house for when it was time for Viola's first heat. My feet were restless and carried me into the library. On the sideboard stood a decanter I kept for guests and for the first time in my life, I poured myself a small glass. Perhaps the alcohol would soothe my raw nerves. My first sip confirmed all my previously held beliefs the stuff was rank and only fools drank it. I spit what I hadn't swallowed back into the glass and banged the whole onto the table. It shattered and I noticed I'd cut myself.

"Dammit," I pulled out a handkerchief and bound it around my hand.

A noise in the hall had my head turning towards the door. A scowling Paxton pushed his way into the library with a smiling Fordom trailing behind him.

"What brings you here?" I snapped. "I'm off as soon as my carriage is brought round."

"We ran into Caroline Wilson. It seems you left Kellingham House with Miss Viola Hartwell," Fordom smirked. "Congratulations are in order... That was a rather spectacular way to claim your secretary. But why aren't you with her? Or do you go to Ayleigh first?"

"How long have you known that my secretary was Viola Hartwell?" I interrupted. I was in no mood for his frivolity or the reminder of how I'd abandoned her on her uncle's doorstep.

Paxton grimaced. "Do not be angry with her until you've heard her reasons... I'm sure she has told—"

"Oh, I am angry with her, angry beyond measure. I am more like to kill you, the real Iris, and her uncle too, for letting an omega, one fresh from the country and untouched virgin, undertake so dangerous a prank. Anything could have happened to her!"

"Angry at me!" Paxton recoiled as if slapped. Pure confusion covering his face. "I tried—"

"You knew," I growled. "You knew, yet you continued to let her spend time with an unmated alpha. Alone. You..."

"I didn't have much choice," he snapped. "I am as angry with myself as I could be. But she would not listen, and I supposed you knew your own business."

"How long?"

"I met the real Iris at a boxing match in February. There is not much difference between them. She is perhaps a bit broader in the shoulder. But one thing they do not share is their eyes. Iris Hartwell's are brown. And Viola's are—well, you know better than any, they are as unusual as the lady is herself."

"I'm going to tie her to that damned nest," I snarled. "Why? Give me one good reason why you let her put herself in so much danger."

"I don't know her motives. I assumed political," Fordom shrugged. He had a hand on Paxton's arm, physically restraining the larger alpha, who'd recovered from his shock and was on the verge of making the mistake of challenging me in my own house.

"At your dinner party, I pulled her aside to lecture her. Then you appeared before I could send her home," Paxton shook his head. "How could you not know?"

"Did you? Until you met the real Iris, did you know?" I threw back.

"No. But I wasn't spending every day with her."

"She masked her smell. And I," I looked to the ceiling realising how easy it had been to trick me. "I lost my sense of smell ten years ago, which she didn't know until recently. Dammit, but she pretended to be herself to woo the countess for me. A farce. She played me for a fool."

"Orley, do not think you are the only one," Fordom interjected. His usually carefree attitude gone. "Beatrice cares nothing for her personal safety. She chases one thrill after another, heedless of her dynamic. So your Hartwell is savvy enough to attempt to protect herself with a false alpha scent. I presume you will be making her your mate and duchess?"

I gave him a stiff nod. "She is already my mate. I'm not so stupid as to let her—"

I froze. I had not made Viola my mate—she'd not been in the thrall of her heat. Too furious, too embarrassed that I had been made a fool. My pride... I shook my head. I had left her.

"Relax, Orley," Paxton took his own advice and shook Fordom off. "As Jack said, Her future Grace has a much better sense of her own safety than her sister. I think we can agree the Miss Hartwells are a menace to society?"

I had not felt any sympathy for the other two alphas until that point. But it seemed they had been dealing with Beatrice far longer than I had been entangled with Viola. "Get out of here," I growled. "Go catch yourself a Hartwell of your own."

"Horne," I shouted. "We stop by Weymouth Street."

I was going to claim my omega and bring her with me to Ayleigh, whether she willed it or not.

"SHE WILL NOT SEE YOU," IRIS SNARLED. "WHATEVER YOU did, it was enough... You made my sister cry!"

I snarled at the younger alpha. Viola had twice the spirit and all the blood lust. "I will see her. She is mine."

"I won't let..."

"Let?" my fury made my voice drop to a deadly stillness. "Let? You presume to decide what I do with my property."

"Viola isn't property! No omega is."

"She is my jewel. I will not let you lock her up. I will have her shine. Now get out of my way this instant before I—"

"Orley! Get out of here, Iris," Viola's aunt pushed her niece aside. She scowled but knew to go.

"Mrs Florey," I bowed.

She looked me up and down with a sneer. And I saw Viola in her disdain.

"Leave her alone. She... She does not need you. No omega needs an alpha. Do not think I will permit you to force yourself on her. I won't let that happen. Not to her. Never to her."

"She is mine."

"Only if she wants to be."

I clenched my jaw unable to argue with her. Viola my violet-eyed secretary was her person. Regardless of her dynamic, because of her dynamic, she deserved more than my feral need to rut her into heat.

"I'm gone to Ayleigh. If she wishes to see me, send her there."

"Arrogant ass!" the omega screamed and slammed the door in my face.

I DRANK ON THE JOURNEY TO AYLEIGH—THE STUFF WAS foul but it drove away some of my darker thoughts. On arriving at the one place I'd called home, I fell into my bed and woke only to drink again. I wanted to chase away every dream of Viola. Not just the ones of an intimate nature with her hand on my cock. Her lips wrapped around it as I fucked her mouth. I wanted to erase the memories of her, dark curls catching the light as she bent over letters, or more likely one of her speeches.

On the third day, Timms insisted on pushing back the

curtains. I squinted in the light, he was holding something out to me as if it would cure all my ills.

"What is this Timms?" I asked.

"Why... It is the omega's gown which you kept in the duchess' nest," my valet hedged. "The one Your Grace has been spending so much time with. We, that is Horne and myself, thought it might give you some peace of mind to have something of hers near while you must be separated. We sent a parcel of your unwashed shirts to Weymouth Street for the omega..."

The delicate fabric of Viola's gown still gave off the faintest hints of her scent and I damned my servants to hell and back for thinking this would bring me comfort. I'd not be admitted to her company again. Her scent would only drive me mad, not bring comfort as the beta had hoped.

"Burn it," I snapped. "That lady is not what you assume her to be."

"But we thought—"

"Do I pay you to think, Timms?" I barked. The beta tipped his head to the side in submission.

"Yes, I mean no, Your Grace. Right away, your Grace."

"Forgive me. I am a bear. In no way fit company for anyone."

I almost didn't let go when he came forward to take the gown from me and I watched in awe the way he handled the garment as if it were made of spider webs and he dare not let a single thread break. I put the dress out of my mind. I could not fixate so entirely on her who invaded every moment of my day with an insidious seduction that with each breath I fell deeper under her spell. Memories of her cursed me with another night of tossing and turning as violet eyes and dark hair curling around a long neck.

The next morning I wrote to Viola informing her of a permanent end to our relationship. I wanted no obligations or formal ties between us when I returned home and claimed her, courted her in earnest. I'd let her free if that is what she wished. I did not write that if another alpha so much as touched her hand in greeting I'd kidnap her and make her mine regardless of her feelings on the topic. She would understand in the end. She had to. But I kept that resolution to myself. If not, I would retire to the country forever and give up on finding a mate or wife. I would look into finding some alpha cousin, no matter how distant, to take my place. Or let the title fall extinct. The legacy no longer mattered to me.

I stared listlessly out across the lawns when an express arrived from London. A letter from Iris—though I would only know for the signature since the handwriting resembled a child's attempt to write. What could she have to say, when my own letter could not have reached Viola yet? Still, I was more anxious to hear from my... I was not even sure what to call her now. But where a name should be was only an ache and anger at the universe for denying me what was mine.

Sir,

I write for there are rumours concerning my sister Viola's name concerning you and the events of the previous week. I realise any connection between our families must be terminated but I write to assure you that any scandal will be scotched. I will not permit my sister's name to be raked through the mud.

Against my better judgement, I also must inform you that Viola has been unwell. I ask you to keep her in your thoughts. Perhaps when you return you could grant her some of your time. For there are things you must know but which only she can tell you.

Your servant
Iris Hartwell

Viola, unwell? I remembered her face as I thrust her from the carriage. How pale she had looked. How she had begged me, apologised, screamed. I'd driven her to her bed. No, I could not flatter myself that I'd such power over her. Some cold... It had to be some trifling cold. But a cold had killed my grandmother. I cursed myself for caring when it would have been so much better to wipe her from my mind. Everything that I had sought to avoid? I was one of those pathetic alphas driven mad by an omega.

$\sim$

I WAITED A DAY BEFORE IMPATIENCE GRIPPED ME AND I ordered the carriage, with word that I would return to London that day and expected the house prepared to receive me by that evening.

The sky was just turning pink and purple when a shot rang out. The coach lurched to a halt, and I was startled from a light doze.

"Hands up and hand over the goods," a crude accent cut through the stillness that followed the commotion of highwaymen stopping the progress of one of the most powerful aristocrats in all of the Islands of Great Britain and Ireland. I swore, furious that anything would stop my progress. I wished to reach London before nightfall. So I might speak with Viola before she spent another night anywhere but with me.

I did not move, but the rapport of my pistol rang loud and the aspiring thief fell back, dead. A shout went up, and I leant out the window and in a minute the other pistol in my possession went off, killing yet another of the men who so dared to hold up a carriage on the King's Highway.

"Pretty friend, you've now injured one of my men and killed the other. That is enough," the woman's voice was polished but full of bite. I heard the familiar click telling me a pistol was ready to blow my brains out.

"Do I know you?" I asked, sitting back against the squabs. The light in the carriage was strong enough to reveal a small woman wearing a black loo mask never her face. She looked as if she was on her way to a masquerade, a ruby ballgown covered by a matching domino with diamonds at her throat and dangling from her ears. Her hair looked red, and there was something almost familiar in the shape of her mouth and chin.

"We've not met formally," the feminine voice laughed. "I'd hoped to meet you under better circumstances. But you've gone and made my little sister cry. Now you have the chance to beg for your life from Hippolyta Hartwell, Queen of the High Toby. Consider it an honour."

Hippolyta. The only thing I could remember of her was Viola describing her as a cat dissatisfied with wherever she found herself. I'd no love of cats, they made me sneeze.

"What do you want?"

"I want you to consider that if I kill you it will hurt my sister. But if you make her cry again, I shall take pleasure in making you a meal for worms."

"You're mad," I shook my head. She was an omega. So much smaller than I, but I knew fear when she levelled her pistol at me.

"Most likely. Perhaps you should just consider this a dream."

"Nightmare, more like."

"As your fancy takes you," she laughed. "I must leave you or be late for my night's revelries. But I am glad to have made your acquaintance. And should thank you for killing John. He was bad for business. Always wanting to shoot people. Guns are ever so loud and messy. One of the reasons I always wear red. Have a pleasant journey. The roads are good."

I waited until the sound of horses retreated before stepping out of the carriage.

"How's it?" I called to John Coachman.

"I'm winged, Your Grace," came the reply. "But nothing to stop us. Can give—"

"I'll take the reins."

"'Tis' a four you aren't familiar with," the old man admonished as I jumped up to see how bad "winged" was.

"And you don't trust me with them? We've got light, and the postboys ain't scared. Eh, lads?" I said. The postboys affirmed that they were right as rain.

The anticipation for a fight had brought the world into focus. I had heard Hippolyta's warning. I'd made a mistake with Viola. Fool. Arrogant fool to have left things unresolved.

Damned fool to have left London. To have allowed her out of my sight even for a moment.

Hippolyta had lied. The roads had been muddy, and it had taken us far longer to arrive than I'd wanted.

On entering my house, Horne gasped on seeing me covered in mud from the road. Horne sent a footman running to prepare a bath. I waved him off. It did not matter how I looked when I claimed Viola.

"Find out where I might find Viola Hartwell," I barked, and a lackey left the house at a sprint.

The man must have wings on his heels for he was back in moments, panting out the information that Viola was at a ball hosted by Viscountess Gale. I growled, furious that my future mate and wife was anywhere near that slippery eel. I didn't bother asking if I had an invitation, I was an unmarried and unmated duke. No hostess would deny me.

I arrived so late that Gale, her omega wife-mate and their beta husband were no longer greeting their guests. I found my omega hostess, a rail thing woman with an oddly plump face. She pressed her lips together and shook her head in the negative when I questioned her about Viola. But of a sudden, I saw Viola dressed in one of the simplest gowns, silk the same colour as her skin, throwing her unpowdered hair into sharp relief. Every fibre of my being responded to her and a fit of possessive anger flared at the sight of her dancing with another man. He was not familiar to me and by his bearing, no match for my Viola. I did not trust myself if it had been an alpha, but this beta was nothing to me.

But Viola, sweet Viola, summoned me like Circe. I carelessly brushed past my hostess in my eagerness to reach my omega's side. For seeing her here, even knowing how things had ended, I knew no doubt. She was mine. She drew me like a lodestone through people I neither cared for nor sought to know, until I stood on the edge of the dancing, biding my time until the music finished. And while I waited, I scanned the other alphas to see if there were any who might try and take my place at her side. I growled at the sight of several alphas following her progress down the dance. By no means the most graceful dancer, Viola radiated a regal beauty that drew the eye.

The music had not ended, but I was already moving towards them. There was a deep, if dark, pleasure when Viola saw me. Brave girl, I thought, for she stood her ground and did not look away. At this distance, I could not say if she was unwell. But that chin! Raised and firmed. That assured me that her spirit was not broken. She had fire still.

"Your Grace," she asked, looking between me and her boring suitor. It was hard to mistake the way the younger man gazed on her. I would not begrudge him those glances. "Did you come to dance? I'm afraid my dance card is full for the evening."

I smiled down into her arresting eyes. As Iris had written, she did not look well. Her normally clear complexion was sallow, and dark circles under her eyes made me frown with dissatisfaction. She was not taking care of herself. Omegas needed to take care of themselves, be taken care of, before their heats. "I am no dancer. Come walk with me instead."

"Miss Hartwell?" the man asked.

"It's fine. I would be happy to join you, Your Grace."

I placed her hand on my arm and covered it proprietarily, glaring at the stranger until he left.

"You shouldn't be here," she whispered. "Syon, please, I implore you. No scandal, Syon. I could not... Yell at me another time. Not here... If my letter angered you..."

I grunted. She misunderstood the situation, but a part of me was soothed that she recognised, bowed to my power over the situation.

"Iris says you are unwell," I replied. People stared at us. Let them. This merely confirmed our connection. "I dislike... Hartwell, you should not be out in society if you are feeling unwell."

"I... I had a fever," she said, looking about nervously. I glanced down at her pale face. Then bent closer than was appropriate—but damn the tabbies—to better catch her scent. There was no illness but a hint of... She'd been in heat. I growled at the thought she had suffered through a heat with no alpha to care for her. For me to see her through it. I wanted to tell her so. In a crowded ballroom, while the polite world watched us, I was more concerned with lecturing her about never going into heat again without me there to rut her through it. More concerned with that than making things right between us. Because there was no forgetting the letter I'd written or what had passed between us.

I swallowed the inappropriate words. The question, demanding why I had not been summoned to rut her. This was not the place. This was not the time. So we walked slowly through the ballroom, acknowledging acquaintances and not speaking to each other.

"Do you and Iris get mistaken often?" I asked as we passed another smiling gentleman who'd met Hartwell at my house.

"Only if I were to wear her clothes... and the light is too poor to see our eyes are not the same," she laughed bitterly but managed a smile and a slight nod of her head as we passed a couple, who acknowledged her with a wave. "She is an alpha after all. It would be a challenge to confuse anyone."

"But you did it. Not just with me," I pressed. While I could only expect the sisters to be close, I did not know how far she had taken Iris into her confidence. "If anyone... You pulled it off. You did with me. With everyone."

"It was easier when we were children," she continued as if I hadn't spoken. "Before we presented."

"Is Iris here?"

Our conversation felt oddly pedestrian as we weaved through the masses of people.

"No. She left town and returned to Oxford."

"Then," I paused. If I wanted to make her mine correctly, I needed to speak with her mother or I could follow instinct and claim her without permission. However, I must not do that in a ballroom without causing the kind of scandal she wanted to avoid. "Miss Hartwell, please do me the honour of having a quiet word. It is... There is something we must speak of. I recognise we did not part on good terms... A moment of your time."

"Is there something wrong? The pamphlet that got published yesterday about the bill? Hippolyta was at fault. I told her not to meddle," she said, her whole attention on me, her hand clutching my arm. "Sy— Your Grace. Yes. If you... We should find somewhere for me to explain. Your name won't be dragged through the muck because of my actions."

I did not correct her. I knew nothing about any pamphlets. Rather, I needed to know if my chances with Viola were destroyed by the letter I'd written. If she read it, if she... I looked down and saw a strange flush that did not look healthy spreading across her face and chest.

"Are you quite alright?" I asked. She'd been unwell. What if she had not recovered? I'd kill them all for forcing her to come to the ball when she was not fully well.

"Enough. I am too hot."

"Find us somewhere," I commanded. She led us to the library, and I held the door open while she slipped in.

"You are familiar with the house," I remarked.

"The Viscountess is a friend." She put a hand on her mating gland, pressing down on it as if it bothered her. "She... You do not care for my rambling. Her son is planning to stand in the next election. They hope I will... Never mind, it will not interest you. She says she wants to help with the Omega Right's Property Act."

"Gale wishes you to marry her son, doesn't she? Didn't I warn you to stay far away from him? I know I did, so don't... You are a hellion," I growled and wrapped my hands around her shoulders. Not enough, I must cradle her against my chest, a hand holding her head to the place above my heart.

"I would never!" she gasped and struggled to get away, but I would not let her. "Why are you growling at me? I did nothing wrong. You are the one who sought me out. Make up your mind. Do you wish to growl at me, or never see me again?"

"I am sorry," I purred. "I know you wouldn't go near that reprobate."

"Syon, I don't feel too well," she closed her eyes as if the soft candlelight was too much. I purred for her, pulling her closer still that she might feel the deep reverberations in her very bones.

255

"You called me Syon."

"You asked me to," she sounded petulant. "And just now I called you many things but you would not respond. Are you angry about the pamphlets? Hippolyta—"

"I know nothing about the pamphlets. I just arrived in town. Do not worry yourself," I reassured her. I wanted to keep her talking. I wanted to forget everything but how her body melded with mine. Difficult conversations could happen later. I had my Viola, nothing else mattered. "Your sister's handwriting is nothing compared to yours," I teased.

"Her handwriting is chicken scratch! Not that of a gentle-woman! But we believe it is because they forced her to write with her right hand instead of her left as Papa allowed me. I speak of nothing. I beg your pardon. My thoughts are all over the place." A fluttering hand was pressed to a trembling mouth that appeared desperate to speak more if it weren't being physically restricted.

But her scent! It spiralled and thickened. Ripe and decadent.

I growled with purpose now. Here before me was forbidden fruit I yearned to taste. I'd done so unknowingly. My alpha purred with satisfaction, but I forced myself to reject the instinct to fuck Viola in this place. To draw forth more of that sweet scent. To provoke her into releasing her slick. But no matter how tempting it was to pull down her gown and suck on her breasts, her clit, until she mewled in pleading, tortured desire. I needed to get her to the duchess's nest first.

"We must leave, Viola. We must leave now before I am no longer in control."

"What do you mean?"

"Sweet innocent. You smell divine. Precious above all things. But I am only an alpha and the—"

A growl was ripped from me as she let out a mewl of

distress. Her scent, however, remained sweet, and I knew slick must be dripping from her hot, innocent cunt. The predator that lurked beneath the surface took on a new interest.

"I cannot," I said even as I pulled her closer, rocking my aching cock into her in a feeble attempt to assuage the need I felt. "Goddess, I want you. But I cannot... Not here."

I groaned into her hair.

"You hate me" she shook her head. "You said in your letter! You said you would give me up."

"I was angry."

"I am angry," she snapped and tugged at the low neck of her gown. Her skin was feverish. Surely, surely she could not be going into heat? Everything pointed to her having recently finished a heat. It would be madness to think she would risk...

"Omega, when was your last heat?" I barked. All thoughts of a proper courting period replaced by the very real possibility that this delicate flower was about to bloom before my eyes and at a ball in a strange alpha's house.

"A week ago."

Everything pointed to there being some problem. Her scent was too rich for her to have finished her heat.

"I took suppressants," she moaned in distress. "How was I meant to come to the ball without them? They insisted I come..."

"Fool girl," I barked. She swayed towards me giving off the soft omega purr in hopes of soothing my temper. "Suppressants cannot be trusted. And if you work against nature, nature will only find its way. Why? Why did they force you to come, knowing your heat could come on you at any point?"

20

VIOLA

"I need to find a mate," I whimpered. My body feeling like it was melting and boiling in turns. "They want me to find a mate. Frederick Gale... He will become the Viscount... political... They say it is the right thing to do. That I should forget you. You rejected me. You wrote that horrible letter."

Syon froze. I could see him restrain himself, restrain the violent feral alpha that did not like the idea of Gale touching me. A small comfort, even if he did not want me. I didn't want Gale touching me either.

"You don't need to do anything while I am here," he purred. I twisted into him, trying to bury myself in him as I might in my nest. Nuzzle through the layers of fabric that kept me from his skin where his scent would be strongest. As long as I could, I wanted to keep him with me. "You are mine."

The air was too heavy with our scents, and I fought for sanity. Yet for the first time in my life, I revelled in my slick. Syon would smell it. Know what it meant and then he would stretch me. It would sting, but my slick would ease his way. It was natural and right. I needed him and his knot. I craved and I demanded his body, as was my right. I shook my head, trying to clear it. There was something wrong with that. He was not mine. He had repudiated me. Rejected me. He had written that horrible letter. I mewled, distressed and confused.

"Syon, please."

"What, little one? Tell me, omega. What do you need?"

"Kiss me," I begged.

"You don't need to ask." His kiss consumed me, forceful and demanding entry. When I was too slow, he nipped at my bottom lip. On my gasp, he moved in. Our first kiss had tasted of him, but now there was the bitter hint of that uniquely alpha saliva that when he bit my mating gland would cause it to scar, change me, and make me his in every way. He was going into rut. That heaviness in an alpha's scent rising even as mine became sweeter.

"Mine," he purred against my lips.

It left no room for argument. In this moment, I was his. I could not hold on to that. Yet each time I came close to surrendering completely to him, the uncertainty would rush back freezing me.

"Wait. Syon, this is a mistake," I pulled back. Horrified that I had let it come to this. Stealing kisses from an alpha I'd lied to.

"There is no mistake. There is nothing but us. As decreed by nature," he said between sinful, sipping kisses. His hands flexed at my waist and his face buried into my hair. He groaned and pulled me into him. His erection pressing between us. I arched trying to get more contact.

"Viola," he growled. "You can't go into heat here."

"Heat?" I asked, confused. "No, I can't be going into heat. I'm... I had a heat... No..." I remembered what my aunt and Mrs Markham had said. My heat had been a false heat. My body craved him, his knot. I needed Syon to rut me through my heat or I would not find satisfaction. I moaned. My body flushing and the slick beginning to gather.

"I must take you somewhere—"

"Yes," I whispered. I couldn't recognise myself or the need building. "I'm too hot. I—"

"We'll find Iris. You need to be.... Not here. I meant to do this properly. I will approach your uncle since your mother isn't returned from France."

His lips wandered down my neck to the lace at the edge of my gown. I wanted to laugh, he would not leave me. I would not let him. "We'll get you somewhere safe. I'll not let something happen to you. I want to do this right, properly. I will declare myself in front of all. But not like this."

My skin flushed hot, ordering my body to claim this alpha.

"Ahhh!" I crumpled as the cramps washed over me and caused my knees to buckle.

"Viola, Viola, I need to get you somewhere," he purred for me. I nodded weakly. "My duchess' nest is close."

Nest. The word snapped me out of the lust filled fog. My nest was empty and lonely. Cold because he had abandoned me.

"No, I can make it home. You said things were over between us. That letter... You can't want me. Not after what you wrote. Syon, why are my thoughts so muddled?"

"Damn what I wrote. I need to take care of you," he snapped. I moaned as another cramp shuddered through my body, but this was a sweet cramp that sent more slick rushing from my body.

"Syon, I need..." What I needed was his knot, damn the consequences to my heart.

He scooped me up into his arms. "Your dresses always get in my way."

"No! It hurts, Syon. Syon, it hurts so bad." The cramps that came with my heats had never left me so weak.

"I know, my darling. Shh..." his purr rumbled, and I buried my face into his neck, seeking out where his scent was strongest. "I'm taking you home. You'll need to walk for a little bit. I'll get you out of your gown as soon as possible but not here where others might see you."

Syon dropped me to my feet and only his vice-like grip on my waist held me upright. It was a blur, but I heard people calling his name and perhaps mine. All I knew was the warm body next to mine had me itching to remove every scrap of clothing from both of us.

Within moments, we were out into the cool night air, and he had to restrain me from clawing at my gown.

"Dammit, you'll rip the thing off, and I'll not them see what belongs to me." Syon threw me over his shoulder and strode across the square to his house. He rammed through the door and began barking orders at his surprised servants.

"Take a note to Weymouth Street. Tell them Viola Hartwell has gone into heat. I'll put her into the duchess nest."

I purred at the thought of a nest. My nest.

"Shall I bring supplies?" Horne asked.

"Yes," I growled. I needed supplies if I was going to be rutted through my heat. My alpha needed supplies too. Nesting materials. Food. Water. But Horne was a good beta. He would know what was needed.

I could feel the tension in Syon's body. Supplies implied that he would rut me through my heat, which he had not agreed to. I growled. He had brought me here, and I'd be damned, but he would be the one to knot me. I would have it no other way.

"Syon," I whined, knowing he would worry and be more receptive to suggestion than if I unleashed my omega temper.

Pained at the thought he would leave me in my time of need. "I need your knot."

"Do it. Bring everything we will need for a protracted heat," Syon called as he carried me upstairs. Good. He was taking me to my nest. My nest... My nest was attached to the bedroom I'd been using for months. Had they known? Did it matter?

I sighed and leant into his scent. Rubbing my face across his chest, marking him as mine, being marked by him in return. Syon stroked my back while the beta servants brought nest material into the duchess's suite. I itched to begin sorting through everything, but he kept me trapped to his chest, nipping at my mating gland and purring for me to be calm until they had finished. I resented this but did not resent being in my first proper nest. I had never been in a room dedicated to nesting before. One where a huge, low platform filled most of the room with a deep feather mattress on top of it. Now, thanks to the servants, there were fresh linens and pillows. At last, I managed to wriggle free from the alpha's grip and tore into the materials to begin the process of sorting and placing them into the perfect mosaic. Somewhere fit for an omega and the alpha she invited to rut her. Syon's scent was not to be found, nor mine, but that would be rectified soon. I did not worry too much. We would make this nest ours.

All the while, Syon prowled back and forth, while I attempted to focus on where I placed each pillow and blanket. Timms brought his unlaundered clothes to the door but no further as Syon had snarled at the poor man. I did not care who brought the precious nesting material so long as there was no scent of omega. No omega but me. I looked over my shoulder to where he stood, in mud-splattered clothing. I scowled.

"Strip," I ordered him.

My alpha didn't respond, but every line of his body tensed as I shuffled to the edge of the nest.

"Strip," I growled. "Get out of that jacket. Give it to me."

Our eyes held as he removed each article of clothing. One by one he handed fine wool and velvets and linens to me so that I could find each its perfect place amongst the sheets and pillows. Until, at last, he was naked.

Syon in all his alpha glory was a sight to behold. My eyes traced every plane of solid muscle that seemed cut from marble. Beautiful. I licked dry lips, desperate to taste and lick and bite and kiss and suck every inch until he was marked and mine.

"Now you," he commanded.

Tonight, I was not wearing a simple gown but a full ball dress that a maid had laced me into. Syon moved close as I struggled to get out of the gown. When he became impatient, he spun me around as if I weighed nothing and ripped the fine satin. Those solid arms wrapping around me and pinning my back to his chest while he licked at my mating gland. It caused another wave of slick. I knew he noticed, for the growl that reverberated through my body and how he ran his teeth down the column of my neck.

My heat was upon me, and Syon, my alpha, had tipped straight into rut. Reason? We abandoned it, returned to bodies embracing and revelling in instincts that demanded we fuck until he had bred me.

I landed on Syon as he tumbled us into the nest. I shifted into a kneeling position to better wriggle free from the gown we had yet to completely remove. Syon reached up to help me but only managed to get in the way. He settled for pushing my skirts to my waist, stroking his hands up and down my legs, rubbing my thighs through the slick soaked silk stockings, but never once touching my sex, mewling at being so denied. Eventually, he became too impatient and, in a demonstration of alpha strength, ripped both the bodice of my gown and my corset in half, tossing it somewhere in my nest. How strange that straddling a powerful alpha in nothing but the skirt of a ballgown should make me feel so powerful.

He cupped my breasts which spilt out of my torn chemise. His thumbs grazed my nipples, driving a keening wail of need as fresh cramps shook my body. My agony pleased him. But it pleased me more to feel his hot and heavy length bumping against my sex. Neither of us had expected my heat. Neither of us had dressed for seduction. But in my innocence, this was the ultimate form of attraction, when a simple cotton chemise, shredded gown, and plain silk stockings felt like the most expensive French negligée.

I didn't have time to worry about my inexperience because I didn't give myself time. As soon as we had tossed my skirts over my head, I was desperate to feel his bare skin against my own. I ran my hands along his strong chest, covered with crisp hair. Syon caught on to my urgency and sat up so that he could strip the fine cotton chemise from my body. I dropped soft open-mouthed kisses on his shoulders. For the first time, I felt his hands clasp the twin globes of my ass. Pushing them together before lewdly pulling them apart. I dropped my forehead to his neck, panting at the luxurious feeling of his hands gripping the flesh of my ass. I mewled as they moved away to knead my bare breasts. His touch was addictive. I could have happily stayed there forever—allowing his hands to roam over my feverish body. But Syon had fallen into rut and was ready to move on. He allowed me one final reprieve before he claimed me. His palms weighed my breasts before coming up to hold my face and pull me in for a deep kiss.

I fell into him as he expertly rolled us so that I was now on my back, staring up into mirrored-gold eyes. Taking in his crooked nose and the faint sheen of sweat on his brow.

"Viola…" his eyes, mirrored gold, had never looked more beautiful. "You are so beautiful."

"Take care of me, Syon," I told him. "Let me take care of you."

"Viola…" he moaned into my neck. I gasped when he lightly bit the sensitive skin of my mating gland. His scent overwhelmed my senses. I arched into him when he stroked my sex with the back of his hand. I knew about how to pleasure my own body—had survived heats with nothing but my slim digits and toys—but the confident fingers I felt were a different kind of pleasure entirely. Through the haze of building orgasm, I instinctively reached out for him. The feeling of his erection and swollen knot on my thigh was tantalising, and I found myself drawn to it. To touch it and hold it in my hand. To measure its weight and length. He gasped when I squeezed him. This was mine. It had been mine for weeks now, ever since he had covered my face with his cum. But now was different. Now he would know that I was the one giving him this pleasure.

"I want to see you," my voice sounded breathless.

"Yes."

He knelt above me and I saw how large he was—before, I'd had an impression of his girth and length, but the warm glow of candlelight multiple a hundredfold made it possible to see every throbbing inch. The pulsing vein that snaked its way from base to tip. The strength of his knot strained against gravity for he was so long and thick that his hard cock bobbed with the beat of his heart. In mimicry of the torture he subjected me to earlier, I stroked his thighs while never touching where we both wanted. I was captivated by what I saw. I wrapped my hand around him, my thumb and middle finger not touching. My breath caught. Could he fit? Would he rip me in half? But those irrational fears fled when he gripped my hand tighter around his shaft. It was hot and velvet-smooth, yet hard and insistent. I could not know how much control he possessed to allow me to explore him with my searching touch especially when my heat rode us so strongly. I glanced at his clenched fist and wondered how far he would let me go before taking back control. When I turned my attention back to his erection I noticed a bead of arousal on the swollen tip. I collected it with my finger and brought it to my mouth. The taste was different and intriguing during his rut, stronger to prove his virility. My body tensed with need. I wanted to taste, but my body wanted his seed deep inside my womb.

"Can I?" I asked, never taking my eyes off the swollen head wet with precum. He didn't speak, which I took for permission. I gently pressed him onto the bed and knelt beside him, tucking my hair behind my ears and bending over to lick him. My hands roamed after my mouth. While I explored, Syon reached between my legs and began stroking my cunt. I could hear the obscene sounds of my slick as it leaked from me and he thrust his fingers deep into my tight channel. I became increasingly distracted from kissing his shaft.

"Alpha!" I threw out a hand to prevent myself from falling. He grabbed my arm and steadied me without once stopping the steady rhythm of his stroking fingers.

"For me, Viola. Look at me."

My eyes blindly found his steady gaze. When my vision refocused, he thrust two thick fingers inside of me. I cried out as my orgasm rolled through me, overwhelmed by the shock of feeling so full. I collapsed on his chest, shallow, shuddering breaths puffing through me as he continued to piston his fingers in and out and in and out, stretching me, preparing me. And all the while he gently stroked my hair and back while I recovered.

"How are you?" he whispered with a light kiss on my hair.

"Yes. Good. I mean, amazing."

"Come here."

I was surprised that he encouraged me to straddle him. Everything I had been taught said that an alpha would mount me from behind or take me while I was on my back, my legs open for him to do as he wished.

"Take your time. I am going to watch you, Viola. I am going to watch you stretch yourself near to breaking as you take my knot. You are going to beg to take my knot," he growled. I felt his hands on my hips slowly bringing me down until the very tip began to nudge at my entrance. The invasion, the expectation, made me hold my breath and tense, but he soothed me by massaging my clit. He teased the bundle of nerves with firm and gentle strokes, which followed no pattern so that I was never sure what to expect. I relaxed into the mounting orgasm, trusting and loving the alpha who could so command my body that he was not unmanned by the fact I was about to mount him. It was my alpha who had put me in control even as he made my body sing. I was going to be able to do this as I wanted and he was there to hold me steady.

"Hold my hands," he said.

When I felt his strong fingers interlace with mine, a surge of confidence enveloped my body, and I lowered myself. I had heard how painful my first time could be, but Syon had prepared me and my slick eased the way so that I only had an intense feeling of fullness.

He did not take the time to let me properly adjust. He did not let me ride him.

Instead, he thrust his knot deep inside my channel in one punishing thrust. Even as I screamed at the abrupt fullness, I locked him in with an omega's strength. The immediacy of feeling his knot inside of me triggered another orgasm that had my body shaking as it tried to assimilate to the intrusion.

Amazingly he grew, pressing back against my spasming sex. The pressure building until he erupted and shot his hot cum against my womb. The knot firmed, catching against my pubic bone, increasing the press against my sensitive front wall. The sensations triggered another round of orgasms, milking him, drawing out his very essence.

"Please!" I begged but didn't know what I wanted.

"Come. Come here," He hugged me, rolled us over, and slowly began to rut into me. "Wrap your legs…"

He kept his thrusts shallow while his knot remained lodged within my tight cunt. I urged him on while I revelled in the mixture of pleasure and pain as his hard knot tested my opening. I cried out his name when he hit something deep inside of me. He granted me pleasures beyond my wildest imaginings.

"Viola," Syon called out my name and again I came as more of his hot seed spurted into me. I pulled him close, forcing him to lie with his body's full weight on my smaller frame.

"Thank you," I kissed his shoulder. The simple fact that he had spilt his seed inside me soothed my heat and gave me, at least for the moment, some of my sense back.

"Am I crushing you?"

"Yes, stay. I want to feel all of you." I held onto him tight and pressed a kiss onto his neck. My sex clenched, drawing out a groan from him. He might be so much larger than I, but lodged in my cunt—I revelled in the word—I had the power. I was the centre of his world as he was the centre of mine. "I want to feel everything."

"Very well," he collapsed with a huff and pressed kisses to my face and neck. "But your heat is only just beginning."

It took nearly a quarter of an hour by the grandfather clock for his knot to shrink enough for him to slip out of me. But even then, he cupped my sex to prevent his seed from leaving my body and littered my body with sucking bites that were sure to leave marks. I purred at the idea that the world would know we were together. Marked and owned.

The cramping began again as my body shifted and altered so that it could better accommodate him. I knew what would happen next. He slid a hand between our bodies to find the little pearl of pleasure which he began to press and rub. The sounds I made were obscene. Words I would never dream of saying out loud came pouring from my lips, begging for him to rut me with his cock, to fill me up and heaven be damned.

When the knot bloomed inside of my tight cunt for a second time it hurt more than when he had broken through my maidenhead. The stretch seemed to be never-ending. In part, I knew that it was my own body locking his knot deep within me. If we had not been compatible I could have rejected it, my omega muscles equally strong and capable of strangling an alpha's cock. But Syon, oh Syon!

I wanted his everything, and when he could not get any deeper I held him there, grinding onto him, arching and shifting my hips to find the best angle.

"You are mine now," he growled. His eyes, which had been closed in agonised ecstasy, flared open. We lay together panting and straining as he began to come inside of me over and over, filling me up until there was a constant pressure on my womb.

I DID NOT KNOW HOW MANY DAYS HAD PASSED BY THE TIME my heat faded and I was once again myself. Myself, but weak and covered in slick and cum and sweat. But above all, infused with a deep carnal satisfaction. I turned my head to see Syon lying on his back, my nest framing his inhumanly perfect form. The broad chest I had lavished so many kisses on now came into focus. It had an enticing amount of crisp hair that I wanted to trail my fingers through and down his firm stomach and below the thin sheet that barely covered his erection. I could see the outline of it still hard despite the number of times he had used it to fuck me. I ached between my legs, knew I would be raw and sore for days, yet if he had rolled over and demanded I take him again I would have gladly.

I dared not touch him. We were out of my heat, and he had not mated me. The delicate skin at the juncture of my neck and shoulder was unbroken. There was no going back and yet no future before us. No matter what he said in the thrall of my heat, he had not come to my nest because he wanted to be the alpha to rut me through my heat. He had accompanied me through my heat out of a sense of responsibility, and by the force of his basic desires and needs.

He still planned to marry some other omega. He must be planning that, or he would have mated me, claimed me as his. If he truly wanted me, I'd already carry his mark. Now I must return to being Viola, no longer his loyal secretary, certainly not his mate or wife. I rolled away looking out blindly unable to focus on the beauty of my nest.

I would not regret my time with him. If this was the only moment of perfection I could ever have, I would cherish it until like every good thing in my life it would be ripped from me.

For now, until he woke, Syon was mine.

21

SYON

The smell of sex and violets and vanilla covered me like a blanket.

Viola's heat had broken sometime in the early morning, and we had both fallen into a deep sleep. My body ached for her still. That elusive scent that had haunted my dreams now lingered in every breath. I needed to have her again. Take her, breed her, and—Goddess forgive me—mate her because my instincts screamed for it. Yet everything else protested—I could not be like those feral alphas perpetuating the rape of omegas lost to their heats. The savage rejected even those basest needs.

From the moment I had seen her at the ball, I had not thought of her deception. But now in the bright light of morning, all I knew was the never-ending guilt of betrayal. I loved Hartwell. But was Viola the same as my enchanting secretary, or was that an act as well? I had rushed back to London heedless of the consequences. Then her heat had come on so fast. Now daylight revealed how very little I knew about this woman.

I turned my head, resting my cheek on a pillow infused

with our scents. All I saw was her back and a mass of black hair. That graceful back I remembered seeing arched and begging. How strong it looked. How perfectly yet delicately muscled. My cock, already hard, throbbed as I took in the marks I had made on the pristine canvas. There was nothing gentle about how I had bitten across her shoulders and along the graceful line of her neck. Except her mating gland which stood out for its untouched perfection.

Until that moment I had never felt worse. The realisation that I had violated her. True, she had been begging, but omegas were needy and vulnerable in their heats. It came flooding back. She'd been at Gale's to find a mate. Her uncle most likely wanted her to marry Gale's heir. I scowled. Even if she did not want me, I could not let her be with a man and alpha I had no respect for—she was too good for him. However at war I was with myself about what to do next, if Viola wanted, needed a mate, that one could only be me. I had ruined everything. I had stolen her and rutted her through her heat, taken her virginity, and done everything but marked her as mine. I regretted nothing. Instead, I swelled with a hunger for her body, a need to have her in the bright morning sunshine. All to remind her that there would be no other alpha in her life. I had not mated her yet, but I wouldn't let her be with another. I was a selfish bastard and I refused to share her. At least not yet. There was time enough for the difficult conversations. I wondered if I had held back, not just out of consideration, but for a greater reason —that after her deception I did not in fact want her beyond her body. A pretty lie to tell myself because I did not like my new self. The one that would gut another alpha for looking at her too long or one who threatened to take her from me.

I reached a hand to trace her spine, but, as my finger made contact, she flinched away from me. I froze. My heart stuttering to a stop as reality crashed in. Outside of her heat this omega, my omega, might yet reject me. Perhaps she would decline to be my duchess, refuse to become my wife. Based on the way she had recoiled from my touch, I had been right to give her the choice rather than take it from her. Thank Goddess. I let out a heavy sigh. If she would reject me, at least there would be no bond there to tear us apart from the inside out.

"Your hands are cold," she mumbled and twisted under the sheets until we were facing. She pushed her tangled, dark hair from her face. For the first time, I was aware enough to study her face—violet eyes, thick lashes, and a little yawn that ended in a murmur of contentment. She blinked away the last of her sleep and chuckled. "I think that means I'm out of my heat if I flinch from cold hands."

Her smile could have made a starless, moonless night as bright as day. My heart released and soared with that.

I had perfection before me.

And perfection didn't hate me or my touch.

"Do you think we might call for some food? I had not expected to be so hungry," she blushed.

I needed to have her again, damn the consequences. Damn the fact we needed to talk all this over.

"Yes. I find that I am starved," My lips found hers. Slow and sinful kisses to make her drunk with desire. I would give her a different taste of alpha this morning. Not that brutal, instinctive fucking we had perfected but something more permanent. I would not rush us to completion. I would take my time. First I would feast. My kisses made a pilgrimage to her neck, nipping where I had already marked her then soothing kisses. I bit, gentle and careful, at her mating glad to test the waters. She rewarded me by pressing my face into her neck. I growled, pleased with her response. But no omega would dictate my seduction. From there, to her breasts, weighing them with my hands, teasing her nipples with my tongue.

"I meant food," she gasped. I would never get enough of those little sounds she made. Would never grow bored with dragging them from her. I pinched the rosey buds, they had been neglected for hours, but that would be rectified when I suckled on her breast, lavishing them with attention as she arched into my touch. Her hands laced through my hair, tugging. My omega had desires, but so did I.

And I desired to taste her slick drenched sex at my leisure. Spending my time, head buried between her thighs, all day if I could. I didn't know what the future held for us, but I would suspend time to spend an eternity with her in her nest.

"This is the nectar of the gods. An ambrosia. There is no need for food," I informed her and licked again from the pucker of her ass—where I had yet to take her—to the sensitive pearl at the top of her sex. After that first deliberate pass, I teased her pussy coated with slick that tasted as sweet as ever. I feasted, reached deep within her with my tongue, and sucked on her clit. Taking my pleasure by giving her hers. Aware that with each moment I drove her closer to the point of no return. And once she arrived there, I would keep going. For it was my pleasure to draw out hers until she was mad with bliss.

"I need you inside me now," she purred with a painful tug on my hair. Very well, I'd satisfy my omega's needs. After all, I'd decided we'd spend an eternity together.

I surged up her body and sheathed myself in a single sure stroke, pushing my already partially swollen knot into her slick cunt. She had taken me over and over the last week but she was as tight as ever.

"Alpha!" She begged. "Oh Goddess, I feel you everywhere."

I growled with that primal satisfaction and began to thrust. I took my time, pulling out until just the tip teased her opening before slowly gliding into her wet heat. Each movement a delicious torture.

My knot swelled and even before it had reached its full size, I could feel her locking down on me with her omega's muscles that completed the seal, preventing my seed from leaving her body. And around me her walls clenched, milking me. The increased pressure sent me back into rut, pulsing over and over into her, filling her with my cum to plant a pup in her womb.

"I..."

"Shh," I kissed her forehead. "Shhh. Be quiet and rest."

"With you pressing me into my nest?" She asked.

"Exactly."

"But I'm hungry," she pouted.

"Then I shall summon Timms, and he can bring us food like this. Or would you prefer for me to carry you, naked and impaled on my knot, to the dining room?"

"Oh," she wriggled beneath me and my knot, which had begun to relax, flared again. I caught her gasp in a kiss. "I am... Oh, Goddess, please. I am so full. I can feel you... How could you be so big? How can my body take you?"

I growled and grew hard again at her words. Her face went slack, her mouth opening into a perfect "o" of delight as another, then another orgasm washed over her. I did not force my knot into her this time. My omega was hungry and needed another kind of tending.

Horne, Timms, whoever had a preternatural knowledge for our needs, brought a feast within minutes of ringing the bell. All foods to help an omega and alpha regain their strength after a long heat.

"How long?" I asked quietly.

"Six days," Timms said equally quietly. "Her family has been by. Shall I send word?"

I nodded, and he slipped out again. Six days. So long? There was no legal requirement for me to keep her, but by now the news that I had taken Viola Hartwell from a private ball and rutted her through her heat would be all over town, if not further. Perhaps not yet to Paris, but it would not be long before Viola's alpha mother was banging down my door demanding my head.

I stood at the foot of the nest and watched her nibble on a piece of toast, a half-empty teacup nestled by her thigh. For all her begging for food, she had barely touched the porridge or baked egg prepared for her.

"Eat all of it," I told her. "All of it."

"The egg is cold," she wrinkled her nose.

"Omega," I growled. "You will do as your alpha says."

She smirked. "Are you my alpha?"

I nearly cursed her for the insolence. I nearly pulled her from the nest to press her up against the windows that overlooked the square to prove to her and to passersby that I was her alpha. But I held back.

"Yes. After the ball, I have every legal right to claim that you are my omega."

"You are doing this because you want to protect my name?" She asked, her jaw clenched. "Out of... Because you compromised me at Gale's ball?"

"That is part of it, yes." I would not lie to her. But how could I tell her that I had been obsessed with her scent from almost the beginning? Before then, I had been drawn to her as Hartwell, my secretary. Even after I'd learnt her lie, I would have done everything to ensure she belonged to none but me. I loved who I remembered her being, back when she had been mine. But my pride prevented me from uttering the words.

"And my deception, what of that? I thought you wanted to end any and all relationships with my family. Isn't that true, Your Grace?" she asked, all emotion schooled from her face. "I've no doubt you returned to town to throw my response to your letter in my face."

She sucked on her bottom lip, glared at me, managing to look murderous and distressed all at once. Such was the power of violet eyes.

"I received no such letter— just one from your sister. I will do the right thing by you," I told her through gritted teeth. "Your prank will not change my mind. I saw you through your heat. You are mine. We will marry."

I had not expected her to move so quickly. She flew across the nest and grabbed the lapels of my dressing gown.

"You do not love me. You wanted nothing to do with me. And now you will marry me? Will you mate me, bind me to you forever, or am I the same as the Countess? A wife and nothing more to you? The omega to give you heirs but never have the security of your bite? You would... No, thank you. I will not submit to that. I would rather be shunned by society than live through the torture of being your wife and nothing more. Is that truly all that you can give me? Can you not find it in your heart to give me more?" she ended in a plea.

In the time since her heat had ended, I had begun to see a vulnerability in Viola that sparked a need to protect and thus overwhelmed my alpha's feelings for Hartwell—for I had still not quite reconciled them in my head. My love for my secretary remained. I could not deny the ache that I would never again see that dark head bent over a speech she scribbled for me, knowing I'd never give it. Or the way she badgered me to eat properly. And yet, when I looked down on Viola, I knew in my bones that she would be everything and more that I needed. She commanded my soul. She would be my mate... If she ever let me into her nest again.

"I will try. I will try with every fibre of my being to be the alpha, the man you need. I will never stop..."

"Try? You will try," her voice broke. "Did those months mean nothing to you? Is your pride so wounded, your skin so thin that you do not understand that I am Hartwell? Viola? All are me and I am all."

"Hush. I will undo this tangle," I purred. For now, at least, I needed to keep her various names and those memories separate. "Let me try to make you as happy as I know you will make me. I just hope you will not hate me..."

I rested my forehead on hers, breathing in her scent. My body shuddered with desire. Not carnal desire, but the desire of a heart which prayed that I could work some miracle.

"I will make you my wife. I will never leave you vulnerable," I promised. "No rough breeze shall touch your cheek while you belong to me... As you already belong to me."

A knock on the door, and Timms' insistence that I come forced me away from Viola before she could reply. Before she protested her hatred... Or that I had not mated her? I was not sure. I would mate her, but cooler heads would make that decision. I could be a coward in small doses, it seemed. Timms had nothing important to say. Just a note from Florey informing me that he expected an announcement in the Times by tomorrow. I growled at the presumption. But instructed Timms to write it up for my inspection.

Viola would be my duchess, but upon returning to the nest I found her hunting about the piles of clothes for something that was not covered in cum and slick. I scoffed. Her everything, mind, body, and soul, belonged to me. She pulled a chemise over her head. It was ripped and hung lopsided on her body in a manner far more enticing than she perhaps realised. When I asked why she needed clothes, she informed me that she could not return home naked.

"You are home," I informed her. "This is your nest. You

will have no other... Except for the one at Ayleigh. There is a nest there. We will have your next heat in that nest."

"We are not yet mated. We are not married. There is nothing that requires me to stay with you. Did you mate me? No," she snarled, baring her neck, taunting me with my civility.

"That is a formality for the law."

"We are not yet mated," she shouted. I smiled at the aggravation which coloured her voice and brought a delightful flush to her cheeks.

"Is that what it will take?" I reached forward to snag an ankle and pull her towards me. "I was civilised and did not mate you during your heat. But I do not need to be civilised now that you have agreed to marry me. It might not take, but if you want me to bite into your mating gland... Trust me, Hartwell, I will gladly put more of my marks on you."

"I have not! You do not make sense, *Your Grace*." Goddess, I loved the way she sneered my title, it made me hard for some inexplicable reason. Everything about her made me hard, had from almost the moment we met. I loved how her eyes flashed. So similar to countless times before when things had been simpler. "I have not agreed to marry you. How can we be happy when you have not forgiven me? *Your Grace*, I will not be subjected—"

"Syon," I bit out. Once was cute, the second was just obnoxious. "You will call me Syon."

"Syon, then," she snapped. "We just spoke about this. I must go home. They will be mad with worry."

"They know where you are. Your uncle just sent a note. I am to send a notice to the Times. And in three weeks, when the banns have been read, we will be married. "

"But it is not where I am meant to be," she began rummaging once again for more clothes.

"Your Graces?" Horne said through the door.

"What!" I shouted, still glaring at my little omega.

"A Miss Iris Hartwell is here."

"See!" Viola cried out and jumped up from the nest, heedless of her near-nudity. "Iris will help me!"

"Put some damn clothes on!"

"Fine," she spat and grabbed a too large dressing gown from the edge of the nest that had miraculously managed to escape her heat clean. She ran fingers through her tangled hair. She looked like she'd been dragged through a hedge backwards. I grinned.

"MY GODDESS, VIOLA!" IRIS STUMBLED BACKWARDS. VIOLA didn't just look fright but she probably smelled of heat sex, and the collar of bruises around her neck was enough to demonstrate exactly what I'd been doing.

"YOU!" Iris glared. "You ruined my sister! Did you mate her? I... Name your seconds."

"Don't be ridiculous. You can't beat him in a duel. And there will be no repercussions. His Grace saw me through my heat but didn't mate me. I'll bathe and return home. An omega can be helped through her heat without the need to then be tied to the alpha even if mated," she glared at me. "This..."

"That is Scottish law! The Act of Union makes those laws... We are in England!" Iris looked at her as if she was mad. "A mating bite means you belong to that alpha..."

"Oh," Viola looked at me a little lost. "Are we in England?"

"Heat head?" Iris asked. She heaved a sigh. "Omegas. Go through a heat, then all they want to do is not eat the food they've asked for and talk nonsense."

I blinked at the siblings. Iris, I was not warming to. She'd come to challenge me but was distracted from her purpose at the smallest diversion. Viola meanwhile had discovered her reflection in the mirror and was throwing surreptitious glances at the rat's nest on her head.

"Shall we agree that Viola Hartwell will be my wife and in her next heat I shall mate her? Next, we can agree that you, Iris Hartwell, can leave?"

"No." Came from two voices. Now that I looked at them they were not so like at all. I should have felt like a fool, but instead I was impressed that Hartwell had pulled it off.

"Very well. Iris Hartwell, I accept your challenge. But informally, I'm not inclined to hurt my future sister in law."

"Ridiculous. It's not a fair fight!" Viola complained. "Iris, I'll fight in your name."

Iris threw her hands in the air. A picture of resignation. "Vi, I've said it since the beginning, you will go your own way to the devil."

"Then it's settled. I'll go home and get some proper—"

"You have clothes here," I told her.

"I want pistols," she snapped.

"You are not the one challenged. I pick swords."

She moved so fast I almost missed the moment her little hand slapped my face.

"Picking a fight with me, Puss?" I grinned through the sting.

"As you see," she glared.

"Would you like pistols, my little omega?"

"I'm neither yours nor little," she huffed, but I could see a little smile peeking through.

"But you are an omega."

"Well, is this happening or not? I promised to pay the countess a call after this to let her know how you are, she has been worried," Iris complained.

"Making up to Lady Clare?" I smirked.

"Yes. You've a problem with that?"

"Take milquetoast if that's to your taste."

"Get out of here, Iris. I can handle this. Tell my aunt I will be home for dinner."

Iris looked at me. There was a little tick at her jaw. I thought her a poor excuse for an alpha to leave her sister like this. How could she believe her sister safe? It proved that none but I could be counted on to protect the hellion at my side.

"Vi. Beat him. Beat him so well he won't forget the name Hartwell."

"Ha! By the end of this, her name won't be Hartwell," I promised the twins.

TWO HOURS LATER, I MET WITH MY HARTWELL IN THE long gallery. We'd negotiated that she could bathe on her own. But she would not leave for fresh clothes, which meant she was in the first gown she'd worn in this house, the one that had been carefully stored since that fateful day many weeks ago, kept my servants even after I'd commanded it burnt. Her hair was still wet, and she'd left it loose falling over one shoulder, causing the fine cotton fabric to turn almost sheer with how wet it was.

"You look lovely, my dear." And she did. Beyond what mere words could say for she glowed.

"You took a bath," she replied. I would have thought her tone provoking except for her one nervous tick, she was playing with the collar of her dress.

"We've seconds." I turned and indicated Paxton and Fordom who'd arrived on my doorstep ready to find my corpse.

"I take Fordom," she said quickly. "He was in the army and smells like family."

"The lady has taste," the alpha smiled. "Let's get this finished. You didn't call for a doctor, Orley..."

"We can fire at a target that isn't breathing," I informed the bloodthirsty omega who was glaring at me.

"That isn't any fun," Viola pouted. "I'd rather put a bullet through you."

"Hartwell omegas and shooting alphas who have their best interests at heart... To be clear, you are all mad!" Paxton snapped. "Thank Goddess, I am not acting for you."

"I hate you," she snapped.

"Children," Fordom growled in an unexpected show of temper from the normally sardonic alpha. "Decorum, please. I think this ancient knight and his fellow will make fine targets."

I looked over at the suits of armour he had chosen. "They'll do."

"How will this work?" Viola asked with a frown.

"Whomsoever hits the target closest to the heart wins."

"That isn't how a duel works!"

"This isn't a duel," Fordom told her, allowing a bit of alpha to colour his words. "You are both letting off steam. Have this as a bet. What is the stake?"

"Whatever you choose," I told her. "Gentlemen, I would like to speak with her before..."

"Of course," Paxton nodded.

I put a hand on the back of her neck and steered her a little away from the other odd duo. I looked deep into her violet eyes while I gathered my thoughts. Each word must count for this was my last chance to convince her with words.

"Viola Hartwell. You are mine. By law and by my will. You passed your heat with me—I didn't bite you out of respect but that don't make you any less mine. However, I will give you a choice now. If you win, you can have whatever you want. I cannot promise the crown jewels, but if it is in my power, it is yours."

"My freedom?" she asked but her eyes did not meet mine.

"Yes." It should have been painful to say that one little word, but I promised her everything. Even if it meant her freedom, I'd give it to her.

"And if you win?"

"You are my wife."

"Is't that simple to you? That you will have me as a wife? A broodmare? Is that... Is that all you think of me?"

"No, my dear Hartwell. I think of you as much more than that. But that is all I will ask of you. If you wish to become my mate in your next heat, I will gladly mark you. All I ask is for your hand in marriage. Anything else is in your power, and your power alone, to give."

"I'm going to beat you," she pronounced so sweetly that my heart gave a nervous kick.

"You can try," I kissed her forehead. She'd be mine. Viola might be a cracking shot, but I was better.

What happened next was like a dream to both Viola Hartwell and Syon, Duke of Orley. They took their positions, back to back with only their clothes between them. Viola leant back a fraction, her body's heat seeping through Syon's shirt. Perhaps this distracted him, for when the guns went off his went wide, and Viola's shot hit the mark with such accuracy that caused Fordom let out a whoop of excitement.

I stood, frozen to the spot, my senses only just returning. I had not fired wide on purpose. I was not a fool. This was my only sure chance of making Viola mine. Perhaps it was that scent of violets and vanilla that distracted me. Or maybe it was nerves. But now the portrait of the second duke had a hole in it.

"I won," Viola said joyfully. "Oh! Syon! I won! Isn't... Aren't you impressed? I told you I was better than you."

"You did. I'll... I'll go and see about ordering a carriage to take you home." Blood rushed through my ears, filtering out any thought but the building dread that I'd lost her forever. "Paxton, Fordom. Good day to you both."

"Do the right thing, lassie," Fordom said, some of his Scottish accent slipping out. "He loves you even if he hasn't said it yet."

"I know my business," she snapped. "I wish to speak with Syon in private. You can leave."

She dismissed them as if it were her own house. But nothing good ever came when an omega used that tone.

"I've already promised to let you leave," I gritted out and refusing to look at the beloved creature, who'd demand her freedom.

"I'm not asking for freedom. I want to be the one who reads my speech before the House of Lords. Perhaps then I will consider marrying you."

22

VIOLA

The gallery was packed with omegas. On either side of me, my sisters. Behind me, our mother, one of the few alphas permitted as chaperones in the omega gallery. Below, the murmur of Parliamentary members taking their seats.

Beatrice, dressed as ever in men's clothes, took my hand in hers. She did not look at me but down to the floor where our fates were being discussed by men and women, who thought they had our best interests at heart without bothering to ask what those interests might be.

"All will be well," she said with her clear voice. "We were born to see this work done. Papa would be proud of you."

"Papa was always proudest of his little politician," Hippolyta sniffed. "You were making bargains before you could walk. Though why you needed to arrive late and wearing breeches when you had that lovely gown picked out..."

"Hush," Mama said as the Speaker stood.

I cannot remember who spoke or of what. My ears rushed as I waited.

"Uncle spoke well," Beatrice observed, and I nodded despite not hearing a word of what he had said.

"Today I speak to the Omegas!" A clear and beloved voice rang through the chamber. Every eye turned in our direction, but it felt as if it was me they were looking at. There were faces on those benches who had known me as Iris. Ones I had dined with, played cards with. Ones who knew my deception and could with a word destroy my reputation.

"It is Orley," Mama said as if I did not recognise the voice I knew as well as my own. I'd been working with him almost daily on perfecting this speech. I did not know what would happen yet. At least not step by step. I would marry him. He would make me his mate. The last weeks had proved to both of us how well we fit. And how difficult it was to maintain some professional distance rather than fuck all over the library. Usually some poor beta servant had to sit with us.

After I spoke my words before the packed house and gallery, his promise would be fulfilled. My only fear is that we would be thwarted... I did not know what to do if that were the case.

"I have a speech, which I will give. But first... Ladies, Lords. I think we can all agree that omegas are the fairest of dynamics. Not just in face and form..."

There was laughter.

"But also in the manner of expressing themselves. They rarely lose control of their tempers or speak above a whisper..."

Ironic silence from the gallery.

"We claim natural superiority when we assert authority over them and their interests. Alphas, Lords, Ladies... and the Gallery! I say to you:

Necessity is the plea for every infringement of human freedom. It is the argument of tyrants... Or so you said yourself Prime

Minister ten years ago... Do you not believe those words today as we discuss the tyranny of alphas?

What necessity when omegas already run your households? What necessity when they can put forth their views so clearly as to convince a room of alphas?" He smiled. "I had the supreme pleasure, the opportunity to expand my understanding when speaking with one such omega. She spoke thus,"

He pulled a piece of paper from his pocket and frowned for a moment. Was he having problems reading without the spectacles I'd bullied him into purchasing?

"This omega said, *Consider, dispassionately, these observations, see the truth through your own reason. First, to see that the human race is equally born male and female and we make no distinction between the two. Wherefore then do we distinguish between dynamics? Second, if you can accept that thought into your thick skull..."*

Laughter rang out. I choked on my laugh and felt a tear fall down my cheek. He had remembered, word for word, our conversation. Had written it down as I spoke... My friend.

"Come! Let me finish! *Second, if you can accept that thought into your thick skull then take this. Amongst all dynamics, sexes, creeds, races, and professed faiths, there are to be found the good and the bad and the middling of society. An alpha might be as weak in thought as you profess omegas to be. And there are omegas whose ability could rival any alpha's in body or mind. If you can agree that there are good and bad alphas, why not the same amongst omegas? You alphas profess that omegas are the rarest dynamic, and like precious stones are hoarded and jealously guarded. But in shutting the omega away, the beauty withers as a jewel left in a box grows dull. To truly be appreciated, a jewel must be worn in the sunlight.*

"I say to you, my fellow alphas. To the omegas who have joined us." He bowed to us, and I inclined my head. Acknowledging every one of his words. "I say that I believe this to be true. Join me today in voting for this Bill which we have rammed down the throats of the government. Consider your omega mates and children who are subject to the whims of alphas, cruel and kind... Now to my prepared remarks..."

This was my cue. I stood on legs that trembled, my speech clutched in my hands, my eyes locked with those of the perfect alpha for me. We'd discussed how he could give me what I'd asked—the opportunity to give my speech before Parliament. Syon, my alpha, nodded, and we began, together in all things, to read out my words. There were no objections —who would dare interrupt a duke? Who would make an enemy of Orley's future duchess?

I wish I could remember those minutes more clearly. That one day I'd be able to tell in vibrant detail how I'd been the first omega to speak in Parliament. But all I remember is the stillness that followed. Syon bowed to me. I answered him with a tremulous nod. Silence. Silence ruled the alphas below me. The Prime Minister caught my eye, a small smile tugging at his lips, a gracious nod in acknowledgement. He knew now who he'd spoken to at Syon's dinner all those weeks before.

"Your Papa would be so proud," My Mama said, the sound of tears in her voice. "Our little politician."

"DIVISION! CLEAR THE CHAMBER! OMEGAS OUT!"

"What does that mean?" asked an omega behind me.

I turned to see Olivia and smiled. I had not seen her enter, had not seen her since the day in her drawing room, but it gave me hope that she was here and speaking to me. "It means that there is hope. It will be close, but they must now cast their votes since there was no clear majority. All we can do is wait."

"He was talking about you, wasn't he?" she asked.

"He was. I will marry him."

She gave me a stiff smile and exited the gallery followed by Caroline, who bowed to me with a small smile.

"Who is that?" Mama asked.

"That is Lady Olivia, Countess of Kellingham... And possibly your future daughter in law," I informed her.

"What has Iris been up to!" Mama hissed.

"More like what has Viola been up to," Hippolyta smirked.

"Lord forgive me for wishing for omegas!" Mama threw her hands in the air as we followed her out. They took us omegas and our alpha chaperones to a small side chamber where they offered us tea. I paced the length and breadth of the chamber, unable to sip the tea or eat the cake that was offered.

"Viola." It was Olivia.

"My lady," I curtsied, deep and unsteady. When our eyes met, hers searched my face as if trying to find the similarities between me and my sister.

"Please, it is Olivia. Otherwise, I shall have to call you duchess... and that seems strange to me."

"Olivia, then. I am not a duchess."

"Not a duchess yet. You and your sister are very like. If it weren't for the eyes, I would not be able to tell you apart."

"I am so ashamed. I abused... I abused your friendship, which meant the world to me..."

"No. Please. It is in the past. Your injury to the duke would be considered greater and if he can forgive... Besides, your sister has explained it to me in a way that... I understand why and am grateful to you and the duke," a deep blush covered her cheeks. "We, that is Caroline and I, have decided to travel to Europe."

"France in incredible turmoil, or else my Mama and sister would not have returned!"

"Italy is our goal," her eyes twinkled.

"Iris has decided to go to Italy..."

"She has told us as much. I am glad that she is to travel with us."

I admired how steady her gaze was. Her eyes had always been eloquent but now I felt as if our entire conversation went from spoken word to eye beams twisting in the space between us. She had not so quickly transferred her affections to Iris, but the similarities in our forms? Iris's more measured temperament, I could see perhaps her affections moving in that direction both naturally and by force of her own will.

"And Caroline is happy with this?" I asked looking at the elegant alpha who was in quiet conference with my mother.

"It was she who suggested the change. She admires you... As you know I do. I think we and your mate have much in common." There it was, Olivia's playful smile peeking through, a meaningful eyebrow raised and my hands flew to my cheeks as I understood her meaning.

"I thought Caroline hated me," I stuttered.

"Hate you?" Olivia snorted. "My dear friend, Caro doesn't hate you. Shall you ask her? Here she comes. Wish us well?"

"Caroline," I flushed.

"Your Grace," Caroline curtsied.

"Please, I am no duchess! Perhaps I should write to the Times and take an advertisement saying I'm not married. Call me Viola. I wish you well. I wish you all so much of my love. Yours... I do not know what to say," I laughed. "But it seems that all is well that ends well."

She was about to speak when there was a shout outside the parlour. The heavy oak door bounced on its ancient hinges as Syon burst in. It took him but a moment to find me.

"You!" he shouted and stormed over his face all frowns.

I bit my lip hoping to hold back tears at the news of our loss.

"You! I have to go hunting you down instead of seeing you hovering outside like a father waiting for the mother of his child to give birth! You did it, you gorgeous little fiend."

I shook my head. "Did it?"

"Yes, my sweet, darling Puss. You precious jewel! Ha. I shall wear you in sunlight," he pulled me to him and buried his nose to my throat to scent me. His other hand slipped down to cup my bottom and draw me close so that I could feel how hard he was. "You won, Hartwell. The bill passed. The Omega Property Act. You brought them to their knees. It will always be yours. Your victory and no one else's."

"Syon? You cannot mean it?" my heart swelled with joy. Perhaps the joy growing exponentially as he continued to call me Hartwell even while he got used to calling me Viola.

Syon wrapped an arm around my waist and hoisted me into his arms. Without acknowledging anyone he strode out of the houses of parliament and into his waiting carriage.

"You have until we reach home to explain why you are wearing men's clothing."

"I left in men's clothing," I told him.

"Oh? I told you to put on your gown."

"I could not... You... you," I swallowed and let out a nervous laugh. "You rendered it unwearable before you left. I wanted to be on time."

"What?"

"It was ripped down the back."

"What should that matter if you were wearing a cloak."

"I thought it would be quicker to wear men's clothing and walk," I shrugged. "I wanted the fresh air. Syon, mark me. Make me yours."

"We will pretend that you didn't walk from Orley House to Westminster in men's clothing."

Which was not the reaction I had hoped for. "But Syon!"

"Not until we are in your nest," he grunted but he shifted

me until I was straddling him. His face grew serious. "When are you going to answer me? No, Viola, look at me."

"Why aren't you angry? I was so sure you would... Spank me!"

"Spank you?"

"Discipline me for dressing like this."

"Would you like to be spanked? Fear not. I'm more like to hide you for putting yourself in danger than wearing breeches that show off your bottom to perfection. Little omegas should not be taking such risks..."

I searched his face for any lingering resentment but couldn't find it. "I lied to you, Syon. Doesn't that mean anything?"

"Did you ever lie to me? Putting the question of your dynamic to one side. Did you?"

"No... I wooed Olivia in your name... I didn't lie about that."

"Only she fell for you?" He chuckled.

"It was a horrible mistake." I blushed. I'd told him the whole and been mortified as he howled with laughter at the idea of the tiny omega professing her love. He laughed at my blindness in not recognising either of their affections.

"You are just too alluring. I'm lucky Paxton and Fordom are so caught up with your sister. They have no problem with sharing."

"Syon. Stop. Please. I do not want to be thinking of my siblings or the people..."

"Come here."

I thought he meant to kiss me but instead used the hand on the back of my neck to bring my head down to his shoulder. Then his deep purr began. As comforting as his purr was his scent. And on him, I could smell myself. He'd fucked me against his desk before leaving to give his speech. I found my own purr rising. Even if I had not claimed him as my mate, there would be no mistaking it. No alpha or omega would be able to ignore our combined scents.

We arrived home and after a perfunctory celebration with the servants, Syon dragged me to the duchess's nest. We'd been living in sin together since my heat, and I loved every moment I spent in my nest.

He dumped me into the nest and stalked to the windows and drew the heavy curtains closed.

"Strip," he commanded.

"What?"

"Strip."

"Don't you want to talk about what happens now?" I prevaricated. Surely the brief conversation in the carriage had not been enough. "The future perhaps?"

"No."

"Why not?"

"Does it matter?" He asked.

"My love, you—" I crossed my arms, while celebrating my victory in a carnal matter had its appeals, I wanted to talk first.

"What did you call me?"

"Love," I huffed, my whole being tense for we had not discussed *love*. I knew he loved me even if he'd yet to tell me... But—damn him—I'd hoped to slip the word in without his commenting on it.

"Do you love me?"

"Yes. But that is not what is important. It is by the by because I have loved you for a long time. We were talking..."

"Here," he grabbed my ankle and pulled me across the nest until my legs hung off the edge, my hands lying by my head, a smile tugging at my lips. "Do not, mate mine, tease my temper by telling me you love me and then act as if you have not said anything."

"Your mate? Where is the proof of that—"

"There is none of course," he growled. "I saw how miserable my parents were. My peers, equally bound in unhappy marriages and mate bonds. You, little mate, little omega, do not get to say the word love and not expect me to take note."

"Oh? Then I love you. Syon. Syon, I love you," I crooned. I purred for him. Telling him I loved him, would always love him and all the while he loomed over me. His body braced above mine, a crooked smile and that crooked nose I'd noticed when I first met him. How I loved him.

"Come. I want you naked," he stood and pulled me to my feet.

"But wait," I held back. "What about you? Don't you love me?"

He laughed. "Little omega... haven't I said as much? Haven't I proven to you that you are mine and mine alone?"

"Yes but you haven't *said* you love me," I pouted. "It isn't that I doubt you..."

"I love you. But I told you. You were just too drunk to remember. Thank Goddess, for you were in a state and bowled me over, for you told me that you wanted to be a perfect omega. There you stood, by all appearances an alpha, drunk and telling me... Do you know how long I have needed you? Loved you?"

"Stop," I begged him. "Dammit. Stop. I..."

I felt guilty. I had sinned against him. The sin of lying. I did not regret what I had done. If I had not dared to dream this mad scheme I would never have met him. But the lie I told? That I did regret. That I kept telling it for so long. That sweet, innocent Olivia had been drawn into the farce.

"My dear, dear sweet girl," he gathered me into his arms and pressed my cheek to his chest. The purr reverberated through my body and little by little my tears stopped, my muscles released until his arms were the only thing holding me upright. "Hartwell, what you did... It was a mad prank.

But no more than that. It ended without anyone hurt. You brought people together. You have done so much. And not one of us who knows the truth blames you. Look at me, omega."

I sniffed and shook my head. He had never seen me cry before and, unlike Olivia, my tears caused my eyes to swell and my nose to run.

A knock on the door startled us. "There is a bath if you would like it," Timms called.

"Let's get you into that, warm and clean. Wash those tears away."

Syon's tub was by far the largest I had ever seen and filled to the brim. He made quick work of stripping and then humphed when he saw I was taking my time. To be fair, I had been distracted by the vision of masculine perfection. He was tall and broad but naked I could see the play of muscles across his back and the strong thighs and the buttocks that I decided I would sink my teeth into at the first available opportunity. Then of course his front. In the haze of my heat, I had not the wits to appreciate quite how large he was. As I watched him, he began to thicken and grow until he was fully erect and his knot had begun to swell.

In the bath, he settled me above him, causing water to splash over the edges.

I moaned at the increasing pressure on my opening as his knot began to press into me. On top, I had some control of how much of him I could take, but my body was more needy now than ever. I'd long lost my trepidation that I could not take his already enlarged knot without heat madness. Instead, I craved how I stretched until I was sure he would split me in two.

"Oh," I cried as of a sudden his knot was lodged deep inside. "Oh, it is..."

"Are you well?" He asked, sucking on my pulse in a way that had me moaning.

"You... I cannot believe that you fit. Every time, I cannot believe how much you fill me."

"You took me so very easily in your heat," he chuckled.

"Yes, but have you seen yourself?" I punished him by clenching my core about him. He threw his head back with a groan and he rutted into me causing the water to slosh onto the ground. "Syon... Make me yours. I cannot wait another year until my next heat. Do it soon. When the child comes. Mark me then as well. And then again in my next heat. But I can't wait a year without your mark."

"Are you pregnant?" he stopped thrusting and held me close. "Do not lie to me."

"I think... I haven't bled since my heat, and it has been a month at least," I paused. "I won't ever lie to you again. So I cannot promise that I am pregnant, but all the signs point to a pregnancy..."

He stood, holding me close, still impaled on his knot, and stepped out of the bath. He walked us to the window and with one hand opened it.

"Let it be known! The Duchess of Orley is pregnant!" he shouted. A few passersby gawped. And I? Perverse creature that I am, I laughed.

VIOLA
EPILOGUE

Some months later…

T rested my head on Syon's shoulder, idly running a finger along his chest.

"I'm bored," I announced. I'd spent the past four days formulating how to broach the subject of ennui in the kindest but most direct manner possible. As expected he stiffened in silent indignation.

"Not with you, Alpha," I purred. If ever I needed to soften him, calling him alpha was as sure a way as any. "I mean you've insisted that I only leave the nest for a few short hours. That I'm not to read too much or write too much or…"

"Puss… Enough games. Tell me what you want," he growled. Oh, dear. He was more put out than I'd imagined.

"I thought we could go to Ayleigh for the summer…" I hedged. "Before I am confined to my nest… Before I'm forced to waddle like a duck."

"And…"

"What do you mean by that?" I shifted so that I might glare at him.

"There is always an 'and' or a 'but' with your schemes," he smiled. Dammit but that smile had me lose my train of thought.

"I want to invite Mama and Beatrice and Mrs Markham and Hero. To keep me company."

"And..."

"Syon you are such a beast! Teasing me like that," I pouted. He rolled us over so that he rested on his forearms above me. One of his hands drifted down my naked body, brushing over a breast, until it landed on my gently rounded stomach where our child grew.

"You've mischief in mind. I'll indulge you so long as I'm not hosting half of Parliament."

"Paxton and Fordom. That's it. No politics."

"Just matchmaking?"

"Matchmaking?"

"You don't mean to mate and marry your sister off to the pair of them?" he laughed.

"Oh! Oh... No. I just wanted to have them make peace. If they just got to know each other, I'm sure they wouldn't *hate* each other."

He lowered his lips to mine for a brief kiss, but I could feel his laughter. My husband was laughing at me! "Syon!"

"I don't think *hate* is the correct word..."

"Well Beatrice hates them. I mean it! Did you know that Paxton after refusing to accept her paintings for the Summer Exhibition offered to buy them? And then Beatrice aimed her gun at him. I don't know if she shot him in the end. I learnt of it the other day. It seems that now I'm a married woman all the family scandals can be revealed."

"My dear if you think being shot would scare Paxton or Fordom off, you greatly mistake the matter. It's more like foreplay, the delicious precursor to something far more intimate... The games afoot, my dear Hartwell."

299

"I'm not Hartwell. I am Orley," I protested. "She'll lead them on a merry chase, Syon."

"All the better..." He kissed what he could of my head. Shifted that he might reach my lips. "My dear Orley... My duchess."

I bit my lip, hoping to suppress the moan when he tweaked my nipple. "You'll agree to my plan then?"

"Your prank? Aye, I'll agree... On one condition... We keep it secret from them until the moment we all meet at Ayleigh."

"Oh, Syon! I knew I could bring you around to my way of thinking!"

THE END

Thank you so much for picking up
Omega's Gambit.

Reviews are one of the ways indie writers reach new readers,
and it would be wonderful if you could take the time to share
your thoughts on review sites like Amazon and Goodreads.

Please turn the page for an unedited excerpt of Omega's
Virtue Part One which is the first book in a completed duet
available on Amazon and Kindle Unlimited.

OMEGA'S VIRTUE: PART ONE

Beatrice

My breath came in fast pants, my heart rushing, ears ringing with shouts of my pursuer. I didn't bother to look over my shoulder, I didn't bother to contemplate what might happen if I were caught. No. I ran. Ran as fast as possible.

"Stop you piece of baggage!" The alpha's bark ricocheted about my body. He sought to use that defining characteristic of an alpha against me. More fool him. I was Beatrice Jane Hartwell and I was no one's meek and mild omega. It rankled to flee rather than tell this pompous ass that he and his whole dynamic were pathetic fools for believing that alphas were superior to omegas or betas simply because of their bark—no need to think about those other things alphas had that had my resolve wavering, my steps faltering.

I took the right hand turning and kept running.

Then the left... Was that correct? I'd been so focused on escaping a room full of alphas that I hadn't paid attention to where I was running. Just get away. Stupid heat. Stupid heat for coming on while I was in the middle of proving to those officious, spiteful, snobbish pieces of filth that my paintings deserved to be presented at the Summer Exhibition. Curse everyone... Them, me, but most especially the curse of being an omega.

I skidded to a stop. In my last turning, I'd come across a dead end. There were two doors to choose from, neither marked, both closed. The pounding footsteps of the alpha chasing me was getting louder. I needed to pick.

Left.

Locked.

Right?

Locked.

Well, that made for an unfortunate solution. I reached inside the pocket of my blue satin coat and pulled out my pistol. I checked to make sure it was loaded and raised it, prepared to shoot whomsoever came around the corner and tried to rape me. It was not a foregone conclusion that the alpha would rape me. Some alphas had enough control of their natural instincts when around omegas in heat—even omegas with mates were in danger. That this alpha had followed me indicated he was as affected by my scent as if I was an unmated, virgin omega. And by now I'd realised that my heat was very much upon me. All I desired was to strip away my clothes, allow the cool air to caress my skin, and then try to give myself as many orgasms as possible. I cursed that I'd been given no choice but come today when they were making the final selection... Goddess, I needed to get naked.

"Omega!" the alpha roared. He was close.

The pistol shook a little. Not from fear but because the cramps that accompanied my heat screamed for my body to crumble into a ball of agony. It was as if my womb was haunted and wanted to leave my body, pulling me apart from the inside out. A cruel trick to be an omega and a woman. My monthly cycles were also accompanied by cramps, though not nearly so bad as these. I wished for my nest, for hot bricks, and ice to suck on. For sips of brandy. For sweets. My mouth watered at the thought of candied orange peel.

No matter that I might be raped by an alpha, I wanted candied orange peel more than anything in the world.

"Omega..."

I looked up to see who held my fate in his hands.

The alpha was easily the tallest I'd ever seen with prematurely grey hair that matched his cold grey eyes. His mouth was beautiful even as he snarlingly prowled towards me. Goddess he was beautiful, an offended angel sent to track down one of his fallen kinswomen.

"Omega, I do not know what you think you are doing, running around barefoot and in the beginning of your heat, but I do not approve."

I wiggled my toes and realised I was, indeed, standing on the cold marble in my stocking feet. The marble felt lovely against my too hot feet.

"It feels lovely," I smiled at him absently.

"Omega," he growled causing a delicious shiver to run through my body.

My free hand absently travelled over my mating gland which pulsed with anticipation. This mystery alpha would bite me, mate me. Oh, he radiated the kind of alpha power that called to omegas. That powerful, dominating darkness we craved... At least in Gothic novels. In reality, alphas with this kind of instinctual power over me usually sent me running. I knew what it meant to be close to an alpha who caused my pulse to throb and my core to clench. One who'd taken everything I had to give—had given freely. Only now I was cornered by one such alpha with no where to go and, like a coward, I wanted to disappear rather than risk my heart again.

"I would be grateful if you escorted me to my coach," I

said, proud my voice sounded husky rather than desperate. Better for him to think I was seducing him, luring him to my nest, than that I wanted him to fuck me in this hallway.

"First, I'd like you to put down the gun," he growled.

"Oh," I looked at the pistol that was still levelled at his heart. "I forgot. Don't come closer! I'll shoot."

"I'm coming closer. Do. Not. Shoot," his growl caressed my body and my nipples ached, my breasts felt heavy. This is an alpha, my omega crooned. He could give us what we need. A knot. He would have a knot to remember. I tried to push the thought of knots away. What should I, a supposedly innocent spinster, know of knots?

"I will shoot," I warned him

"You've a single bullet."

"I only need one."

He stopped, the frown he wore did n't not take away from his beauty. No, not an angel to bring me back to the light. He was an avenging angel—one sent to drag me where he willed, into the light or dark I did not care. It made sense in my head even as the words fell over each other in my mind.

"My Goddess, you are beautiful," I murmured.

"While I can return the compliment, I would like you to drop the pistol," he purred.

THE HARTWELL SISTERS SAGA

Omega's Gambit
It is a knotty problem, and it will take some slick moves to mate these two together.

Omega's Virtue Part One
The heat rages when two possessive alphas and a fiery omega mate up.

Omega's Virtue Part Two
It Is out of the heat and into the fire for these protective alphas and their feisty omega.

Omega's Dream
When a proud omega craves domination, knot even these deadly alphas can stand in her way.

Planned
Beta's Triumph
Alpha's Prize

BADLANDS ORC MC

Property of the Green Bastards

He is the monster who rules the Badlands.
Her humanity makes her fragile, her past tells another story.

Planned
Old Horde's Pride
Fury of the Green Bastards

About the Author

~

Flora Quincy is British-American author currently living in Glasgow with her Scottish Terrier, collection of stationery, and a daily pot of coffee. She fell in love with books at a young age. Reading romance, fantasy, and science fiction to escape into worlds far more exciting than real life.

With an overactive imagination, she had dozens of stories begun and discarded, before she decided to take writing seriously. Now those characters and worlds are finding their way to the page.

When she isn't reading or writing, she has a *healthy* relationship with the characters inside her head. So far she hasn't been alarmed too many people while conversing with imaginary men and women as she takes the dog for a walk.

Follow Flora for extra epilogues, teasers, and frolicking fun.

Email
    floraquincyauthor@gmail.com

amazon.com/Flora-Quincy/e/B093HDTL5M
bookbub.com/profile/flora-quincy
instagram.com/__floraquincyauthor
tiktok.com/@floraquincyauthor
twitter.com/FloraQ__Writes

Printed in Great Britain
by Amazon

76912495R00194